ALF

DEATH BEFORE WICKET

Abduction, intrigue and death – it's just not cricket! Phryne Fisher has plans for her Sydney sojourn – a few days at the Test match, a little sightseeing and the Artist's Ball with an up-and-coming young modernist. But these plans begin to go awry when Phryne's maid discovers her thoroughly respectable sister has left her family for the murky nightlife of the city's seamier side. And Phryne is definitely not the woman to say no when two delightful and handsome men come to her on bended knees, begging for her help in finding their friend innocent of theft.

DEATH BEFORE WICKET

DEATH BEFORE WICKET

by

Kerry Greenwood

Magna Large Print Books
Long Preston, North Yorkshire,
BD23 4ND, England.

British Library Cataloguing in Publication Data.

A catalogue record of this book is
available from the British Library

ISBN   978-0-7505-4481-8

First published in Great Britain in 2016 by Constable

Copyright © Kerry Greenwood, 1999

Cover illustration © Beth Norling

The moral right of the author has been asserted

Published in Large Print 2018 by arrangement with
Little, Brown Book Group Limited

Magna Large Print is an imprint of Library Magna Books Ltd.

Printed and bound in Great Britain by
T.J. (International) Ltd., Cornwall, PL28 8RW

*This book is dedicated to the remarkable
and excellent Helen Gordon-Clark.
Never a Xword between us.*

ACKNOWLEDGEMENTS

With thanks to Jean Greenwood, Paul and Cassandra Franklin, Iriellen (Paddy) Duane, Ian Johnson and his father A. E. Johnson, Dr William Cochrane, David Greagg, Jenny Pausacker, Sue Tonkin, Dennis Pryor and Richard Revill, as always.

I might be swimming in a crystal pool
I might be wooing some delicious dame
I might be drinking something long and cool
I can't imagine why I play this game.

A. P. Herbert *Ninth Wicket*

One

Stinking Yarra: a contemptuous phrase addressed to Melbournites by Sydney folk in return for Melbourne's sardonic comment on 'Our Bridge' and 'Our Harbour'.

Sidney J. Baker,
A Dictionary of Australian Slang

Sydney struck Phryne Fisher, quite literally, in the face.

Up to then, the journey had been uneventful. She had alighted from the train at Central Station, collected her maid, her baggage, her two attendant young men, Jocelyn Hart and Clarence Ottery, and her shady hat. She had surrendered her ticket and was standing in the street while one of the young men found a taxi. The heat was oppressive. The air was heavy with dust, smoke and incipient storm. Phryne was scratchy from lack of sleep and the difficulties consequent with washing and dressing in a confined space. The city seemed crowded, noisy and more than a little grimy and she was not disposed to like it.

Then a beggar woman, hefting a whimpering baby, whined for a penny. Phryne obliged, and the woman, laughing, thrust a handful of flowers into her face. They settled on her bodice, yellow and white.

The sudden sweetness was a shock. They were frangipani, seen only in florists in Melbourne. They were scented like lemon chiffon pudding and, ever after, when Phryne thought of Sydney, she smelt frangipani.

The day began to improve. The square black cab drew up and Phryne and her party were whisked away, tracking round a rather pleasant green park and up a narrow street.

'This is Pitt Street,' volunteered the first young man, Joss. 'We thought that you might like to go to your hotel first, Miss Fisher, and then we could take you for a bit of a tour after lunch.'

'Very kind,' murmured Phryne, who wanted a bath. Sydney appeared to be composed of be-grimed yellowish stone. The side streets were steep and crooked. She was passing theatres – the Ascot, the Lyceum – clearly built by people who really appreciated decoration and couldn't have enough of it. The taxi came to a sudden halt in a pre-cipitous street lined with blocky banks.

'What's happening?' asked Clarence of the short, sweating man at the wheel.

'Arr, they ain't got the sense God gave to geese,' snarled the driver, mashing his cigarette butt between his teeth. 'Moving a thing like that at nine in the morning!'

Crossing Pitt Street was a truck carrying what Phryne was sure was the biggest bronze bell she had ever seen. It proceeded with casual grace, un-concerned at the increased level of tension in the city, which could almost be smelt like ozone after lightning. Taxis revved engines and swore. Omni-buses seethed. Passing small boys gaped.

'It's a church bell,' she commented.

'I can see that, lady, and they didn't ought to be moving it at this hour!' returned the driver. 'A man's got a living to make!'

Interesting, Phryne thought. A Melbourne taxi-driver would never have spoken to her so freely. The bell trundled on to its destination and the cab resumed the road with a jerk. Sydney went past in a cloud of oily dust and Phryne decided she could see it later.

In all, it was something of a relief to be deposited alive at the solemn doors of the Hotel Australia. A young man paid the driver and Phryne ascended the steps to receive the bow of the bemedalled individual who minded the door.

He saw a slight, small woman in a natural cotton dress with a dropped waist, pale stockings and shoes, a natural straw hat with a harlequin scarf in pink, black and green and the set expression and black fingernails of those who had recently detrained from the Limited Express. He estimated her ensemble at more than a year's pay and deepened his bow. Phryne nodded and went past, trailing an unmistakeable maid carrying a soft leather vanity case and three hotel porters bearing her luggage. Monogrammed, of course, thought the doorman.

The expression did not noticeably relax until Phryne was lying full length in a bath scented with Rose de Gueldy, scrubbing her neck. She twiddled a gold-mounted tap with one foot.

'I don't know how one gets so filthy travelling on a train, but one does,' she remarked to Dorothy Williams, her personal attendant. 'How are you,

Dot dear?'

'Hot,' replied the young woman. 'But this tea's a treat. Nothing like a nice cuppa. And this is a real nice apartment, Miss.'

'It is rather spiffy. You can rely on the Hotel Australia – or so they say.' Phryne gazed complacently at her splendid bathroom, built in the days when having a bath was a major and possibly life-threatening event. The bath was raised on a platform of polished marble. The walls were tiled with marble in a soothing dark grey and the cool floor was as smooth as ice. A bank of mirrors reflected Miss Fisher's admirable form, getting cleaner by the minute. A marble Roman boy stood on a plinth, taking a thorn out of his foot. Ferns sprouted from a brass jardinière. In addition the water was hot and the feeling of ground-in grit was leaving Phryne. A multitude of the fluffiest towels awaited her emergence. Bliss.

'Miss, I can't find the present for the Vice Chancellor,' called Dot. Phryne rose, shedding foam. The Roman boy would have recognised Venus Anadyomene. 'Now, what did I bring?' Phryne asked herself, reaching for a towel. 'I was tossing up between the Roederer Cristal – the '22, of course, and the Laphroaig single malt. The whisky, Dot, it's packed in its own box. Try the trunk. I decided that the champagne might get bruised by travelling. I'm a little bruised myself.'

'Me, too, Miss. I know I've stopped moving but my feet think they're still on the train.' Dot laid aside a shoe-bag and found an oblong wooden box. 'Here's the whisky, Miss. That's a relief.'

'Even more of a relief that someone hasn't

pinched it. Well, here we are, Dot. Sydney.'

'Yes, Miss.' Dot was dubious about the merits of the journey and of the city. It had seemed too big, too loud, too noisy and too thickly inhabited to be really respectable or safe. In any case, out of her own area, Dot felt acutely uncomfortable.

'Cheer up, Dot dear! This ought to be fun. What could be more pleasant than a few days at the Test cricket, dinner with the Vice Chancellor, a little sightseeing, a trip on a ferry, and the Artist's Ball with that up-and-coming young modernist Chas Nuttall? A pattern young woman could not occupy herself so politely.'

'And no murders, Miss,' said Dot cautiously.

'No murders at all,' Phryne assured her. 'Now, a nap, a little light lunch in due course and Joss and Clarence are coming to take me for a walk around the city this afternoon. It will be all right, Dot, you'll see. A nice, peaceful holiday.'

Phryne flung herself down onto linen sheets on a well-sprung double bed, cast a bolster onto the carpeted floor, and was asleep in seconds. Dot looked at her.

'I do hope so, Miss,' she replied. She went to close the shutters against the roar of traffic in Castlereagh Street preparatory to taking her bath.

An hour later Dot was still leaning on the windowsill, staring at the harbour. It was fascinating. She had consulted the *Guide To Sydney*, which the Hotel Australia supplied to all its first class patrons, and was beginning to have a rough idea of both history and geography.

From her view above the warehouses of Circular Quay she could see constant traffic moving on the water under the half-built claw shape of the bridge. Devastated areas attended each end of the structure, which was crawling with life. Dot supposed that they must have demolished a lot of houses both on her end and at Milson's Point. She was not deceived by the statement in the *Guide* which told her that this was 'a much-overdue slum clearance'. Dot herself came from a slum. Where did the people go when they tore down all of those little houses, she wondered. Were they living in the street, like the beggar woman with the baby? Sleeping on the beach? Banished to the bush? Who cared about them, now that everyone was hungry? Who cared about them, now that Sydney was building a bridge?

But the bridge *was* interesting. It vibrated with activity. The ant-workmen moved all the time in ordered lines, pushing barrows and hauling steel joists. At The Rocks she saw lines of matchbox-sized trucks and even drays, bringing in more timber, more steel, and drums of metal cable. Hanging on strings like spiders, the riveters dangled over the edges, held up by cobwebs above the barely wrinkled satin cloth of the harbour.

Across that fabric moved the green ferries, puffing white smoke, their wakes following behind as straight as set-square lines. Pleasure craft wafted effortlessly under the black iron claws. A steamship butted in, its black funnel embossed with a golden bear, pulled by a yellow tug sitting down on the water like a duck.

'It's a patchwork quilt,' thought Dot, elbows on the sill. 'A huge, beautiful, complicated appliqué that changes every minute.'

Taxis hooted bitterly in the street below and carters bellowed. A newspaper boy screamed 'Extra' in a voice which suggested that he had some internal amplifying system. 'Yuxtry!' yelled the newspaper boy. *'Sinny Morn'n Hairoild!'*

Dot was reminded suddenly that she was dirty and tired and now she had black grime on her forearms as well, and she really needed a wash and a bit of a lie down. Even then, she was reluctant to close the window and shut out the harbour. Promising it that she would be back, she released the shutters, closing out the noise and the light.

Miss Fisher had picked at a poached trout in the Luncheon Room and was engaged in cutting up a peach and watching Dot struggle through a mountainous roast beef salad which she had decided she needed and now would rather die than waste. Jocelyn Hart and his best friend Clarence Ottery came in, doffing panamas, wiping foreheads and exclaiming about the heat.

'Is it often this hot in Sydney?' asked Phryne, smiling slightly as Dot managed to swallow the last mouthful and sat back, laying her cutlery across a triumphantly empty plate. 'You must have taken all those sermons about the starving children in China to heart, Dot dear.'

'And I had to put a penny in the Missionary Society box every Sunday, Miss,' Dot agreed. 'So many people hungry, it's a crime to waste food. Especially food like that,' added Dot, as the beef had been tinged pink and moist, the salads appropriately crisp, the pickles piquant and the bread

23

and butter so good as to almost reconcile her to a foreign place.

'It's summer, Miss Fisher,' Joss pointed out. 'And you're a lot further north than you're used to. We were thinking, being as it's so steamy and all, perhaps you'd like a trip on a ferry. What about that? Cooler out on the water, and we can go to Manly and buy an ice-cream and have a stroll on the shore.'

'Sounds lovely,' Phryne agreed. 'Would you like to come, Dot?'

'No, Miss, I've got to call my sister. I've got a telephone number for the shop she works in. If she can get away early I might go and see her.'

'Take a cab there and back, Dot dear, or you are welcome to bring her here, there's plenty of room.' Phryne stuffed a crumpled banknote into Dot's hand. 'We'll dine in tonight, order whatever you like. Don't know when I'll be back. We don't have any engagements until tomorrow, which is the Vice Chancellor's dinner. A little cricket and a nice trip on a ferry is just what we need, eh?'

Dot smiled. Despite this strange anthill city, she didn't think that even Phryne could get into much trouble on the Manly ferry. She handed over Phryne's shady hat and went off to reason with the telephone, an instrument which she viewed with grave distrust. It didn't seem natural to carry voices over wires.

Phryne took the arms of both young men as they stepped down into Castlereagh Street. 'Well, gentlemen, here I am, as you wanted me to be. I am in Sydney and I am dining with the Vice Chancellor at the Great Hall tomorrow night.

While this street is full of people I don't think any of them are listening, and I have even ventured forth in your company without my confidential maid. Now, perhaps, you can tell me what this terrible event was, why you went to the trouble of finding my dear Peter Smith in his cane-fields and getting a letter of introduction, and why you wanted me to come to Sydney and scrape acquaintance with the University elite?'

'It's complicated,' began Joss, avoiding a clanging tram.

'A bit difficult to explain,' agreed Clarence, as they gained the other side of the road.

Phryne looked into each sweating, desperately earnest face and relented.

'Very well, then, let us get to the quay, find a ferry, and you can tell me when we have somewhere to sit down. Which way?'

'To the water,' said Joss. 'Circular Quay.'

They crossed several smaller streets, a patch of green with a large sandstone monument and an anchor on dead grass, and then emerged into a broad sweep of quay and an expanse of water. That's Sydney, thought Phryne. The harbour is an imperative; one must see it. And even then it always catches us by surprise.

'There's a ferry,' exclaimed Joss. 'Come on – we'll just get it.'

Much against her will, Phryne grabbed for her hat and ran, pacing her escorts and diving between a man with two greyhounds and a stout woman carrying a basket of pineapples. Phryne paid for tokens and they raced through the turnstiles, up the gangplank and landed on deck out of breath and scarlet with exertion just as the steam whistle shrieked and the *Dee Why* pulled out of her mooring.

They found a seat at the prow, where the smoke poured back over the ferry's roof and the brass rail was smeared by thousands of hands. They had been right. It was cooler on the water and it was pleasant to be moving. Seagulls flicked effortlessly past, hanging for a moment as though they were on wires: clean and perfect from curved beak to fanned tail.

'She's bigger than the K class *Lady* ferries,' commented Joss. 'She has to cross the Heads, which are open sea, so she has to be stronger. The *Lady* ferries are confined to the inner harbour. Though I don't know what'll happen to the ferries after they finish the bridge. All go out of service, I expect.'

'That would be a pity,' commented Phryne, fanning herself with her hat. 'What about the bridge? It's huge,' she said, as the *Dee Why* puffed importantly past the open spans of the uncompleted structure. They looked like claws made of black iron and they made Phryne uncomfortable.

'Been trying to build it for decades,' chuckled Clarence. 'Sir Henry Parkes declared: "Who will stand at my right hand and build the bridge with me?" Took so long to get it going that the wags reckon someone was standing *on* his right hand, all right. But they call it "the iron lung".'

Phryne cocked an eyebrow.

'Because it keeps so many people breathing,' explained Clarence. 'Four thousand men work on the bridge, and then there's the feeding, lodging and clothing of them and the horses and the mechanics and all their wives and children. God knows what'll happen to the poor labouring classes when it's finished. We've already got slums worse than anything you might have seen in Fitzroy,' he said, almost complacently.

Phryne had seen slums in Paris and London which she thought the equal in squalor of anywhere in the world, but she did not reply. The movement of the steamer was comfortable, gently swaying on the flat calm, but the air was getting heavier and heavier and clouds were building up behind the claws of the bridge.

'Surely it's going to storm,' she commented.

'Before evening,' agreed Joss.

'And me without an umbrella. I wondered why so many people were carrying them. Oh, well, never mind. I'm waterproof enough. Now, gentlemen, if you please. The story. However complicated, however difficult.'

They exchanged glances. Nice young men, Phryne thought, one blond, one brown, with frank blue eyes and loose linen coats. Jocelyn tall and slim with a slightly hesitant air which was most attractive. Clarence dapper and alarmingly self-assured, languid and graceful, very conscious of his beauty. Both, she knew, students of the arts. Both a little disconcerted, now that it had come to the point. Fluent, polished, their public-school voices still a little foreign to her ear. They didn't seem to know how to begin, so she spoke.

'You are both at the University of Sydney,' she began. They nodded. 'You are both studying Arts.' They nodded again. 'Good. Now, has this something to do with the University?' Nods. 'With the Arts Faculty?' More nods. 'Tell me it isn't a murder,' she implored. 'I promised Dot, no murders.'

'Not a murder.' Joss made a huge effort and began to speak. Once he started, he did not seem to be able to stop and delivered himself of the whole problem in one lump. 'You see, it's like this. There's been a theft. From the safe in the Dean's office. It's a great big green-painted safe. In the office of the Dean of Arts.' Phryne waved a hand to indicate that she had grasped the essential point, that the safe was in the office of the Dean of Arts. Joss crushed his hat between his hands and went on. 'There were a lot of things in the safe. The Dean's wife's garnets. A bit of papyrus from Arabia. A lump of rock from the Northern Territory, some sort of Aboriginal weapon, belongs to Anthropology. An old, illuminated book belonging to some queen. Some money, not much. But the thing is, you see, there were the exam papers, the final exam papers, Greek, Latin, the notes for the viva voce, and they're all gone.'

'Well, then, the professors will just have to write themselves new papers,' said Phryne, unable to see the problem.

'Yes, of course, that's all right,' said Clarence easily. 'I knew you'd mess this up, Joss, old man, you don't have any talent for extempore exposition. It's always been my main skill, as well as bluffing my way through exams with the minimum of effort. Effort is so bad for the complexion.' He took Phryne's hand confidingly. Phryne smiled. The affectation was practised and

28

pretty to watch. Clarence continued. 'It's our friend. He's been accused of the theft and is likely to be sent down. We know he didn't do it, but we also know that the University Senate are very set against him because he's a disciple of Anderson the philosophy prof. The University gods think that Anderson is very unsound indeed. He doesn't even stand to attention when the carillon plays "God Save the King" at noon. Sort of radical chap who might tell his students to steal exam papers.'

Phryne might have been annoyed by being brought to Sydney merely to recover a lost exam paper, but her companions were deadly serious. Both faces were turned towards her. Joss's hand, hanging loose at his side, clenched, and then he snatched off his hat. Even the lazy Ottery was keyed-up and tense. There was clearly more to it.

'See, our friend hasn't got our background. He's a scholarship boy with a bit of a chip on his shoulder. Radical sort of chap, too, come to think of it. But he's staked everything on graduating. He's going in for academia. Just the sort of person we need, too, shake the place up. Everyone says he has the makings of a real scholar.'

'What's his name?'

'Harcourt,' said Joss, mangling his innocent panama. 'Adam Harcourt. You see, we can't call in the police, the University won't allow it, and in any case they'd just leap to the same conclusion. And the U doesn't have scandals, of course, so the Senate will just send Adam down and deprive him of his chance at a degree and there will go his chance of a career. And we're afraid – he's so serious, you know, not like us – I mean, the Pater'd be cross if Clarry failed or was rusticated, and my father doesn't want me to go to University anyway, but if Harcourt is thrown out he might do something ... silly.'

'I see. Does he know that's why I'm here?'

'Of course not!' Clarence was shocked. 'You haven't agreed to help yet. No use getting the poor chap's hopes up.'

'What do you expect me to do, Joss?'

'Why, find him innocent, of course. If the U knows you and you've dined with the VC, then you've got the entree and can go wherever you like, carrying out your investigation and drawing your conclusions. It'll be very educational to watch you,' added Joss, seriously.

Phryne was about to instruct the young men to read more Greek and less Sexton Blake when she caught sight of a shore approaching. Manly, if she was any judge, source of a nice walk below the pines and, with any luck, ice-cream. The crossing of the Heads had been accomplished with such skill that she had only just registered the change of current.

'How did they know – rather, why do they think that Adam Harcourt stole the exam papers?' she asked as the landing stage, emblazoned with an advertisement for Fry's Malteasers, slid into view.

'They found them locked in his carrel at the library,' said Clarence reluctantly.

'Oh.'

'Will you help us?' asked Joss, taking up her hand and kissing it.

'If you buy me an ice,' said Phryne, 'I'll think about it.'

Two

'Bonfires? Strewth, we'd burn anything! Matteresses, make good smoke, matteresses, get rid of the bugs and the cockroaches ... once we pinched Quong Kee's laundry cart and threw it on the flames, up it went ... then the fire brigade would come. Killjoys! And everyone what was dancing round and singing ... would poke borak. Names! Make yer teeth turn black. But sometimes we'd cut the hoses, turn the water on the firemen ... great days. Yer don't get days like them anymore.'

Ruth Park interviewing an old man in the
Argyle Cut in *A Companion Guide to Sydney*

Phryne had eaten her Neapolitan ice-cream under the disinfectant shade of the cypresses, walked slowly around the small resort of Manly, and was about to suggest that they board the *Dee Why* for home when the sky broke open and all the water which had been idling about as droplets in the overheated air said the equivalent of 'the hell with it' and let gravity win.

'This isn't rain,' she called through a curtain of water, 'this is a deluge.'

'Clarry, did you put in that order for gopher wood?' yelled Joss.

'They were out of stock; we'll just have to swim home,' replied Clarence.

31

'We'll get soaked,' commented Joss. 'What are we going to do?'

'The pub,' said Phryne.

'It's shut,' said Joss.

'Is it?' asked Phryne. She walked – running would only make the drops collide at greater velocity, with her already drenched frame – across the street and banged on the door of the Steyne Hotel.

'Bona Fide Traveller,' said Phryne to the huge red-faced man who allowed the door to grind open an inch. 'Find the book and I'll sign it, and bring me three towels, a gin and tonic and two beers for my escorts.'

She shoved the door heartily, it opened, and she was inside out of the rain, which was increasing to a torrent, drumming hard on the pavement and splashing back knee-high. The landlord, who had to stoop to see Phryne's face, yielded to superior force and led the way to a small plush parlour designed for the accommodation of ladies. She dried her hair, arms and hands and signed the Traveller's Ledger as Phryne Fisher – London. Which was, if only historically, true. The gin and tonic was well made and the air was beginning to lose its stifling quality.

'Well, that's an improvement,' she said, looking out of the heavily curtained window at the streams flowing down the street outside. Joss and Clarence accepted their beers and drank them in dazed silence. Eventually Joss said to Clarence, 'I never, *never* managed to get into a pub which had closed its doors before. I think we made the right choice of detective, eh, Clarence?'

Clarence nodded, appearing to be much cast

down by the rain, which had ruined his carefully arranged coiffure. He slicked down his hair with the palm of his hand and studied himself dolefully in the fly-flecked pub mirror. The sight of the dapper young man appearing between two Staffordshire dogs distracted Phryne for a moment. It was quite odd, almost surrealist.

'I like your cheek,' said Phryne without heat. 'I haven't agreed to help you yet.'

'What more will it take to convince you?' asked Clarence, unenthusiastically. 'I bet this fabric will spot. I don't like rain!'

Phryne smiled and offered him her comb. He accepted it with a graceful bend.

'Hmm. Not sure. What have you got so far?'

'Well, there's the introduction from the anarchist, he was hard to find.' Joss had rubbed his head dry and his hair was beginning to curl. 'Fortunately we've got a friend in the Australian Workers' Union, he goes out to the cane-fields and he knew Red Pete; he said that this Smith man got a letter from you, so we asked our friend to tell him all about it and he agreed to introduce us. You have to give us marks for effort.'

'I do,' said Phryne.

'And I suppose that everyone in Melbourne knows that you're an anarchist?' asked Clarence, insinuatingly, handing back the comb with another bow.

'I don't care a straw if they do,' replied Phryne, looking the young man in the eye and daring him to continue with anything which even remotely resembled blackmail. He subsided into gloomy meditations on the subject of rain and linen suits.

'What if we just beg?' asked Joss, dropping to his knees at Miss Fisher's wet bare feet. 'Come on, Clarence. Stop sitting there arguing.' He dragged his friend down to kneel beside him and put up his hands, palm to palm, like a good child.

Phryne had defences against almost any argument, but not against two pretty young men at her feet. Very decorative they were and she might have uses for them. They both looked up into her face with an identical expression of lamb-like faith. They do believe that I can solve this, thought Phryne. And although I did promise Dot no murders, this is just a theft.

'Please?' asked Clarence, and Jocelyn echoed, 'Pretty please?'

'All right,' agreed Phryne, and called for another drink.

The landlord considered that they had all, self-evidently, had enough.

Phryne returned to the Hotel Australia in time to change for dinner to find her clothes laid out neatly on her bed and a note from Dot: 'Gone to see Joan back soon' propped on the dressing table. Joan, Phryne knew, was married to an ironmonger who had a shop somewhere in Woolloomooloo, a name clearly made up by a printer with a lot of surplus letter 'o's. She sat down in an easy chair to read the paper. The *Sydney Morning Herald* was extending itself in the matter of cricket.

The team is definitely ageing, Phryne thought as she ran a pearly fingernail down the list of English players. Hobbs was over forty, and so were Tyldesly, Hendren and Phillip Mead. Of the bowlers, Geary's nose had been broken at Perth but he would play in Sydney. White was a slow left-hander who bored batsmen out, Staples and Tate medium pace stock bowlers who were very hard to score from, and there was also the young man Larwood, of whom great things were expected. Wally Hammond could bowl as well, but he was such a magnificent bat that no sensible captain would risk him injuring himself while bowling. Of the Australians, the old guard predominated also. Woodfull, Richardson, Ponsford and Hendry as batsmen, Grimmett, Ironmonger and Blackie (a newcomer at forty-six) bowling slowly. It didn't look good for the Australians, especially in view of the Brisbane Test. The Australian fielding had been sloppy, the bowling inaccurate, the batting disgruntled, and the Test lost by the dreadful, unprecedented margin of 675 runs.

It didn't look like interesting cricket, thought Phryne, but even the most tedious match was worth watching for awhile; one never knew what would happen, a fact which differentiated cricket from all other forms of sport. Phryne had never been interested in football, except as a tribal ritual, nor in tennis, motor racing, horse racing or athletics. But as a small girl, she had started playing cricket amongst brothers, across a cobbled back lane with a fence for one wicket and a kero tin for the other, and the feeling of excitement had never left her. Phryne still felt the fierce pleasure of thwacking the cloth and cork ball solidly with the paling bat, even though such a shot was inevitably over the fence, six and out. In summer the sole outing for the Fisher children had been a train trip to Altona Beach, where they had played cricket on the greyish sands and her brothers had repeatedly struck the ball into the sea, whence it had been retrieved by a large mongrel dog called Rags.

Phryne's newspaper slipped from her lap and she closed her eyes. Those had not been good days, as the family had been very poor. Phryne had salvaged bruised fruit and veg from the pig bins outside the Victoria market, had been frequently hungry and infrequently beaten by her drunken ne'er-do-well father, had watched one of her sisters die of diphtheria, had never been really warm or really full. Her mother had worked all the hours there were cleaning houses – but it had been fun, playing cricket on Altona Beach with Rags, drawing lots for who got to be Victor Trumper...

She woke with a start as a gentle tone sounded. The Australia provided a dressing gong to inform its guests that it was time to prepare for dinner. Phryne duly dressed and dined lightly on salmon mayonnaise and salad, drank a few glasses of champagne and went back to her room expecting Dot to have returned. Dot was not there, no message had been left by a deferential switchboard, and Phryne was beginning to worry. There were a lot of perils in a foreign city for a good looking young woman, especially if she was foolish enough to appear at all lost or vulnerable. Especially if she did not know the rules, which streets should not be walked down during certain hours, which pubs sold sly grog, which Push ruled which area.

It had been the same in the beginning, when the colony had been established on raw alcohol and flogging, when the Rum Corps – a regiment so corrupt that it disintegrated in a high wind – had ruled the roost and expelled the governor. A city in the old days of mud and disease and reeking poverty; where blood and flesh from the triangle had blown back into the faces of the witnesses.

Phryne shuddered. She was glad that she had not been there when gentlemen hunted kangaroos across the Domain. Life then had been far too solitary, poor, nasty, brutish and short. What would it have been like, to come up from the stinking hold of a ship and see – what? The harbour, the barren shore, the endless wastes of scrubby grass and – to their eyes – colourless forest. No familiar plants, strange animals, birds with no song, but the same old lash, the same old lice and rats and starvation, the specially imported filth and injustice. They must have felt utterly lost, abandoned on the edge of the world, and angry – yes, very angry. So they had behaved like a conquering army, but never one who meant to stay. Cut down the trees, ugly untidy things, tear down the forests, destroy the wildlife, murder the hapless original inhabitants who had lived here for thousands of years without harm. Wipe out a language? Why not? All heathens, anyway. Didn't even make good slaves...

Some of the buildings were still standing: the barracks, the hospital. There was a flavour in the city of its convict past, its brutal origins, which underlay the high Victorian buildings and the air of gentility. Like the tank stream, it ran underground. Little Chicago, Jack Robinson called it. It had been the same in the 1890s. Sydney seemed to have more gangs of vicious criminals, more violence, more murders, than quiet peaceful Melbourne where the last criminal excitement had been Snowy Cutmore shooting Pretty Dulcie and Squizzy Taylor. Probably Melbourne was just as crime-ridden, but there crime had no element of display; there was something about Sydney that made its crooks advertise their talents. It had been the same in Henry Lawson's day. He had produced a very clean version of the gutter-ballad Phryne had heard in Melbourne:

'Would you knock him down and rob him?' said the Leader of the Push.
'Why, I'd knock him down and fuck him,' said the Bastard from the Bush.

It was said that Darlinghurst and Woolloomooloo were impassable after dark. Tensions between Catholic and Protestant were high, there was the admixture of degraded, detribalised and terribly treated Aborigines in Redfern, returned soldiers in the much-rumoured White Army, communists of all stamps and dyes, artists and whores and poets and thieves and the downtrodden desperate poor, out of work and out of place.

A nasty brew, thought Phryne. A very dangerous cauldron bubbling next to the peaceful harbour.

Phryne had not asked Dot for her sister's address. She had in all probability been asked to stay for tea and was presently playing with the children in a respectable ironmongery somewhere while Joan's husband got on with his iron-mongering and Joan made tea for her sister. It would be premature to call out the guard.

Phryne opened her travelling book – Mary Kingsley's *Travels in West Africa* – and sat down to sip cognac and read. A light breeze blew through the open shutters and brought her the distant noise of traffic and a whiff of salt air. She was just laughing at Miss Kingsley's statement that it was only after falling into a leopard trap and emerging unscathed from a pit lined with spikes that one realised the usefulness of a good thick serge skirt when she heard the door click and Dot came in.

'Hello, Dot,' said Phryne, looking up from the book. 'Did you have a good...' her voice trailed off. Dot's face was drawn, her hair coming unplaited; she slumped wearily in her chair and she smelt strongly of beer, cheap scent and tobacco smoke. Phryne knew that Dot rarely drank, certainly did not smoke and never used any perfume other than Potter and Moore's Lavender Water.

Phryne picked up the telephone and ordered tea to be brought immediately if not sooner. Then she filled a glass and took it to her maid.

'Drink some water, Dot dear, and tell me what's wrong. I've sent for tea, it should be here directly.'

'Oh, Miss, it's awful,' Dot whispered. She took the glass and drank.

'Your sister, Dot, has something happened to your sister?'

Dot gave Phryne such a sorrowful look that she drew an instant conclusion.

'Oh, Dot dear, don't say that she's dead?'

'Better if she was,' said Dot with unexpected

vehemence, and burst into tears.

Phryne rallied around with handkerchiefs and cool water and after ten minutes Dot was sitting at the table, red-eyed but with dry cheeks, sipping very strong, heavily sugared tea to which a judicious quantity of Phryne's good cognac had been added. Phryne did not ply her with questions, but after awhile Dot began to talk.

'I telephoned this afternoon, Miss, and Joan's husband answered, and he said she wasn't there. He's a bit of a rude bloke, Jim is, anyway, and I didn't take no notice and said I'd come and visit at six, and he didn't say I couldn't, so I took some cakes and went to the place, it's a shop in William Street, I think he's not doing too good. The shop was open and I walked in and there was little Dottie tied by the leg to a desk at the front, tied up like a dog! And little Mary sitting in the gutter, splashing in the gutter, in the filthy water. So I heaved up one little one and released the other – and there was a raw red ring around her poor little ankle! – and I promised them cakes if I could wash them, and we went into the smithy and there was Jim sitting yarning with some mates of his, and I asked him where my sister was and he stood up and yelled at me, "She's run off!" and I couldn't imagine Joan doing that, not leaving her kids, and I said so, and he said, "You're another, all sluts, all the Williams girls are sluts and so is their mother," and I just took the children, who didn't ought to hear things like that, into the house behind the shop. It was filthy. Joan would never leave it like that. I didn't know what to do, Miss.'

'How awful, Dot. What *did* you do?'

'I made a fire in the copper and washed the babies and changed them and made tea and fed them the cakes like I promised, and they told me that Mummy had gone away and hadn't been back for a long time. There was a light in the little house next door and I went there and an Irish-woman answered, Mrs Ryan. She had two kids herself and her house was real clean so I asked her to mind my nieces and I gave her a pound and told her I'd be back tomorrow to talk to her, and the kids knew her and she took them in.'

Dot paused to take a long sip of tea, gathering her thoughts. Even when shocked and exhausted, Dot tried to tell a connected narrative. Phryne looked at her with deep concern. Dorothy would not be forgiving of a sister who had taken to the bad, and this sounded like the respectable wife and mother led comprehensively astray.

'Then I called my brother-in-law out of his shop and into the street to try and get some sense out of him. All he would say was that Joan was in Darlinghurst and hadn't been home for a week, he always knew she was a tart and he was right, and I could take the little bastards and drown them and he didn't care. And a lot of other things.' Dot blushed red. 'So I went into Darlinghurst to try and find her.'

'Dot, you are a brave girl!' exclaimed Phryne. 'I would have thought twice about doing that.'

'But I didn't find her,' confessed Dot. 'And it was awful. Men kept on making ... suggestions to me, and it was all smoke and beer and girls with cheap clothes. I gave it up for the night when someone tried to pinch my purse and I had to

41

dong him. Then I had to catch the last tram because I'd given my taxi money to Mrs Ryan. What are we going to do, Miss Phryne?'

'We are going to find your sister, retrieve her children, and manage the situation as well as it can be managed,' said Phryne firmly. 'Have you any clue as to where she might have gone?'

'I found her box,' said Dot. 'Her papers and things. I felt funny about taking them but...'

'Good. Have some more tea and I'll have a look, so you won't have to feel funny. Have you a photograph of your sister?'

'Only the wedding one. I took that, too.'

Dot poured herself some more tea and Phryne spilled the paper bag of Joan's possessions onto the floor and sat down to sort it. This was an unexpected turn of events. Two mysteries now to solve: the exam paper theft and the flight of Dot's sister. It looked like being a more interesting visit to Sydney than she had expected.

The photograph was large, expensive, and evidently taken out of a frame. A big bruiser of a man stood next to a seated woman in trailing draperies. Her veil had been put back from her wreath of orange blossom. She had Dot's face, round and girlish, and lighter hair, shingled. Phryne expected that her eyes would be blue and her hair blonde. The paper bag contained a marriage certificate, the 'lines' which no respectable woman ever allowed to pass out of her hands, a collection of receipted bills clipped together, a dance card with attached pencil, several visiting cards including one of Phryne's which Dot must have sent her, three birthday cards and a few postcards. Not

much for twenty-three years of blameless existence.

'I'll take the wedding group to a photographer's
tomorrow to have him make a separate picture of
the face,' she said. 'Then we can show it to
people who might know Joan. What do you think
has happened to her, Dot?'

'She's been kidnapped,' said Dot, bursting into
tears again. 'She's been white-slaved. She would
never have left her children else. Men can't look
after children. He had poor little Dorothy chained
up like a dog, and he couldn't have cared less if
Mary had been run over by a truck. And he called
her a slut! And me,' added Dot, who had no
doubts as to her own purity. She might or might
not marry that nice policeman Hugh, who had
been courting her assiduously, but in any case she
would go to her marriage bed as virginal as the
Queen of Heaven Herself.

Phryne knew that white-slaving was largely a
myth. She was considering the receipted bills. Mrs
James Thompson had paid large sums for rent, for
materials and for cartage. Where had Mrs James
Thompson, wife of an ironmonger who was 'not
doing too good', got seven pounds for solder and
miscellaneous piping, twenty for stock delivered
and eleven pounds for rent? Although women did
run away from husbands and children, Phryne
suspected that Joan's extra-curricular activities
had been going on for some time – at least six
months, to judge by the receipts. And then – what?
What precipitating factor had driven her out,
leaving her babies to be neglected by her disgusted
husband? Where was she? Was there something

which Jim Thompson wasn't telling Dot?

There was always the likelihood that the husband, discovering that his virtuous wife had been prostituting herself in order to pay the bills, had strangled her in a fit of outraged propriety and burned her body in the smith's fire, for which he had a good chance of being acquitted. The law did not care what happened to worthless whores.

Better not mention that possibility to Dot.

'Yes, well, nothing more we can do tonight, Dot. Now you are going to take another sup of my good brandy and then you are going to bed, and you are going to sleep – don't argue with me, Dorothy,' said Phryne sternly. 'We'll get the photo tomorrow and then we can go to Chas Nuttall's digs – if anyone knows Darlinghurst, it will be that most Bohemian of young artists. We'll find her, Dot,' she said gently. 'I promise.'

Dot drank the brandy and went to bed biddably. Phryne gathered up the documents and replaced them in the paper bag. She looked into the face of the bride and said quietly, 'Joan, I'm afraid I'm going to have to find you. I do hope that you want to be found.'

Phryne could not see any end to her investigation of Mrs James Thompson's disappearance but disillusion and pain for Dot, of whom she was very fond, and she very quietly cursed the name of propriety. She might have added husbands of whatever cut and stripe wherever found, but her eyes were closing and she put herself to bed instead.

Joss might well have been right about Sydney having slums worse than any to be found in Fitzroy, Phryne reflected, and the fact that they were not as bad as the lower arrondissements in Paris or the East End of London did not say much for them. Rows of terrace houses, built in a fine flourish of slum clearance in the 1890s, were crumbling and leaning and falling slowly down. The streets, though paved, were cracked and unsafe. The roofs were cocked like hats over one eye. The streets of the 'Loo stank of bad drainage and oysters for supper and vomited alcohol in front of the lavatory-tiled swill houses which, every day at six o'clock, disgorged a horde of drunken wretches into the street. This was a place where all the landlords lived far away on the North Shore and never came into such a dangerous area. This was a place of moonlight flits, pavement evictions, bruised women and undernourished children.

Yet bougainvillea poured red and purple down the cuts and steps which connected one level to another. Jacaranda trees flowered azure as a Mediterranean sky in neglected gardens. Jasmine twined with roses over broken fences and terrible outside privies. Everywhere children quarrelled and fought and played cricket across the streets. Washing flapped on lines. Brawling, yeasty, unconfined life went on in the tumbledown houses and sheds and a thin dog chewed pineapple rinds in the gutter at Phryne's feet.

It was exotic and lively though, at ten in the morning, subdued. Dot and Phryne knocked at the door of Mrs Ryan's Old Clothes Shop and heard a voice scolding, 'Play nice, now,' as the

45

door was opened.

Mrs Ryan was about thirty, a stocky woman in respectable black, hair neatly coiled on the nape of her neck, standing easily with a baby on her hip. The shop smelt musty, but the widow was redolent of yellow soap and the baby she was holding was shining with health, though dressed only in a washed-thin nappy and a sunbonnet. Two identical sets of dark blue eyes regarded the visitors.

'Miss Williams, come in and have some tea, I'll mash it directly. This is your Miss Fisher? Pleased to meet ye, Ma'am,' said Mrs Ryan, making a suspicion of a curtsy. She led the way into a large kitchen, which was full of children, noise, and the smell of soup.

Two infants detached themselves from a game involving a ball passed from hand to hand around a circle and ran yelling to Dot, colliding with her knees. 'Auntie, Auntie!' they cried. Phryne stepped back, inspected each indistinguishable infant as it was presented to her, and gave each of them a large lollipop, coloured red and green. Both Mary and Dorothy plugged these into their mouths. As the lollipops were passed around, silence fell in the kitchen.

'Nice to hear yourself think,' commented Mrs Ryan. 'I've washed your two again this morning, Miss Williams, and little Dot's ankle I've mended with some iodine – terrible to think of the poor creature being tied by the leg like a calf! But men will be men,' she sighed. Phryne sat down at a scrubbed table and observed that this was true and would Mrs Ryan continue to mind the children until their mother returned?

'To be sure,' said the widow promptly. 'I would have taken them in myself had I known that Mrs Thompson was away.' She mentioned her terms, which seemed hardly enough. Phryne inquired politely. Mrs Ryan explained.

'I've got the house, see, Mr Ryan finished paying for it before he was taken from me, and there was the Bridge money that the company paid because he fell while he was working for them, twenty pounds it was, I've got that put aside for a rainy day and the Burial Club buried him nice and proper with a stone and all. I just have myself and my two to feed. Not many people around here have any silver to spare.'

Phryne, who did, added a sizeable payment to cover emergencies and Mrs Ryan closed a hand over the notes and stowed them in an old-fashioned petticoat pocket. Phryne made a mental note to obtain a couple of these admirable articles as soon as possible. None of her clothes had any pockets and she hated carrying a bag.

'Now, Mrs Ryan, can you tell me anything about my sister?' asked Dot, who had waited with ill-concealed impatience while the tea was made and poured into three matching Coles cups.

'I didn't know her well,' said Mrs Ryan slowly. 'She seemed a nice lady. That's all I can tell you.'

Phryne could take a hint as well as the next woman.

'Dot, wouldn't you like to take the children into the garden?' asked Phryne. 'It seems a pity to waste all this sun.'

'Yes, take the little darlings to see the chooks,'

said Mrs Ryan. Dot went out obediently, shooing six toddlers out onto the back steps.

'Now, tell me what you didn't want Joan's sister to hear,' said Phryne, laying a pound note on the table. Mrs Ryan scanned Phryne's face. The widow laid a workworn hand over the money.

'God love you, you're fast on the uptake for all you're a high-born lady. I think Mrs Thompson took the bad path. I saw her collected from here every night for a week by Tithe Devine's motor car, and she came home God knows how late. Her husband knew, too. Pleased to take the money, maybe, though he beat her for being a whore. Where she is now I don't know, but you could always ask Tillie, though she's a wicked strong brawling woman. Hush! They're coming back. She's lucky to have a devoted sister who is a good girl, anyone can see that,' added Mrs Ryan. 'But I don't know that she wants to be found.'

That was Phryne's fear, also. But she said nothing to Dot: she would find out soon enough. If twenty pounds was the price for a man's life in Sydney, what could a woman possibly hope to realise on her own virtue?

Three

But this measure [to establish the University of Sydney] this which is to enlighten the mind, refine the understanding, to elevate the soul of our fellow men; this, of all our acts, contains the germ of immortality – this, I believe will live.

William Charles Wentworth, speech to the Legislative Council

By the time Phryne arrived at the lodgings of that advanced young Modernist Chas Nuttall it was already three o'clock and she was getting tired. The slums were oppressing her spirits and what she had heard about Tillie Devine had not elevated them to any degree. She had come a long way from the East End slums where she had been born. Somehow, Phryne doubted that she had a heart of gold. In fact, she was reputed to be even more dangerous than Kate Leigh, Queen of Sly Grog, who ruled the other vices in the Cross. No one seemed eager to assist Phryne in her inquiries as to where the elusive Miss Devine could be found and she had been tracking in circles all afternoon.

'Dot, I think I need some advice before I go any further,' she said to her maid.

'Advice, Miss?'

'Yes. I need to talk to a cop; I'll ring Jack

Robinson and get him to find a useful one for me, and I'll comb the dens of iniquity tomorrow. If Chas and his friends haven't seen Joan, of course.'

'Miss Phryne, you don't think my sister is in any danger, do you?' asked Dot. 'If you did, you'd go and find her right now, even if you do have to dine with the Vice Chancellor.'

'Sorry, Dot dear, I really am sorry,' said Phryne. 'But you're right. I don't think she's being held against her will, no. I think she's fallen into bad company. That doesn't make her any less your sister, nor am I less concerned about her. But I'm not getting anywhere asking questions from the outside. I need an insider – perhaps Chas, perhaps someone else. I need the equivalent of Bert and Cec. This looks like the bell,' she added, and pressed it.

A window opened far above and a female voice called, 'Who's there?'

'Phryne Fisher,' Phryne yelled back. 'Looking for–'

'Don't say it!' urged a male voice behind the woman. 'Cop this and come in, Phryne. Third floor.'

A key tied to a celluloid baby doll bounced down the flaking blue paint of the facade. Phryne caught it. The kewpie had been filled with sand and was quite heavy.

Phryne and Dot mounted the hollowed sandstone steps through a peeling blue door and climbed stairs. The house smelt strongly of frying onions and old mattresses. They avoided a pram on one landing (it contained a collection of news-papers and bottles) and a dismembered bicycle on

50

the next, finally arriving out of breath at the third floor attic. The landing was gritty with fallen plaster and Phryne was out of humour. When the door opened and she could speak again, she demanded, 'What's going on, Chas? You knew I was coming today.'

'The landlady's been around,' whispered Chas through a face full of stubble.

'That's why you are growing a beard?' Phryne was amused.

'It's all right for you capitalists,' exclaimed the young man bitterly. 'I get five shillings a canvas if I'm lucky and the canvas itself costs a shilling, not to mention the paint. I've moved so often that my furniture's got wheels. Meet my model. This is Blonde Maureen.'

'Hello,' simpered Blonde Maureen, taking Phryne's hand, holding it for a moment and then dropping it. She was undeniably blonde, listless and pretty. 'Well, hoo-roo, Chas. See you tonight at Theo's.'

'Wait a moment,' said Phryne. She produced the picture of Joan Thompson. 'Do you know this woman?'

'Why, what's she done?' demanded the model.

'Nothing. I just want to talk to her. Do you know her? There might be a few shillings in it,' hinted Phryne.

'Nah,' decided Blonde Maureen. 'For a moment I thought she looked like Darlo Annie, but now I ain't sure. Sorry.'

They heard her clatter down the stairs.

'Well, Chas, how about you?' Phryne offered him the photograph. 'If you can find her for me,

I'll pay your rent.'

'True dinks, Phryne?' exclaimed the artist eagerly. 'Give us a look.' He took the photograph over to the light. This was provided by a large gap, innocent of glass, which might have been meant to have a shutter in the days when this house had been clean, respectable and ordered, fifty years ago.

Chas Nuttall had always been a thin young man, careless of haircuts and dressed in old flannels and whatever shirts came to hand. He was still under-fed, scruffy and badly dressed, and his nascent beard accentuated his resemblance to a sun-downer who had been on the wallaby far too long. Phryne liked him because, however poor, he had always resisted the siren call of work. Chas Nuttall was devoted to his art and, like all artists, was always ready to shamelessly sacrifice everyone else, as well as himself, to his Muse.

It was a pity that his Muse did not inspire him to paint anything recognisable. His canvases were splashed with roughly cube-shaped bridges, houses and nudes, garishly coloured and carelessly drawn. Phryne was leafing through the paintings stacked against the wall – the frying pan might have disgraced a stockman's camp and the bed might not have been made in the present century, but his paints were all laid out in meticulous rows and his palette was exact – when she heard him exclaim, 'Cripes! It *is* her!'

'Is who?'

'Blonde Maureen was right, I think,' said the young man, biting his lip. 'I think this is Darlo Annie. Looks a good bit younger here and ... er

52

'... not so glamorous, but I reckon it's her.'

'Good. Where can I find her?'

'She'll be at Theo's tonight. She's always at Theo's. Though come to think of it I haven't seen her for a few days. Works out of Palmer Street, usually.'

'One of Tillie Devine's women?' asked Phryne.

'Maybe. I don't ... I haven't got the money to ... and in any case I don't like to...' stuttered Chas.

Before Dot could say anything, a nasal voice and a sharp knock interrupted.

'I know you're home, Mr Nuttall, you come out here! If I don't get my rent then it's out of my house you'll go neck and crop and all your nasty paintings. You owe me seventeen and sixpence and I'll have my money!'

'The landlady?' asked Phryne.

'How did you guess?' asked Chas, scratching his bristling chin.

Phryne opened the door and smiled at a scrawny woman in a wrapper and down at heel slippers. 'Hello, here's the back rent.' She counted it out into an astounded hand. 'Here's an extra month.' She counted that out as well, then instructed, 'Leave the receipt on the hallstand. Goodbye,' she said and shut the door.

'Now, Chas dear, you don't need to grow a beard; have a shave, there's a good chap, or even the Artist's Ball will be shocked. You look like a swaggie. Now, Chas, listen carefully. I've paid the rent and I won't ask for it back. Are you sure that the woman in that photograph is Darlo Annie?'

'Like I said, fairly sure. She's pretty, isn't she? Bit like Nellie Cameron. Darlo Annie's got blonde hair and big china-blue eyes – that help?'

Phryne looked at Dot, who nodded.

'Might have helped, at that,' she agreed. 'Thanks, Chas. I'll see you tonight at Theo's – where is Theo's?'

'Thirty-four Campbell Street – only gets going after about midnight. Any cabbie'll take you there,' said Chas, searching for a razor amongst a mess of belongings. 'If I see Darlo Annie I'll try and keep her with me – if you can give me a pound for her time. I'm a bit short this week. Though now I don't have to worry about the rent I can buy a new tube of cerulean blue.'

Phryne handed over a pound, returned the kewpie doll she had been holding all the time and escorted a very miserable Dot down the stairs.

'I'll go to Theo's after I return from the University,' she said. 'I can at least find out if Darlo Annie is your sister Joan. If so, what do you want me to say to her?'

'You aren't going to take me with you?'

'No, Dot dear, I think I'll get on better on my own.'

'Tell her – tell her I still care about her and ask her to come home,' said Dot, dragging in a huge breath. 'Whatever she's done, she's still my sister.'

'Bravo, Dot. Now let's get out of here. If I'm going to be trawling Bohemia tonight, I'll need a nap.'

The Hotel Australia seemed even more of a cool, clean haven after Woolloomooloo, Darlinghurst, heat and dirt. Phryne bathed and lay down to sleep, and Dot sat up to watch the harbour and worry. The children would be all right. If Jim

54

Thompson had abandoned them Dot could afford to pay for their keep until they could be conveyed to Melbourne and lodged with her mother. She knew that Phryne would lend her the money. But how could a good girl like Joan have been transformed into Darlo Annie, leaving a good husband and two innocent little ones for a life of vice?

And even if she had done so, where was she?

The harbour was transformed into one great mirror by a flash of bright sunlight, and Dot's eyes filled with tears.

Phryne woke refreshed, drank coffee, and dressed for the Vice Chancellor's dinner. Her gown, in deference to academic sensibilities, was modest, for Phryne. The loose lines of a sapphire-blue silk Poitou tunic swooped decorously to the floor, leaving her slim arms bare. Phryne slid one thick silver bracelet above her elbow. It was a copy of one found in a grave at Mycenae, figured with gorgon faces, and might amuse the Professor of Classics. She donned dark stockings and shoes and long sapphire earrings. Dot laid a silver fillet with a panache made of peacock feathers on her sleek black head. Phryne surveyed herself in the glass. The eyes of the feathers reflected her own green gaze. She blew her reflection a kiss. A pleasant ensemble, she considered: not daring, but delightful.

She had managed an invitation to this dinner in honour of a retiring professor through three telephone calls and one rather boozy lunch. James Cobbett, the Reader in English Literature at the University of Melbourne, had succumbed to her wiles with gratifying speed, bolstered by Phryne's undoubted social position and wealth. The University was a closed community, Phryne knew, and one to which she had no natural entree. She had attended no university herself. She had no academic bent. She was, however, beautiful, intelligent, well-read and rich, and the Reader had wondered what Sydney would make of her. He hoped that it wouldn't be an endowment of a chair. After all, her namesake had already given Sydney a library.

Phryne left Dot with firm injunctions to call Room Service, dine well, and drink two glasses of wine. The VC's Daimler was comfortable and scented with cigars. Phryne was content to add her own Gauloise Gitane fumes and a dash of Jicky to the ambiance.

The car left George Street West, took a road which crossed a paddock and some building works indistinguishable in the half-dark and passed through large iron gates attended by a sweating keeper dressed in the standard Australian costume: boots, shorts and a dustcoat. He waved the car through and shut the gates again.

'Excuse me, Miss? Miss Fisher?' The driver, who had not spoken a word, allowed the car to slow a little as they climbed toward a massive Gothic pile on a hill.

'Yes?'

'Miss, can I ask you a favour?'

'Ask,' said Phryne.

'Could you sort of not mention to the VC that the gatekeeper's improperly dressed?'

'Was he? I didn't notice. It's not likely to arise

in conversation,' she assured the driver.

'Thanks, Miss.' His voice was so heartfelt that Phryne was curious.

'Could the gatekeeper really get into trouble for his costume? I mean, he's only there to open and shut the gate. One wouldn't think...'

'Oh, no, Miss, he could lose his place, and it's a good job. He ain't been the same since he came back from Villers-Bretonneux. He got blown up. He's married to my sister. He's supposed to wear what they call livery, like what I'm wearing, but he says it was wearing a uniform which got him buried in mud and anyway it's too flamin' hot to wear a uniform on a night like this and I have to agree with him.'

'Me too. But I gather that the VC wouldn't. What's he like, then? You ought to know him better than anyone.'

'He's all right,' said the driver slowly, running the car along the frontage of what looked like one of the larger Gothic churches. 'But he's set in his ways and he's mad on the dignity of the University. He wants us to be like Cambridge and Oxford, and he's disgusted by these lax Aussie ways.' A suspicion of a grin was seeping into the driver's voice. Phryne smiled into the rear-vision mirror.

'Not a word,' she promised. 'Lord, what a building! There's miles of it!'

'Built by Sir Edmund Blacket, Miss, pride of Sydney. He also nicked the best land. The VC'll tell you all about it. I'll escort you in, Miss,' said the driver, 'and I'll be back here at eleven to pick you up.'

'Any tips?' asked Phryne, allowing herself to be

helped out of the Daimler.

'Drink the sherry, not the madeira,' said the driver. He was a middle-aged man with a gentle smile. 'Don't touch the fish.'

The entry of an unescorted, exceptionally stylish woman into the Great Hall attracted a gratifying amount of attention, and Phryne was immediately grabbed by two gentlemen eager to make her acquaintance. She smiled benignly at each.

'Miss Fisher? I recognised you immediately. James Cobbett asked me to look after you, introduce you around and so on. My name's Bisset. Jeoffry Bisset. Reader in European languages.'

'And the Vice Chancellor asked me to look after you,' snapped a sharp voice. 'M' name's Kirkpatrick. Professor of English.'

'Delighted,' said Phryne, 'and I shall shamelessly retain both of you.'

'Sherry or madeira?' asked Bisset, who had been well trained in what a young woman required of an escort. Professor Kirkpatrick, who hadn't, snarled something under his breath. The server stood poised with his heavy silver tray – of little glasses. It appeared that sherry or madeira comprised the only beverages on offer and Phryne, forewarned by the driver, chose sherry. It was dry and young but perfectly pleasant.

'Glad you chose the sherry,' said Bisset. He was a tall, shambling young man with shaggy pale hair and vague blue eyes. 'We'll be introducing you to the VC soon and he thinks that women who drink madeira are...' He subsided into silence, horrified by what he had just heard himself say, and Professor Kirkpatrick took the advantage.

58

'Let me point out some of the interesting aspects of the Great Hall, Miss Fisher,' he said smoothly, offering her his arm. 'It was built by Edmund Blacket in 1859 in a style he called Tudor Perpendicular Gothic. The dimensions are based on the Guildhall in London. You really need to come during the day to see the windows at their finest; the glass was made in England and shipped out here, though the actual stone is from Pyrmont.'

Phryne admired the marble statues of two bene-factors, William Wentworth and John Challis, and then stood under a magnificent window depicting Schoolmen and considered the angel roof.

'Wonderful,' she murmured with perfect truth. Wooden secular angels crowned with gold leaned out from the hammer beams, each bearing a book. Forty-five feet above her head was Poetica, flanked by Dialectica and Grammatica.

'They constitute the Trivium; that is, the three subjects which gave a scholar in the Middle Ages the rank of Bachelor of Arts.' Jeoffry Bisset, re-covered from his gaffe, was at Phryne's left hand. 'Then we have the Quadrivium – Arithmetica, Geographica, Astronomica and Musica – that would make the scholar a master; they are the seven liberal arts. The angel with the scroll says, *Scientia inflat, charitas aedificat* –knowledge puffeth up but charity ... er ... edifieth. We think they are rather fine.'

'They are beautiful,' agreed Phryne, wishing that the server had also followed. There seemed to be nothing for it but to continue the tour, so she ad-mired the grey and white marble floor, the bosses and corbels, and nodded respectfully to William Shakespeare in his window, hoping that he would get along with his companions, John Ford, Francis Beaumont and his colleague Fletcher.

'What's the symbol on Grammatica's book?' she asked.

'A roll of papyrus – oh, my hat, I haven't reported to the Dean yet about the Oxyrrinchus papyrus, I just remembered.'

Phryne wanted something else to talk about.

'The Oxyrrinchus papyrus?' she asked sweetly, laying a hand on Bisset's arm.

'Yes, you see, there was a huge find in Egypt a few years ago, a stone pit absolutely full of papyri, gigantic job to get it all translated, so they decided to send some to every university which has a Classics department, and you'll really have to ask John Bretherton about it, he's done the work. Massive task.'

'But why are you reporting about it?'

Jeoffry Bisset blushed red. 'Oh, I've been searching my own archives for it. It's ... excuse me.'

'Professor, are all your Readers so precipitate?' asked Phryne as Bisset fled through the chattering crowd.

'Poor Bisset,' said Kirkpatrick with what could only have been extreme malice. 'There was a burglary, Miss Fisher, probably a student prank, and several things went missing. One of them was the papyrus. Nothing to do with any of my students, of course. Bisset has no system and his secretary has given up trying to impose one. All of his papers are in a large heap on his floor – I recall Ayers the Archaeologist saying to him,

"Young man, you have there a proper midden and one could conceivably date the layers." No matter, Miss Fisher, There's the Vice Chancellor. Let me introduce you.'

Phryne allowed herself to be escorted through a fascinating rabble. Delayed by the dignified slowness of academic movement, Phryne had time to listen in to a babble of what sounded like very satirical gossip.

'They say that he's to be sold up, positively sold up, poor dear fellow,' brayed one man above the roar of voices. He leaned forward, allowing Phryne to pass, and said in a confidential undertone, 'It's that expensive wife of his, you know. Always bring a chap undone, expensive women. Gimme girls, they call them. Can have a fur coat out of a wooden statue of James Cook faster than you could say "extravagance".'

'I always thought s-she was rather nice,' protested the first speaker.

'Oh, nice enough, I grant you, but ... hello, Kirkpatrick! Who's the lovely lady?'

'The Hon. Miss Fisher,' replied the Professor abruptly. 'Might I mention'– His tone was reluctant, but social forms constrained him to continue with the ritual; but he was cross, so this was not an introduction and neither could claim any acquaintance with Phryne afterwards – 'Assistant Professor of Engineering George Budgen and Doctor Edmund Brazell.'

'Anthropology,' explained Dr Brazell. 'Very interesting s-subject – are you at all drawn to anthropology, Miss Fisher?'

Phryne noted that he did not make the common error and call her Lady Fisher, and that he had very bright eyes and a charming Cambridge stammer. She also noted that Assistant Professor George Budgen was gulping in the sight of her with an expression only previously seen on cod that had just met their maker unexpectedly, but she was tweaked through into another part of the crowd by Professor Kirkpatrick before she could comment further.

There a very thin young man with the burning eyes of the consumptive was discussing the morality of ownership so intensely that he did not even notice the vision of loveliness at his side. She heard him say in a thick Lanarkshire accent, 'One must consider whether all property is no' theft,' when Professor Kirkpatrick nudged a stout academic aside and Phryne was through to the Vice Chancellor, Charles Waterhouse.

A nice man, she immediately thought on meeting his honest brown eyes. He was large, red-faced and balding and his suit was a poem in thin dark wool. Phryne diagnosed a wife with very good taste. The VC was not very bright, perhaps, and probably very conservative, but nice. He shook her hand heartily and bellowed 'Sykes! The gown!' and a flustered elderly man struggled to his side with an armload of serge.

'Have to wear a gown, eh, Miss Fisher!' puffed Waterhouse. Phryne could detect a quip approaching with elephantine tread and prepared a suitable giggle in advance. 'Decided by unanimous vote to make you a Master of Arts, though you would always be a Mistress of Arts, and Hearts, too, eh, ha, ha!'

Phryne giggled dutifully, the ring of sycophants around the VC chuckled lightly – clearly this was not even up to the usual Waterhouse standard – and Phryne allowed herself to be draped in a scholar's gown, her hood a chaste blue. Phryne bowed experimentally and the VC tipped his Tudor bonnet, beaming approval. He liked a young woman with no pretensions to learning who would play along with a little harmless flirtation.

Dashed decorative, too, and apparently of fabulous wealth.

The gown, Phryne considered, was a wonderful garment. It dragged pleasurably from the shoulder, producing the academic stance which kept both hands on the bands. Its billowing folds would disguise the defects produced in the figure by far too many faculty dinners and it flowed gracefully as one moved. Making a mental note to borrow one and show it to her favourite dressmaker, Phryne accepted another glass of sherry and asked, 'Who is that young man?'

The VC stopped beaming. 'Professor Anderson. Philosophy. Comes from Glasgow. Heard the accent, eh, Miss Fisher? Uncomfortable sort of chap. Now you're one of us, Miss Fisher, expect to see you around the old place. What do you think of my Great Hall, hmm?'

'It's marvellous,' said Phryne, without having to exaggerate. 'More beautiful than the Guildhall, and I shall enjoy dining here a good deal more because it isn't freezing.'

She had said the right thing. The VC filled with pride as a balloon fills with helium. 'Students complained about it being too dark to see in here

63

on dull days,' he said. 'So I put in electricity, though my committee thought that it might be too harsh for the hall, remove the glamour, y'know, but I'm bucked about it. You can see the angels' faces now. I like to see their faces.'

Phryne looked up. Geometrica was smiling severely down on the gathering. Phryne took the VC's arm when he offered it.

'Come along, m'dear, they've all drunk quite enough of my sherry, let's go and sit down. The University cooks have been slaving all day on this meal – be a pity to keep them waiting.'

Phryne found herself at the head of a procession as the gowned figures fell in behind the VC, two abreast, and paced decorously towards the tables and the dais, passing the illuminated windows and the bosses and corbels. She matched her pace to her escort's and enjoyed the swing of her gown and the patch-and-glow of the hanging lamps. It was very beautiful, like a medieval dance, and the gowned procession cast shadows of itself as it passed on the grey and white marble of the floor.

'Now, m'dear, do sit down,' said Charles Waterhouse frankly, 'because I can't until you do and I'm a bit weary.'

Phryne sat as the server shoved her chair forward. The VC and the Senate followed, and the silence was broken by the scraping of chairs and the scurrying of liveried servers who were hauling in tureens of soup and decanting it into the University's expensive white china.

The Reverend Doctor of Divinity (Dublin) James O'Malley stood and began to intone a grace from a card he held partially concealed in his hand. Phryne, having very little Latin but a lot of French and Italian, grasped that they were thanking the lord for his mercy in providing bounteous meats. The soup smelled delicious. Beef bouillon, if she was any judge. She surveyed the mob in the hall to take her mind off how hungry she was.

There was the 'uncomfortable chap', Anderson, still haranguing his neighbour despite the silence required for grace. There was the anthropologist with the beautiful eyes, Dr Edmund Brazell, a picture of piety. She was seated between the VC and a tall man with silvery hair who was listening to the Reverend Doctor with barely concealed loathing. When the Irish voice had intoned the last word he snapped 'Amen,' and added, 'Nice to meet you, Miss Fisher. I'm John Bretherton, Classics.'

'And you don't like the way the Reverend Doctor reads Latin.'

'No. He's read it often enough, why can't he recite it? He's got a card in his sleeve, you can see it. And entire social classes would have been exiled from Rome for massacring the tongue as he does. No one cares about Classics nowadays – I put it down to the war. What was your university, Miss Fisher? I observe you are wearing an Arts hood, but it might be the spare – last week it was Veterinary Science.'

'Neither. I have no university. I'm here as a guest.'

'Very kind of you to alleviate the masculinity of this assembly.' He recovered gracefully. 'All chaps together can get very crude.'

'I shall do my best to provide an example of the purity of womanhood,' said Phryne with a very creditable straight face. John Bretherton looked at her for an astounded moment then gave a short bark of laughter.

'I'm glad to have made your acquaintance,' he said, picking up his spoon.

'"How pleasant it is to stand in the marketplace, taking notes on one's neighbour's behaviour,"' she quoted, and he put the spoon down again.

'You knew that he was my favourite Roman, how did you know that?'

'A satirical cast of expression and a very discerning eye,' said Phryne. 'Who but Juvenal would really speak to you? You can do me a service.'

'My gifts, such as they are, are yours,' he said, fascinated.

'Tell me all about your fellows,' she said, and Professor John Bretherton grinned. 'And tell me all about the burglary of the Dean's safe,' she added, and the grin widened.

'Such a scandal,' he began. 'But, Miss Fisher, do eat your soup and I shall eat mine, and we shall discourse further. Old Charlie's engrossed in trying to talk to even older Charlie, so we shall not be overheard.'

The VC was indeed bellowing conversation into the wrinkled ears of a gowned man of fabulous antiquity. Phryne was going to hear the whole story of the theft in what amounted to decent privacy.

Four

Game of all games, than Olympian, Roman, serener;
Cricket I sing!
Here is no bloody barbarian dyeing the sward;
No thumbs turned upward or down.
Only verdure and pipe-clay and silence perfect;
The sacred silence of the game!

Stephen Phillips, *Cricket I Sing*

'Arts is not a large faculty,' began John Bretherton. 'We have one secretary, the Dean Mr Gorman, Professor Kirkpatrick, the Bursar Mr Sykes and us academic rabble. The University doesn't work like one of those city offices, you know. Anyway, a number of things were put into the Dean's safe. Because you knew that I liked Juvenal, Miss Fisher, I am not asking you how you came to hear of this, or why you want to know.' He paused and Phryne nodded. 'Well, the safe is a huge great Sheffield-steel thing. In it were the Classics examination questions, the faculty books, the Dean's wife's gewgaws, some bit of rock belonging to Brazell, an illuminated book, the petty cash, and the Oxyrrinchus papyrus, which is in Greek, unmistakeable and important.'

'Important to whom?'

'Why, scholarship, Miss Fisher. Scholarship, to be sure. I can't see it having a great value except to

67

a collector. Someone's probably told you that there was a great find of Aegypto-Hellenic papyri, and each university is responsible for translating and publishing their allotment.'

'And have you translated yours?'

'Oh, yes, got on to them as soon as they arrived. All the others are in the library, but I was keeping this one by me. That's why it was in the safe. I feel very badly about that. It was a rather curious manuscript.'

'Oh? Why?' Phryne allowed a waiter to remove her soup plate.

'Er, well.' Professor Bretherton looked uncomfortable for the first time. 'It was a curse. The Egyptians were rather inventive when it came to curses. Greek is such a good language to curse in. Anyway, it's lost, which is a pity. Where was I? Ah, yes. Picture the scene. There we all are, in the faculty office. I was talking to Dora, the typist, a stupid girl who cannot copy what is in front of her, about the number of errors in the very simple prayer she was typing for the Bishop – you've heard of the trouble at John's College? Refused to let the Archbishop in? I was thinking I ought to let it go, and see if the cleric would detect the difference between *Domine te regamus* and *Domine te rogamus*, meaning that he was declaring that God should worship us rather than the other way round, you see...' He paused in case Phryne was going to laugh, so she smiled obligingly. 'The Dean was shouting at the Bursar about some irregularity in the bookkeeping, the secretary went to open the safe and lo and behold, nothing in it. The cupboard was bare. Nothing at all, upon my

68

word. And my papyrus gone along with my examination papers and all the other things.'

'Was the safe damaged?'

'Scratches around the lock and so on, you mean? Not that I saw. Of course, the Bursar might have forgotten to lock it. Such an idiot, Sykes. I fancy that may be the explanation, you know. Someone just walked in, found the room empty, and helped themselves – to my papyrus!'

'But why take everything in the safe? If they were after your papyrus–'

'Oh, no, they were after the exam papers. Took the rest of the stuff to cover up what they were really after. Anyway, there was a flap to end all flaps, the Dean bellowing, the Bursar whimpering, Professor Kirkpatrick going all Scotch and rigid with fury. Each and every one reverting to type. If I hadn't been so worried about my papyrus I would have enjoyed it even more. It's probably on some rubbish heap even now, being taken away by the Municipal van and dumped in the tip.'

He brooded darkly while plates were laid and the waiters returned in a group, bearing huge salvers of roasted beef and tureens of vegetables and gravy. A young man leaned over Phryne and filled her glass with dark red wine.

'Sorry, Miss Fisher, I should have asked if you preferred a light hock,' apologised Professor Bretherton. 'Server, another glass for Miss Fisher.'

'No, I would rather have red wine.' Phryne sipped. It was robust and a little raw and tingled on her palate.

'Good, eh? We laid down dozens of the new

Tahbilk vintage in '20 and it's come along well. Shiraz. The wine of the ancients. Only place the phylloxera didn't get to, mainly because the place is so far from a road it would have had to be a very athletic little beast indeed to plod all that way. The Vice Chancellor believes that we should support our own vignerons, and that is one point on which I agree with him. A country that doesn't grow its own wine grapes has no claim to civilisation. Also, of course, it's cheaper than imported burgundy.'

'And better,' agreed Phryne, sipping again. 'Did you find your examination papers?'

'Yes, the papers – and they were no advantage, you know. Poor little tick who stole them was some scholarship boy, Harcourt. The Dean instituted an immediate search of all the students' carrels and there they were in Harcourt's. The boy absolutely refuses to answer any questions about where the rest of the stuff is, drat him. Those Andersonians are tough. I don't care about the examination papers: I can easily fudge up another set with my fellows. But I want my papyrus back. I say, Miss Fisher.' He leaned a little towards Phryne. 'You're an investigator, aren't you? You wouldn't consider a little investigation on my account, would you?'

'I promised not to investigate anything.' Phryne was wondering just how much Professor Bretherton wanted his papyrus back. 'I'm on holiday.'

'But you've an interest in this matter, haven't you? Otherwise how would you have heard of it and why would you ask me about it?'

'It's no use trying to pull the wool over a Juvenalian's eyes,' sighed Phryne. 'If you can get me an interview with all of the participants, I'll

70

see what I can do.'

'Nothing simpler, my dear Miss Fisher.' The scholar's eyes gleamed with mischief. 'I'll just mention that you are very wealthy and childless and thinking of a bequest. Then your only problem will be drying off your shoes.'

Phryne raised an eyebrow.

'Wet with all that drooling,' he explained. 'Perhaps you might call at the Faculty Office tomorrow? And tell me,' he added, as the Vice Chancellor's conversation with the aged academic died away, 'why did you favour Sydney with your presence, Miss Fisher?'

'I came to see the Test match,' Phryne replied.

The old man on the other side of the VC quavered, 'Test match? Waste of time. Bludgeoners. Butchers. They don't have the sort of games we had when I was young. All killed off in the war,' he said sadly.

'You must have seen some great games,' said Phryne gently. Her voice was clear and the old gentleman had no difficulty understanding her.

'I saw the greats: F.E. Woolley of Kent, C.B. Fry and Rantjitsinhji of Sussex. Used their bats like a conductor's baton. Elegance, m'dear!'

'Miss Fisher, might I introduce our Emeritus Professor of Engineering, Mr Jones?' The VC, after a moment's astonishment, picked up the social thread.

'Nice to meet you,' said the old man. 'That was the Golden Age, depend on it. Fast. Nothing for a batsman to score over a hundred runs an hour. Beautiful to watch. Now they're just boring them out. I remember bowlers who terrified batsmen

71

out – you should have seen the Demon Spofforth. Ran like the wind. Delivered a ball so fast you couldn't see it in the air. I was there on the day when Ernest Jones fired a ball right through W.G.'s beard. But it's not common to see one of the fair sex interested in the great game,' he added, his voice rising to a question mark.

'I went to Leeds in 1921 and saw Lionel Tennyson's innings,' explained Phryne with pardonable pride.

'Ah, yes,' Professor Jones nodded. 'They say it was glorious.'

'He came out, broken arm in a sling, with a child's bat in his other hand. We held our breath,' said Phryne. 'He made sixty-one. And that was off McDonald and Gregory, too, not some weak county attack.'

'Cannon to the right of him,' murmured Professor Bretherton sardonically, 'volleyed and thundered.'

'All the world wondered,' agreed the old man, completing the quote from 'The Charge of the Light Brigade'. 'Tennyson was a great captain. Hampshire and England. They say that he backed Hants at one hundred to one against Warwickshire after they made fifteen in the first innings. Then they went on to make over five hundred in the second and it was champagne all round on the proceeds. Of course, he had Mead. They say he has an honest face, for a left-hander. Great days,' sighed Professor Jones. 'Now these damned professionals have ruined the game. Cricket's simple. As W.G. said, all you have to do is lay the bat against the ball.'

'And you don't like the present Test team?' asked Phryne.

'Pounders, and they're all too old. Half that team are over thirty and some of 'em are over forty. Need some new blood. Young man's game, Test cricket. Look what happened in Brisbane. Disaster. Larwood, Jardine, Tate, Farmer White – fair bowlers and disgraceful Australian batting. And our bowlers can't seem to make any breakthrough against Hendren, Hobbs and Hammond.'

'A fair summary,' commented Professor Bretherton, who was interested despite himself.

'So I fear that the great days have gone,' said the old man. 'I'm not likely to see any batsman again as good as the men of my youth.'

He closed his eyes and appeared to enjoy a short nap; dreaming, perhaps, of the Croucher, Jessop, greatest office-emptier in the history of the game. Phryne drank more wine and attacked the mound of meat and vegetables in front of her. Talking always made her hungry.

The college meat was tender, the college vegetables correct, and the college plate remarkable. Phryne asked about it as yet another heavy silver salver was hauled past by a sweating waiter.

'Oh, well, you see, Miss Fisher, if some chap is retiring, he might donate a piece of silver. The heavier the plate, the greater the importance, is the rule which many of 'em seem to have stuck to. My college is rather big on loving cups.'

'Loving cups?'

'You'll see later. You really are interested in cricket, aren't you?'

'Yes,' said Phryne, her mouth full of beef.

'Well, in that case, most of the faculty will be at the Test tomorrow,' he said. 'Perhaps we can invite you into the Members? The ladies' stand is quite comfortable. I could call at your hotel at about nine in the morning?'

'Thank you,' said Phryne, swallowing. 'That would be delightful.'

The plates were cleared again. Cheese and biscuits were distributed. Phryne was suddenly as sleepy as a boa constrictor who has greedily tucked into its second coolie and drunk deep of an intoxicating mountain spring. The Vice Chancellor stood up, settled his robes, and gestured for silence.

'We are here,' he announced, 'to say farewell to our good Professor Jones, who is now leaving the hurly burly of the academic life and devoting himself to his other loves, apart from engineering: gardening and cricket,' and there was a scatter of applause.

'Master of the obvious,' murmured Professor Bretherton.

'Goes with the job, I should think,' returned Phryne.

Her mind wandered. Why should someone steal all the things in the safe? To cover up their real object. Quite sensible. Though she would have thought that someone with that level of planning would not keep the stolen papers in his carrel. She discounted the wandering thief hypothesis. The safe was probably quite impressive, and even if Sykes the Bursar had failed to lock it, it was very unlikely that he would fail to shut it. Phryne had met a number of burglars and could not see them trying the handle of a safe on spec, because she could not see them passing unnoticed in the University grounds, much less a faculty office. It was just possible that a thief might have walked in on business, a tradesman's assistant, for instance, but what would he be doing in the office? It sounded unlikely, though it had to be investigated, as did the timing of the theft. The loss had been discovered in the morning, of course, but when had the contents of the safe been stolen? That went on Phryne's mental list as well.

She was just speculating on John Bretherton's strangely evasive response to her questions about his papyrus when the Great Hall broke out into cheers and everyone rose to their feet. Phryne did likewise.

'What are we doing?' she asked Professor Bretherton.

'Cheering,' he replied, demonstrating his own mastery of the obvious. 'Now, Miss Fisher,' he advised as they resumed their seats, 'this ritual ought to amuse you.'

A heavy two-handled cup was presented to the aged Professor Jones. He stood up, and the VC and the Bursar rose as well as the old man drank. He passed the cup to the VC and immediately Professor Bretherton stood up.

Phryne was intrigued. Each time the cup passed, the passer stayed on his feet and two new people stood up, so that the one with the cup was always flanked by two standing men. It produced a charming ripple effect as the loving cup moved down the table, but it was a mystery to Phryne.

'I would really like to know what gives rise to

this strange procedure,' she said to Professor Bretherton, who grinned.

'In the bad old days, life was not safe for a man to let his hand stray too far from his sword,' he said. 'So anyone who takes a two-handled cup is vulnerable to attack. Therefore...'

'Therefore his fellows stand to guard him while he is drinking. How medieval,' said Phryne, as the ripple effect reached Professor Jones again. 'And I, of course...'

'Being most emphatically and delightfully female...' put in Professor Bretherton.

'Don't drink because I could not possibly guard you or Professor Waterhouse from attack by, say, a student maddened beyond bearing by the imperfect subjunctive,' she reasoned.

'They are more likely to be driven insane by Greek verb forms,' he agreed.

Professor Jones, however, was determined to use his Emeritus for something useful, like honouring a young woman with sound ideas on the summer game, and he beckoned to Phryne to stand. She did so, wondering if she was about to commit a social solecism which would see Waterhouse demanding pistols for two and breakfast for one on the morrow.

'Miss Fisher,' said the old man, and handed her the loving cup.

With Bretherton and the VC flanking her so that she was safe from hypothetical assault, Phryne raised the cup and drank. The cup was extremely heavy, doubtless being donated by a fellow with importance to underline. It contained very good port. Phryne lowered it to find that she was being applauded. There seemed nothing to do but bow, so she bowed, gave the cup on to Professor Bretherton, and the ripple effect passed on again.

'Well, that will give them something to talk about,' said Bretherton, shaking Phryne's hand.

'For the foreseeable future,' added Professor Kirkpatrick, on Bretherton's other side. He had been occupied all through dinner with a discussion on certain early English grammatical borrowings from Old Norse with Jeoffry Bisset and had withdrawn his attention from Phryne, allowing Professor Bretherton to monopolise her.

'Gosh, yes,' exclaimed Bisset. 'Unprecedented events don't happen very often here, you know. You'll go down in history as the first woman to drink from a loving cup.'

'Honoured,' murmured Phryne.

'Only Jones would have dared,' marvelled Bisset.

'One can dare a lot if one is Emeritus,' said Bretherton.

Phryne cut herself a lump of blue cheese and took a long sip of port from a conventional glass. When the VC announced, 'Gentlemen, you may smoke,' she assumed that she was an honorary gentleman for the evening and accepted a rather good cigar from the old man, who had clearly taken a shine to her.

'I remember when I first saw a cricket match,' he said, settling back and smiling. 'E.M., G.F. and W.G. – the Three Graces of Gloucestershire, they called them. I was eleven and a schoolboy and my father took me to the cricket – my first grown-up match. Cost sixpence to get in. Had a curiously high-pitched voice, W.G. Bowled a slow flighted ball at the leg stump, and his brother E.M. used to field a bare yard from the bat and even the batsmen worried about killing him, though it was Fred who was killed, tragically, but not on the cricket field. Took lots of catches at deep long leg off his brother's bowling. Strange how one man can change history, Miss Fisher. Before W.G., the Players won nineteen in a row against the Gentlemen. Professionals always beat amateurs. In the next ten years the Players only won once. Just one man turned it around, from disaster to victory.'

'Did you really see Jones part his beard, Professor?' asked Bretherton.

'Certainly. And what did the great man do? Ruffled his beard back into place and took guard again and struck the next ball over the fence.'

'There were giants in those days,' said Phryne, without marked irony.

'Golden days, they were. All dead now. You will come and see our own cricket match, Miss Fisher?' asked Professor Jones.

'I certainly will,' said Phryne. 'When is it to be?'

'On Friday,' Professor Jones told her. 'Faculty against students. Relying on you, Bretherton, to get a hundred.'

'You said,' Professor Bretherton pointed out, 'that cricket was a young man's game.'

'Test cricket *is* a young man's game,' the old man corrected. 'If we have you and Bisset opening the batting, and that chap from Edinburgh bowling, we might give the students a surprise.'

'And you will be there?' asked Phryne.

'Certainly. I've seen every University match since the year '12, and I'm not going to miss this one. Come and sit with me, m'dear. You can tell me about Warwick Armstrong's last hurrah. The Big Ship, eh? He was a man, not like these namby-pamby modern ones. He knew he was a Captain and the artists – Trumper and Mailey – flourished under his leadership. Knew what he wanted, see? He wanted to win. Nowadays Australia's lost the will to win.'

'Delighted,' said Phryne. The faculty showed signs of enthusiasm. The annual cricket match against the students might be amusing, after all.

At eleven precisely Phryne was escorted to the door by Professor Bretherton and handed into the VC's Daimler. The driver did not blink an eyelash when she asked him to take her to an address in Chinatown.

'Theo's, is it, Miss? Lots of my gentlemen go there. Interested in poetry, Miss?'

'Yes,' murmured Phryne, who was very sleepy. 'Very interested.'

She slept lightly until the door opened and she was escorted across a hot pavement. The driver rang three times – one long and two short – at a bell in a dingy green door. A peephole slid, there was a pause, then the door swung open. A door-keeper surveyed her without a word and allowed her to pass. Phryne climbed some stairs into a very noisy cafe and immediately felt herself begin to rouse. Universities were foreign to Phryne; her natural habitat was a cafe. She knew how cafes worked.

Theo's was an unremarkable room in the top

half of an unremarkable building in a depressed bit of the city. The Campbell Street address was on the corner of Pitt Street, in Chinatown, and very unrespectable. The room was whitewashed and decorated with a few Chinese lanterns that had seen better decades. Two full-sized sketches hung on the wall: a female satyr and a cartoonist's charcoal of a tall man. A large washing tub stood on a kitchen table in the middle of the floor, around which were ranged an eclectic assortment of tables and chairs and an even more eccentric collection of people, some drinking from china teacups, some dancing in whatever space was left between the furniture. A sinister woman in a turban raised her eyes from an array of Tarot cards and gave Phryne an unfriendly glance.

'Yes! We have no bananas,' sang a gramophone. 'We have no bananas today!'

Phryne stood by the door, trying to see through the fog of smoke generated by a kero stove cooking sausages, the fume of boiling spaghetti and a lot of people smoking cheap tobacco. Experience in Paris had taught Phryne that one didn't just stride boldly into a strange cafe. Paris had thousands of cafes, all with their own clientele, who could get noticeably unfriendly to outsiders who walked in at the wrong moment and rapped a coin on the wrong zinc counter. Therefore she leaned on the wall and groped for a cigarette. She could not see any woman who bore a resemblance to Dot's sister Joan.

A large man loomed before her, flourishing a match.

'New here?' he asked through the side of his mouth.

'Chas Nuttall,' said Phryne, providing a name to support her presence. The huge man nodded slowly. He had all the earmarks of a professional chucker-out (broken nose, split eyebrows, and ears which any greengrocer might have exhibited with pride amongst the cauliflowers) and Phryne did not want to be chucked. At least, not just yet.

'Chas ain't 'ere yet,' said the bouncer. 'You know artists. You po'try, paintin' or slummin'?' he wanted to know.

'I expect I'm poetry,' said Phryne.

'Poets're in that far corner,' said the chucker-out, looking a little disappointed. He stood back, allowing her to pass, and Phryne walked slowly across the room, collecting a teacup and some punch and leaving a shilling in the saucer next to the washing tub. She had no intention of drinking the foul concoction and insulting the University's port, but it was protective colouration.

She put a hand on the back of a chair at the furthest table and said, 'Mind if I sit down?'

The whole table stopped in mid-word and stared.

'Bet you a deener I fuck you in a week,' said a young man with a very conscious grizzled beard and locks of hair straggling into his uncollared neck. Phryne assessed this as an opening bid.

'I wouldn't put any real money on it, but I'll watch your progress with great interest,' she promised. She sat down. The chair was paint-stained and rickety, thrown out by some respectable kitchen. Phryne leaned both elbows on the table

81

and said, 'Nice to meet you,' to the grizzled beard. 'My name's Phryne Fisher. I'm thinking of establishing a magazine, since *Vision* has gone down the drain. What do you think?'

This was a demand bid and she was not disappointed.

'Who sent you here?' asked the beard.

'Chas Nuttall,' she answered. 'Why, do I need a sponsor?'

'You do to come into Theo's, unless you're just slumming amongst the gay Bohemians. Don't mind about Jack, he says that to every new woman he meets after it worked once in 1924, even though it never worked again. I'm Bill, this is George, and Christopher Brennan is ... er ... not entirely with us at the moment.'

He referred to a large man who was snoring, face down, in a puddle of punch.

'But doubtless he'll be back,' added George.

'I'm from Melbourne,' said Phryne. 'Via Paris. This is the first cafe I've seen which bears any resemblance to Bohemia. Smoky. Contentious. Noisy. Colourful. Not, however – despite Jack's sporting offer – very salacious.'

'Night's young. And the girls from Tillie's haven't knocked off yet. They usually come in here after the evening rush.'

'I'm looking for one of them,' said Phryne artlessly. 'I have a job to offer her.'

'Who?' asked the bearded man.

'Darlo Annie.' Phryne handed over her photograph. 'If this is her? I've got a friend who wants to photograph her. At quite a reasonable fee, if I could find her very soon.'

'Haven't seen her for a week,' said George. 'You sure you're not a cop?'

'Quite sure,' said Phryne. They all looked at her again, and decided that she really couldn't be. Then they looked at the picture.

'Looks sorta like Darlo Annie,' confirmed George. 'Younger, but.'

'Well, if you could come back tomorrow night, I reckon we could lay our hands on Darlo Annie, we can go round and order her from Tillie and you can hardly do that, can you? We'd like to do Darlo Annie a favour,' offered Bill. 'Especially if you are in the market for some poetry.'

'I might be,' said Phryne. 'What have you got?'

'Some pretty hot stuff,' promised Bill.

'"The loveliest whore in Darlinghurst was in the family way,"' announced Jack. '"In spite of her diamond pessaries and the jewelled whirling spray…"'

'No, no, not that sort of thing!' protested George. 'She wants to buy good poetry!'

'And who are you to disdain the poetry of the people?' demanded Jack. 'The poetry of the workers? You and your Symbolism!'

'Symbolism,' said someone, 'is the only way to make a pattern out of Fate, dust, and time.'

Phryne located the voice. Christopher Brennan had spoken without moving from his puddle of wine. She waited, but he seemed to have passed out again.

'You! You'd do anything to get into *Smith's Weekly!*' accused Jack.

'And you wouldn't?' Voices were rising. While a fight would be amusing, Phryne thought, she didn't have time to wait until it had died down. Grabbing Bill as he started to his feet, she said firmly, 'I want some good poetry, by which I do not mean either réchauffé T.S. Eliot or what sounds like an Australian version of the "Ballad of Eskimo Nell", which I have already heard.'

'"Oh, the harems of Egypt are fair to behold..."' began Jack hopefully.

Phryne squashed him. 'And that one,' she snapped.

'How about: "In her breasts' rise and fall/I felt the mighty ocean of desire/Swell to the calling Moon.../Her impulsive thighs/Pressed tighter to my side like petals that close/About a trapped bee venturing too far"' quoted George.

'Hmm. Whose is that?'

'Jack Lindsay. He's the boy for erotic verse! But there's lots more. We're all poets here.'

Phryne felt a hand slide onto her knee, and the beautiful voice of the great poet pronouncing '"All mystery and all love beyond our ken/She wooes us, mournful 'till we find her fair:/And gods and stars and songs and souls of men/Are the sparse jewels in her scattered hair/Jewels in her hair..."' Phryne looked full into dark, deep and agonised eyes as of a wounded deer before Brennan fell back into his puddle and subsided.

'He's comparing you with Lilith,' commented Bill. 'He must like you.'

'As I recall, Lilith was the demon who mated with Adam before Eve came along. She was dismissed for being too forward,' said Phryne.

'Are you forward?' leered Jack.

'I'm probably so far ahead of you, my dear, that

84

you could run all day and never catch up with me,' Phryne told him. 'Is Mr Brennan always like this?'

'Sometimes. He's a great poet, you know. But ... he's got his troubles. Annie, for example.'

'A stupid slut,' said Jack. Phryne liked him less and less as their acquaintance festered and lit another cigarette to stop her fingers itching for his ears.

'Venus of the Gutters, they call her,' said Bill consideringly. 'There was a terrible scandal. They said...' He leaned nearer and whispered in Phryne's ear for some time. Against her will, her eyebrows rose.

'Really?' she asked. Incest was not new, perhaps, but surely close to the last taboo. The advanced age in which she found herself demanded free money, free love and free beer – not that it got them – but incest seemed too extreme even for the more altitudinous of the *fauves*. And that was in Paris.

'That's what they say. That's when his wife threw him out. And we don't know how long he'll last with the University, either. They don't appreciate what he does.'

'What does he do?'

'He shuts himself in with his students and they can't leave until they have undergone self-examination. Not to go out of someone's sight, to pee in a bottle and use a wastepaper basket for a lavatory, never to leave the others, until they have it. The university don't like it. They have to call in cleaners. They don't know what he's doing for us, making us see.'

'See?' asked Phryne.

'Yair.' Bill's face was radiant. For a moment, he looked like a cheap religious lithograph and the blurred lighting cast a glow around his head like the halo of a saint. Then Jack nudged him and said, 'You're talking to a sheila. She can't understand.'

'I can't?' asked Phryne, resisting the urge to stub her gasper out on the young man's hand. His venom was catching. Another womaniser who didn't even like women, she thought. There were a lot of them about.

'But there are sheilas here who do understand,' protested Bill. 'Don't be such a woman-hater, Jack. Jeez, I dunno. Nice lady wants to give us money and you're putting her off. But they're stuffed shirts, up at the University. You won't find any real poets up there. Remember the *Hermes* scandal? The University magazine published a poem by one of our friends, Bert Birtles. Real nice. A remembrance of how his girl lay in his arms with the moonlight coming in through the window and the birds cooing on the roof.'

'"Lie still, dear, and rest awhile,/Contented, our longing now appeased..."' quoted a man behind Phryne. 'Best thing that ever happened to me, that scandal. "Move not dearest. Unfold not your warm limbs from about me." The U summoned the *Hermes* editors and warned them with the utmost academic severity not to do such a thing ever again, and the craven scoundrels haven't, either. No balls at all.'

'Hullo, Bert,' said George. 'Miss Fisher, Bert Birtles.'

Phryne shook hands with a brisk young man.

86

He grinned.

'What happened to you, then? And your lover?' she asked.

'Oh, well, you see, they really got on to poor Dora because she'd written a poem in much the same vein, and she was rusticated for two years and I was flung out, neck and crop. She'd enjoyed that night as much as I had, so we got married and started a magazine. You might have seen it. Called *Vision*. Didn't last but it was good.'

'Miss Fisher's thinking of starting a magazine,' put in Bill.

'Wonderful,' replied Bert Birtles warily. 'Takes a mint of money and a lot of work,' he added. 'You might want to think about it, Miss Fisher, before you let these blokes bully you into anything.'

'Possibly,' said Phryne, suddenly exhausted and tired of the smoke and the smell of spilt punch. 'Well, see you tomorrow night, fellows,' she said briskly. 'If you want to ascertain my bona fides, you can find me at the Hotel Australia. Phryne Fisher. Goodnight,' she said, and walked out of Theo's as Dulcie Deamer danced on the table to a gramophone which lamented that, regrettably, he had absolutely no bananas at all.

Five

There has always been a certain dourness about Australian cricket, an unashamed will-to-power, with no 'may the best man win' nonsense. Even the brilliant Victor Trumper was an Ironside in Cavalier's colours, his bat a conquering sword, not a lance in tournament.

Neville Cardus, *English Cricket*

Phryne slept heavily and awoke to demand aspirins, black coffee, and suitable clothes to wear to the cricket. As she breakfasted she tried to reassure Dot.

'What you can do today, Dot dear, is to go and see that nice policeman whom Jack Robinson recommends and tell him all about Joan. If Theo's is a sample of how Australian Bohemia behaves, no one with a particle of resolution would stay in it if they didn't want to – it seems to have none of the unfortunate aspects of the Parisian version. I haven't seen a single *souteneur*. Though there are undoubtedly bullies. If Joan is there it is because she has a reason to be there. Tonight we shall see what we shall see. This morning I've got to go to the cricket with the faculty and see if I can get anywhere with this odd theft and ... now what?' she exclaimed. Dot went to the door and unfolded the note, offered to her on a silver tray.

'Your two young men are waiting downstairs

88

and would like a word, Miss,' replied Dot.

'Oh, very well, send them up. I'll just have a quick wash. It will be all right, Dot dear,' she said and vanished into the bathroom.

She emerged muffled in a huge towel to find Joss and Clarence sitting on the end of her bed, side by side, looking startled. Though Phryne was actually more clothed in her towel than many young women were in their street garments, they were ill-at-ease. Phryne looked on them with little mercy.

'I am going to the cricket with the faculty this morning. I may elicit something interesting. It is very odd that all of the contents of the safe vanished and the only parts that resurfaced were the exam papers.'

'We thought that was strange,' agreed Joss.

'Professor Bretherton has asked me to try and find his papyrus,' she added, allowing the towel to drop and reaching her stockings. She was clad in complete undergarments and could not understand the shock on her interlocutors' faces. She looked down.

'Oh, good lord, and you call yourself Bohemians. Turn your backs if the sight of a stocking offends you. I'm in a hurry. Professor Bretherton will be arriving any minute. Have you anything else to tell me?'

'Yes, we have a small confession to make,' said Clarence, staring fixedly at a marble urn on a marble plinth and trying to ignore the silken rustle of stockings sliding up a slim leg towards a destination which he would not imagine.

'That Adam Harcourt pinched the papers?'

'No!' cried Joss. 'They were shoved in his carrel to make it look like it was him. But we've not told you something and now we think we should.'

'Well, get on with it,' said Phryne, fastening the stockings and settling the silk blouse and linen skirt which Dot had provided as suitable cricket-going clothes.

'It's about the papyrus. It's...' He stuck, and Phryne cut in.

'A curse.'

'Did Professor Bretherton tell you that?' asked Clarence.

'Of course he did.' Phryne buttoned her new petticoat pocket and slipped it beneath the skirt where it hung, not noticeable, at her thigh. 'Nice work, Dot dear. What an excellent invention.'

'My grandma used to wear them,' said Dot.

'You see, there's a group of people who might want that curse,' Joss was saying uncomfortably. 'They're followers of the Great Beast, Crowley. Come back from some temple he's established on an island.'

'Cefalu, yes, it got a lot of publicity. The Abbey of Thelema, Temple of Do As Thou Wilt, which of course meant Do As Crowley Wilt,' said Phryne shortly, slipping her feet into sandals.

'They're magicians,' said Clarence wretchedly. 'And they're saying that they magicked that curse out of the safe, and they're going to use it.'

'On whom?'

'Their enemies, I suppose.'

'One of you?'

'Or Harcourt. He laughed at them when they...'

'When they? Come on, boys, out with it, time

90

is passing.'

'Harcourt works with the Bursar, you see, helps him with his figures. He's always in the faculty office and they got very dirty on him when he refused. They asked him to steal the papyrus because they want the curse.'

'It's been published. Photograph and translation. Why didn't they just buy the book?' asked Phryne impatiently.

'They want the actual papyrus; apparently it has secret writings on it.'

'Hmm. I need to meet Harcourt. Do you know where Theo's cafe is?'

'Yes,' said Joss. 'The er … magical people will be there, too.'

'Will they indeed? Who are they?'

'A woman called Madame Sosostris,' said Clarence. 'Chap called Marrin.'

'Bring Harcourt to Theo's tonight about eleven,' ordered Phryne. 'Tell him that no one magicked anything out of that safe. If he baulks at seeing Madame and Marrin again, tell him that I've got an amulet which will preserve him against any magical attack, given to me by the Masters of the Golden Dawn. I was at the Invocation of Isis in Paris,' she added. 'Tell him that. Now off you go, gentlemen. I've got a cricket match to attend.'

They left biddably.

'Miss?' asked Dot, very uneasily.

Phryne paused while trying on a panama hat at the rosy mirror and raised an eyebrow.

'Did you really see that … thing?'

'What, the Invocation? Certainly. Interesting performance. While I am out, Dot, after you've talked to the policeman, buy me a yard of thin white cord, a silk handkerchief of the strongest purple you can find, and pick up a handful of wormwood and some dried rosemary.'

'Why?' asked Dot.

'Obviously, we have to make an amulet which was given to me by the Masters of the Golden Dawn. Crowley – well, I really don't know about Crowley, but I do know that his followers aren't him, and most of their effects are obtained by hypnosis, drugs and fear. If this boy was a Christian, we could give him a crucifix drenched in holy water and it would work just as well. As it is presently fashionable to be an atheist, I have to do a little sleight of mind. Fear is a very powerful motivator. I think I saw this woman last night at Theo's – Madame Sosostris, telling tarot fortunes in a turban. Has to be a fake. Even the name is pinched from a T.S. Eliot poem, and what T.S. Eliot didn't know about magic you wouldn't be able to stuff in a tea-chest. Do you follow, Dot?'

'No, miss,' said Dot.

'Ah, well, there it is. I'm off to the cricket. Toodle-pip.'

Dot gathered up the towel and found the address which had been scrawled down in Phryne's bold hand from a telephone conversation with Jack Robinson.

Detective Inspector Tom Rawlings. Darlinghurst.

She could buy the amulet materials at the Strand Arcade afterwards.

Professor Bretherton, in mufti, looked younger

and more unsure of himself. He showed Phryne into a taxi and she was thrown against him as the cab screeched into the road and aimed itself at the Sydney Cricket Ground without apparently making any allowances for traffic which might intrude unwisely into its path.

'"Lo, his name is Jehu,"' she quoted, extricating herself from his impromptu embrace.

'"For he driveth furiously,"' agreed Professor Bretherton, attempting to untangle hair like black silk from his blazer button.

''Ere!' yelled the driver. ''Oo you callin' names?'

'Just a quote, my dear sir,' soothed the Professor. 'Excuse me, Miss Fisher, I believe that I have it now.'

Phryne sat up and shook her head. 'I've been hearing about your papyrus,' she said provocatively.

'Have you indeed?' His voice was level and even a little amused. It was hard to pull wool over a Juvenalian's eyes, Phryne recalled. She decided to demand some information.

'What sort of curse is it?'

'Just a curse. You see, Miss Fisher, the essence of most curses, and we have quite a lot of them, especially the Roman *tabulae defixiones*, is that they are very specific. One had a ritual to follow and any mistake could leave the fates a chink into which they could insert their claws. For example, a prayer to various demons to strike down with disease the drivers of the Whites, the Blues and the Reds had to have a special clause which told the demons not to lay a paw on the driver of the Green chariot, on which one had wagered one's toga virilis, wife's jewels and favourite slaves.'

'Yes,' prompted Phryne.

'But the Egyptians had a general sort of curse, one which would strike down anyone who did a specific action, such as opening a tomb, defiling a temple or desecrating a monument and, unlike the curse on the drivers of the chariots, it was meant to last forever.'

'I understand you,' said Phryne, hanging onto the strap as the taxi squealed around another corner.

'So various so-called magicians are interested in Egyptian curses, and they've been trying to buy – or perhaps they have stolen – this one. Assuming that it is still as efficacious as the day it was written.'

'Do you think so?' asked Phryne.

'I believe that it is just as likely to work now as in ancient times – in fact, it would never have worked. However, superstition is rampant. Especially now. And yet – even so, Miss Fisher, even so. I do not like the idea of someone being able to blame an Egyptian curse for some evil-doing of their own.'

'That sounds murky,' said Phryne lightly. 'How does the curse run?'

'I can't recall it off-hand,' muttered Professor Bretherton.

Phryne did not believe a word of this. This was only one page of writing. Professor Bretherton had been studying it. Perhaps he did not want to offend the taxi-driver's ears. She did not persist; there would be time. And in any case, the papyrus was translated and in the public record.

Unless there was something on the document which he hadn't put into his translation, of course. The occultists' 'secret writing', perhaps?

The Sydney Cricket Ground was thronged with cricket lovers, anxious to see some revenge for the humiliation at Brisbane. The day was clear and hot, most of the faculty were there, and Phryne was seated in the Ladies' Stand with a glass of lemon squash in her hand and surrounded by university men in a remarkably short time. She had a reasonable view of the proceedings and a learned commentary from Bisset (in front of her), Bretherton (at her left), Kirkpatrick (at her right) and Emeritus Professor Jones (behind her, seated on a cushion and staring through a pair of opera glasses).

The two captains walked out with the umpires and a coin sailed skyward. One captain shook the other's hand, and then gestured to the dressing room.

'Famous!' said Bisset. 'We've won the toss and elected to bat.'

'Might not be a good decision,' grumbled Jones. 'They've got some dashed good bowling.'

'They've also got some dashed good batting,' Bretherton pointed out. 'Depressing to stand there and watch them belt the cover off the ball to the tune of six hundred odd runs before we get a chance at it.'

'These men have forgotten how to win,' snapped Jones. 'But there is one chap in the side whom I'm rather looking forward to seeing again. Saw him make a rather good century against these tourists. Made eighty-seven and one hundred and thirty-two not out for New South Wales. Larwood simply couldn't fox him. Though he didn't do any good in the disgraceful Brisbane Test. Eighteen and two, I believe. Funny pouncing, pecking style he had. Bradman. That was the name.'

'Sorry, Jones,' said Professor Bretherton, reading the team displayed on the scoreboard. 'He's twelfth man this Test.'

'Drat,' commented Professor Jones, and settled down to watch.

The game began and Woodfull applied himself well and began to make some headway against the English bowling, though the day was hot and the runs hard to come by. Richardson was bowled by a ball from Larwood which streaked through his wicket, Kippax fell to Geary for nine, and when Ponsford was hit on the hand and retired hurt for five, Phryne began to feel that this was not going to be a triumphant game for the Australian side.

'They're bowling at the stumps,' snarled Professor Jones through his teeth. 'Just nice, neat, competent bowling.'

'Lunch?' asked Jeoffry Bisset hungrily. 'I've brought a hamper.'

'Hamper? Nonsense. I'm lunching in the members, as I always do. Join me, Miss Fisher?' asked Professor Bretherton.

'I think I'll stay here,' said Phryne, and was deserted by the gentlemen in favour of roast beef and potatoes.

'"The sincerest love is the love of food",' quoted Bisset, loading Phryne's plate with chicken salad. He poured a glass of champagne for her and leaned back, sipping.

The crowd had largely dispersed in search of beer (and possibly hot pies which the boys had been crying incessantly) and Phryne swung her feet up onto the hard wooden bench. The sun was bright but under the high galvanised pavilion it was agreeably cool.

'Have you travelled much, Miss Fisher?' asked Bisset. 'I was in Italy last year.'

'And how is Signor Mussolini faring?' asked Phryne idly.

'Much better than could be hoped. But I was there to practise my Italian and to see some paintings. Ah, Miss Fisher, Florence and the Uffizi, Venice and the Accademia!'

'Indeed,' agreed Phryne, forking up a mouthful of salad.

'I've seen paintings in some of the Scuola which no one else has seen – especially Raphaels. The houses are locked up, the owners are elsewhere. The buildings are sound enough but no one cares about the pictures. It's not right. Art should be free. A beautiful thing can only justify its existence if it is free to all-comers.'

'Possibly.' Phryne was feeling too lazy to quarrel. 'But the world is full of lovely things and one lifetime wouldn't be enough to see them all. Just Venice, for instance, it would take twenty years to properly appreciate all of it. But you know how tired travellers get. I always know that if I look into a room and say wearily, "Ah, five Botticellis", I need a sit down and a nice cup of coffee and probably an ice. And maybe a ride in a gondola with a pretty gondoliere and supper after the opera at night.'

'Ah, it is only the very decorative that dare to be so hedonistic,' sighed the young man and Phryne looked at him for the first time.

He had fearless blue eyes, blond hair with a suspicion of a curl and the thickening middle of one who has always regarded sport as an interruption to finishing a chapter and has given it up the second that they could. Jeoffry Bisset was not going to be volunteering for his college's old boys' cross country run, though it appeared that he played cricket.

'Thank you,' said Phryne. 'I also approve of your chicken salad. Did your wife make it?'

'Good God no, I can't afford to marry,' said Bisset, shocked. 'I'm living in Coll. The kitchen made up a hamper for me and since I told them that I was lunching with a beautiful lady they put some effort into it, it seems. Ideal life for a chap, Miss Fisher. Someone makes my bed and does my laundry and cooks my meals and I just have to be civil to 'em if I meet 'em.'

'Not entirely ideal, perhaps,' returned Phryne. 'There are the tortures of the flesh.'

'There are indeed,' said Bisset, eyeing her admiringly. 'But they can be relieved by some complaisant person for a small sum, or ignored if the risk is too great.'

'Where do you go for your complaisant persons?'

'Oh, Theo's, the Cafe Royale, perhaps, why on earth do you want to know?'

'I'm curious about Theo's. I went there last night.'

'Miss Fisher, if you are looking for complaisant

98

company, you don't need to go to Theo's,' said Bisset, insinuatingly. 'If nothing better is on offer, there is a person not two feet from you who would be both delighted and honoured to assist in any way he could.'

'I'm sure,' Phryne grinned wickedly and Jeoffry Bisset's delicate flirtation suddenly became as reflexive as 'Elle s'amuse'. He sat up straight. 'I will remember your charitable offer, which does you great credit,' she added, leaning down to kiss him very lightly on the cheek. She felt a shock run right through the young man. He was not as blasé about the lusts of men as he sounded by a very long chalk, Phryne considered, having a lot of experience in these matters.

'Miss Fisher,' said Bisset nervously. 'I never meant...'

'Yes, you did, my dear. You're just disconcerted. I didn't react as you expected a well brought-up lady ought to react, but I just don't blush like I used to and allusive conversations bore me. If I want you, I'll tell you, and if you are willing, I'll take you. And then I'll give you back to your College. Clear? Now, tell me about Theo's. I saw a sample of Bohemianism last night and if it was representative, it's a pretty wishy-washy imitation of Paris. I didn't see one suicide, they were all drinking punch, not a suggestion of the under-world and no occultists.'

'Then you didn't stay until Tillie's girls came in and Madame Sosostris and Marrin weren't there.' Bisset recovered his poise with some difficulty.

'A woman in a turban with a most unfriendly stare? Yes, I saw her. Reading tarot cards. I'll go

99

back to look again, perhaps I have misjudged them. That Jack Lindsay does a fine line in erotic verse, I have to say. But it wasn't precisely roistering, you know. More like a safe little chap's club which only admits women if they are "complaisant" or decorative. I couldn't see someone like Gertrude Stein presiding there.'

'An off night, perhaps,' muttered Bisset. 'Try it again.'

'I shall. Besides, I'm looking for one of Tillie's girls, or at least, I believe I am. I have a commission for her, worth quite a lot of money if I can find her quickly. Darlo Annie, they call her. Do you know Annie?'

'Yes, well, yes, I ... know her.' Bisset squirmed and Phryne diagnosed his discomforture with unnerving speed.

'You've purchased her company? Tell me, is this her?'

She handed him Joan's photograph. He held it up to the light, turning away to hide his own blushes. He had never met anyone like Phryne before, and one of the things he had not expected to be discussing at the cricket was the demimonde.

'It looks rather like her,' he told Phryne. 'Younger, you know and less ... hardened. But I don't know where Annie is. I haven't seen her for a week at least.'

That would fit with the calendar of Joan's disappearance.

'Where could such a girl go?' asked Phryne.

'Well, she might have gone back to her husband. That's a wedding photograph, isn't it? Wreath of orange blossoms and all. Or she might be in hospital. Or dead. Suicide is a possibility, likewise an overdose of veronal or alcohol. She might be in jail. There was a raid on one of the properties last week. Apparently Tillie Devine was ropeable. She'd bribed all the coppers in Sydney, she reckoned, but these ones had slipped through her net. They usually give people "found in a common bawdy-house" fourteen days without the option, because the fine would be paid out of the very immoral earnings which they have been arrested for making. That's why I always go to Theo's to meet the girls. The faculty might overlook a little boyish high spirits, but not a jail sentence.'

Phryne filed all these suggestions away. It should not be difficult to ascertain if any of them were true. She hoped not. Surely if Joan were dead, her family would have been notified? Not if she was lying anonymously on ice somewhere. 'So cold, so blue, so bare.' Phryne dismissed the verse of 'St James' Infirmary' from her mind. If necessary, she would view all the unidentified corpses in the mortuary herself.

'But she'll turn up,' said Bisset complacently. 'Those girls always do. Have some more chicken salad. So will you go to Theo's tonight?'

'Yes. Tell me, do you know the student who stole the exam papers?'

'Adam Harcourt? Yes. I can't believe he would have been that stupid. He would have passed any examination without needing to cheat. He's brilliant. Now he's ruined his life, quite needlessly.'

'Has he been expelled?'

'Not yet. The University Senate has to meet next Monday and they'll make it formal then.'

'When do you think the safe was cracked?' asked Phryne. 'The theft was discovered on the Monday morning, but do we know when it was accomplished?'

'Not precisely. Harcourt refuses to talk about it, beyond saying that it wasn't him and he didn't do it. I know the Book of Hours was there on Saturday morning. I was in the Secretary's office and Sykes dropped it when he was putting his books in the safe, clumsy bloody fool ... I beg your pardon.'

'What Book of Hours is it? I have seen some splendid ones in the British Museum.'

'It's the Hours of Juana the Mad of Castile. It's only an octavo, made to carry to church, but especially beautiful. The colours, particularly, are as fresh as the day they were painted. And it has a macabre tale attached to it.'

'Pour me more champagne and tell me all,' instructed Phryne.

'One of our graduates was in Spain – he was thinking of writing a book on Catalan and a marvellous novel called *Tirant Lo Blanc*. He must have picked up the Book of Hours in a junk shop somewhere and he had it in his pocket when he was killed on the mountains by a bandit. The Embassy packaged up his property and sent it home, and his parents found a will which left everything to the University, so they gave it to us.'

'That was generous of them,' commented Phryne. 'Isn't it very valuable?'

'To a collector, perhaps, but they didn't want it. We haven't even cleaned the blood off the binding because it might damage the gilding. And that idiot Sykes just let it fall to the floor and then stuffed it back in again as though it was one of his wretched ledgers. However. Poor Sykes, I suppose. His accounts have all gone missing and what he's going to say to the auditors I don't know.'

'Apparently he isn't one of nature's accountants,' said Phryne.

'Good God no, he has to take off his socks to count to more than ten. Only a university faculty would have made him Bursar. In fact, only the Dean would have done so, because he likes having someone to yell at. Terrible man, Gorman. Makes everyone who comes in contact with him feel tarnished, because one feels like a coward trying to avoid him and yet one has to, because he never gives up once he's got his fangs into a chap. Then he runs him ragged.'

'In what way?'

'He's a bully,' said Bisset. 'He likes tormenting people. He likes knowing things. He will then drop little hints, wife happy to see you, Bretherton? when he knows that Bretherton likes the ladies. Rather too much, perhaps. He twits Sykes on his accounts and Kirkpatrick on his Scotch accent, though Kirkpatrick gives as good as he gets. He's always telling Brazell that he only wants to get back to the desert because of the native women, and God knows that isn't true – Brazell really loves his Coast Murring, a good deal more than he loves civilisation, but that small fact wouldn't trouble the Dean. In fact, truth isn't important to him. He's loud and obnoxious and flashy and has no taste, but we could put up with that if he was a good chap, but he isn't. He'll drive someone to suicide one of these days. For instance, on Friday he says to Ayers, saw your slides on Cairo, Ayers, uncommonly handsome boys you always seem to find, when Ayers ... well. You see what I mean.'

'And what does he say to you?' asked Phryne.

'Whoops, here are the others, back from their roast beef and apple crumble. Better give me the glass and we'll pack up. Professor Jones doesn't approve of people turning serious games into picnics.'

Phryne drained the glass, it being against her principles to waste good champagne. 'So who would have been in the faculty office over the weekend?' she persisted, noting Bisset's avoidance of the Dean's accusations. What would the Dean have on Bisset? Communist sympathies? Some scandal about love? But these matters could wait.

'No one,' said Bisset, hurriedly stuffing the remains of the feast into his hamper and shoving it under his bench. 'The office should have been locked, so should the safe. Only the very dedicated go into a faculty office on a Sunday.'

'What about a Saturday night? Was there a social function, perhaps, and might someone have decided to seek a little privacy there?'

'An interesting suggestion,' muttered Bisset. Phryne wondered if it was a trick of the light or whether he had actually paled to the colour of vellum. 'A good lunch, chaps?' he asked the returning lunchers.

'Very good,' said Professor Bretherton, sitting down as the umpires walked out onto the field again, 'eh, Jones?'

'Not as good as it used to be, when my digestion

104

was also younger,' grumbled the Emeritus Professor, taking up his opera glasses again. 'Who's bowling? Geary, I believe. I don't know why they can't cope with him. Perfectly ordinary seamer. Just aims at the wickets, that's all he does.'

'More than we can do,' said Kirkpatrick. 'Did you have any lunch, Miss Fisher?'

'Some salad, thank you, quite delicious.' Phryne was watching the bowler.

'Rabbit food,' grunted Kirkpatrick. 'Howsat?'

'Out,' said Bretherton sadly. Woodfull walked off the ground.

'That was never LBW,' protested Bisset. 'Would have missed the off stump by a mile.'

'My dear young man, in all my years of cricket, I have never seen anyone more plumb in front of the stumps,' said Jones. 'Definitely LBW. Ah, me, that's the end of our resistance, I fancy.'

He was right. When Professor Bretherton dropped Phryne at her hotel, the score was not very much for a lot of wickets and Australia was on the skids again.

'You might dine with me,' suggested Professor Bretherton, diffidently.

'I might,' said Phryne, 'if you can show me the faculty safe.'

'An interesting request,' he replied.

'And your response?'

'At your service,' he bowed.

Six

*Be he poor, be he friendless, here he may acquire
distinction, the reward of merit alone. Knowledge to
him will here unfold her ample page; all the spoils of
time, all the treasures of thought, and all the bright
domains of a glorious future, may here become his.*

Sir Charles Nicholson, *On the Ideal Student*

Professor Bretherton walked boldly up the steps
to the faculty office and surprised a rabbity man
who was blotting a pile of papers with his sleeve
and staring into the distance with an expression
of deep despair.

'Sykes, what are you doing here?' demanded
Professor Bretherton.

'The Dean thought that I might be able to reconstruct the books,' said Sykes. 'I thought if I had
no distractions I might be able to remember what
the last transactions were, maybe even extract a
trial balance. But I can't remember. This isn't
going to work.'

'Do you have any notes?' asked Phryne, sym-
pathetic to Mr Sykes' wild eyes.

'They were all in the safe,' wailed Mr Sykes, then
he put his head down on his blotted manuscript
and began to sob.

'There, there,' said Phryne, putting a slender
arm around the fallen man. 'The auditors can't

106

blame you, Mr Sykes. This isn't going to work, as you say. Why don't you pack it in for now and go home?'

Mr Sykes, overwhelmed first with grief and second with the closeness and intoxicating scent of an unexpected lady, broke down entirely and cried like a child. Professor Bretherton made a subdued noise which sounded like 'Tcha!' and stalked off into the corridor, to return later with a cup of tea. He found Mr Sykes had recovered some of his equilibrium and recalled his scattered wits.

'Now, Sykes, you drink this, sit up straight, and tell the lady what she wants to know. This is the Hon. Phryne Fisher, you know. She's famous as an investigator. She's promised to help me find my papyrus, and that means she will have to find out what happened to your books.'

Inhaling fragrant and brandy scented steam – Professor Bretherton had clearly added some of his own cognac to the tea – Sykes did as ordered and quavered, 'I put the books in the safe and locked it – I'm almost sure that I locked it! – on Saturday morning. Just as usual.'

'What time?'

'Noon. I always lock up and leave at noon promptly, because my wife and I attend the meeting of our garden club at two. We wanted to see the new azaleas.' Sykes' lip quivered again, and Phryne patted him on the shoulder. 'Everything was there then. Bisset bellowed at me for dropping the Book of Hours, it was an accident, then the Dean started in on me for the mistakes in the Day Ledger, and it was all too much, so I just shut the safe and went home.'

'I hope you enjoyed the azaleas,' said Phryne gently. Poor Sykes. He was a furry man with greying hair and spectacles and he was liberally spotted with ink. If he had been a stuffed toy rabbit, he would have been threadbare with one bent ear. A nice little man, perfectly adequate for ordinary tasks, thrust into the unordinary and quite unable to cope with it.

'Yes, they were beautiful. We ordered three for that shady spot near the roses. Frilly pinks. My wife was very taken with them. They've been working on a new azalea for some time. Pure white. Lovely things. But how I'm going to survive if the Dean dismisses me without a reference, as he is threatening to do, I don't know, I don't know at all...'

He was about to burst into tears again and Phryne did not want to expose Sykes to what Professor Bretherton was evidently about to say.

'Now, Mr Sykes,' she said firmly, 'brace up. If I find Professor Bretherton's papyrus I'm quite likely to find your books. You are sure that the contents of the safe were all tickety-boo at noon on Saturday?'

'Er ... yes, Miss Fisher, perfectly, er ... tickety-boo,' replied Sykes.

'Good. Now cast your mind back. Look at the office. Someone who took all that stuff out of the safe would need something to carry it in, wouldn't they? Is there a box missing? A case?'

Sykes surveyed the office. It was cluttered. All the walls were lined with bookshelves stuffed with miscellaneous volumes. Sykes' desk was loaded with papers. In the inner room, the Dean's was bare and polished, carrying only an inkstand, a tray of pens and the broad white expanse of faultless blotting paper. The safe hulked in a corner. It was large enough to store a small rhinoceros.

'No, nothing missing, as far as I can tell.'

'Interesting,' commented Phryne. 'All right, now, off you go, Mr Sykes. Leave it to me and enjoy your garden.'

'Yes, push off, Sykes, that's enough emotion for one evening,' said Professor Bretherton.

Mr Sykes, seemingly heartened, abandoned his papers, collected his hat and left, babbling apologies for his loss of control. When he had bowed his way out, Professor Bretherton shut the door. Phryne inspected it. It was not a deadlock but needed a key, and did not appear to have been forced.

'How many keys are there?' asked Phryne.

'We've all got one, and I suppose that the porter has one, and the cleaners, and there would be a master key as well,' said Bretherton. 'In any case poor Sykes probably forgot to lock it.'

'I notice that there is a couch and a door which can lock,' said Phryne. Dousing the anticipatory light in Professor Bretherton's eyes, she added, 'So someone could have come up here in female company for purposes quite unconnected with theft, couldn't they?'

'Well, yes, I suppose so, such things have been known to happen,' agreed Professor Bretherton grudgingly, 'youth and all that. But much better to take the lady into one's own office, of course. More private and less likely to be noticed. One could always explain that one was working late.'

'Could one take a lover to one's room if one lived in College?'

'Oh, no, my dear lady, impossible unless one smuggles her up the stairs, though there are climbing possibilities in the ivy in one of the Colleges, I believe. No women in the rooms after ten, that's the rule. And that rule, if broken, will get one rusticated.'

'Expelled?'

'No, not necessarily, but there would be a filthy scandal and the unfortunate man would find himself thrown out for a couple of years to repent. If one could use one's office, that would be better. No couch, perhaps, but there are rugs on the floor and youth makes nothing of discomfort in the service of Venus.' He grinned. Phryne suddenly liked Professor Bretherton.

'Not that I'd be doing anything of the sort. Married man and all that. The scandal does not bear thinking of.'

'I'll keep that in mind,' promised Phryne. 'I observe that there is a large coat cupboard in which the lady might be hidden, in fact it's big enough for two if one's tastes ran that way.'

'Extravagant,' murmured Professor Bretherton. Phryne closed the coat cupboard on a faint whiff of ... what? She sniffed deeply. She had smelt that before. Not unpleasant, faintly sweet, but not a common perfume. Odd. She was presented with a picture of a church in Venice. San Barnabo, as she recalled. She shook her head and filed the scent for future reference.

'And there is the couch.' Phryne sat on it, then lay back. 'Quite large enough in an emergency,' she observed. Professor Bretherton drank in the sight of Phryne in her blue dress reclining on the couch and said nothing. She leapt to her feet and continued prowling.

'Nice safe,' she commented, kneeling down in front of it.

'It was bought from a deceased estate, I believe.' Professor Bretherton was pleased to find his voice quite level, even though Phryne had plucked her gown above her knees so as not to crease it. She got up abruptly, spoiling the picture.

'Yes, and this is why they sold it. Pass me my bag, please.' Phryne took out a German steel nail file, which she had found invaluable for picking locks, adjusting the spark in her Hispano-Suiza, turning screws and occasionally even filing nails. 'Very impressive front, see? Heavy door and great big combination lock. But this safe was meant to be set in a wall, so no one has bothered about the back. Observe.'

She set the nail file into the peeling back of the safe, gave a wrench and a twist, and the whole thin steel plate lifted off its rivets.

'Good God!' exclaimed Professor Bretherton, sitting down rather abruptly in the Dean's chair.

'It's hard to tell, but I think that someone has done this recently. There are scratches here that look quite fresh. So the only bar to getting into the safe is whether or not the office door was locked. It's not a deadlock. It would be quite easy to pick.'

'Miss Fisher, I am appalled!' Professor Bretherton fanned himself with one hand while groping for his pocket flask with the other. 'But that means that it needn't be one of us. I mean, if any passing thief could open the safe so easily...'

'Have a heart,' begged Phryne. 'What thief would be "passing" here? This is a closed puzzle, Professor. Now, I'll just have a look at this window,' she said as she examined the catches, which were complete and even dusty, 'and you can take me to dinner and tell me all about your fellows.'

John Bretherton looked uncomfortable. 'I don't know that I'm going to enjoy this as much as I thought,' he confessed.

'Do you want your papyrus back or not?' asked Phryne.

'I want it back,' he said.

The Hotel Australia put on a splendid dinner, and Phryne intended to enjoy it; investigation made her hungry. She felt exhilarated. Out of her own milieu, with none of her own helpers, in a foreign city which became more foreign by the moment, she was getting somewhere. Or so it appeared.

'The Dean,' she suggested, and Professor Bretherton chuckled into his vichyssoise.

'Old Gorman? Surely you jest. I'd put the chances of him escorting a lady to his office for a little dalliance at three hundred to one. More. He's very respectable.'

'And is it your experience – or Juvenal's – that the very respectable are also the very virtuous?' asked Phryne. The cold soup really was remarkable.

'No, of course, every man is basically rotten, both Juvenal and I agree. But the Dean wouldn't dare. He might want to. I suppose all men have lusts, disgusting thought when one considers Gorman, but I admit the possibility. But he wouldn't put his academic position in jeopardy for any woman. I don't think he even likes women much. One only has to look at his wife. And he would never put himself in the position where he might be refused. Far too much of a risk. Actually, more of a certainty, when one considers Gorman.' Professor Bretherton shuddered slightly.

'He might steal the contents of the safe for another reason,' Phryne suggested.

'Possibly, but why? He's independently wealthy, his family owns half of the Northern Territory, mines and so on. I doubt he'd want a Book of Hours. He has all the artistic appreciation of a hog. His own wife's garnets went and she's a formidable woman who would make her lack of appreciation sting. He wouldn't take the books, surely, he knew what a state they were in, though there's not a particle of harm in Sykes, poor chap. Never seen him break down like that.'

'Sykes, then?'

'Would never have the nerve,' decided Professor Bretherton. 'You saw him. Falls to pieces at a touch.'

'But his nerves may have something to do with him systematically stealing from the faculty. Has he been getting worse lately?'

'Well, yes, now that you mention it, yes, I suppose he has. But no, Miss Fisher, I could believe that he has some guilty knowledge, perhaps, but he could never have stolen something. He's very honest. Small things cost him sleepless nights, poor chap.'

'Is there a lot to steal?' Phryne had chosen lobster, and was now confronted with a scarlet shell containing delicate meat folded in mayonnaise which had never seen the inside of a condensed milk tin.

'Not by the standards of a bank, though we have a lot of scholarships and there are several bequests. But they are paid out, you see, the faculty pays its own fees out of the bequest. There would never be a lot of money just sitting in the safe. The trustee pays the faculty and the faculty pays the University, all in the one day, usually. And there were only three pounds, seven shillings and sixpence in petty cash, not enough to risk a two year sentence for burglary.'

'No. But that relies on the passing thief and as I have said, I don't believe in the passing thief. Consider what problems your thief would have. He's got a bundle of heavy ledgers which he can't understand, a necklace which he might sell for a fraction of its value provided he knew a fence, a papyrus – please excuse me saying this – of no value except to a collector, and a Book of Hours which he can't exactly take down to the pub and sell to one of the boys. Profit from a horribly risky undertaking – three quid, seven and sixpence and maybe a couple of pounds for the garnets. No. I really don't think so.'

'But if a passing thief did do it, then he would have dumped all the other stuff in the bushes and taken off with the saleable items,' put in Professor Bretherton.

'Yes, so he would, if he troubled to take them out of the safe in the first place. Have you searched the bushes?'

'Extensively.' Professor Bretherton was as downcast as a man could be when he was dining with a beautiful woman at the Hotel Australia.

'Nothing?'

'Many things, but none germane to the issue.'

'Well, what about your fellows, then? How about Bisset?'

'An idealist. An eye for a pretty face. No private income, but he's fairly entrenched in the faculty. A shark on European languages and well liked by the students.'

'Kirkpatrick?'

'Wouldn't give a penny to a blind beggar. Mean as a rat but honest in that spare Presbyterian way. I can't see him stealing anything. John Knox would not approve. Married to a woman fully as miserly as he is and entirely respectable. Not a whiff of scandal, as far as I know.'

'How about Brazell, was that his name, the anthropologist?'

'Spends most of his life wandering around observing the beastly customs of the heathen.' Professor Bretherton laughed quietly. 'That's why he's so well-mannered. Says one gets that way if the penalty for lack of decorum at dinner is likely to be a thorough spearing. Charming feller, funny he's never married. No money, of course. He has a permanent feud with Ayers the archaeologist, he's a fanatic about Egypt. Ayers says that there are more things to be discovered, not at the Valley of the Kings, but at a village nearby where the artificers lived. He's petitioning for funds to excavate. Brazell wants the money spent on Aboriginal remains, middens and so on. He says we should learn about our own country before we start digging up other people's. Ayers isn't at all interested in Stone Age cultures and finds that the Egyptian climate agrees with him.'

'The climate or the people?' asked Phryne, observing a glint in the professorial eye.

'Ah, well, you see, people with Ayers' tendencies in Australia have to travel. I mean, they can't just pop over to Tangier to find...'

'...Complaisant company?' hazarded Phryne. 'So he likes Egypt's beautiful girls?'

'Not precisely.' Professor Bretherton paused until Phryne got the hint. 'But a dear good chap after all. I like both of them. Ayers is very funny about foreign customs, and Brazell has a pretty wit. They can even beguile a faculty meeting.'

'So Ayers wants to head off to Cairo with a copy of André Gide's latest in his pocket and Brazell wants to go back to his desert,' Phryne mused. 'I can't see a lot of common ground between them. Who's winning?'

'It's hard to say. The project is in the Dean's gift. He hasn't made up his mind. Gorman always says things like, "I will give you my decision on Thursday at eleven am," and he does, on Thursday at eleven am and not a minute before. He thinks that is being decisive. In fact he makes up his mind at ten fifty-nine am on the Thursday largely based on which side his mental coin lands. It works as well as any other method, I expect. Dreadful fellow, that Gorman. Juvenal would recognise him instantly. He wants clients, you see. He would love to have poor scholars and relations clustering around his door every morning for their

116

dole. But he's got nowhere with me and most of the other chaps ignore his nasty insinuations. Don't know how much longer poor Sykes will last, though. And it's funny about chaps like Sykes. A nervous wreck most of the time and then one day they up and do something very unlikely.'

'Such as emptying the safe?' asked Phryne.

'Slaughtering the Dean, is what I was going to say. Banish Sykes from your mind, Miss Fisher. Although put him on your list if Gorman is found with an axe in his head. Even worms turn in the end. Well, then, this is refreshing. I seldom get a chance to gossip about the faculty with – excuse me – an outsider, especially a brilliant one who happens also to be one of the most beautiful women I have ever met. Who's left to suspect?'

'You,' said Phryne.

Professor Bretherton smiled a smile which Juvenal would also have recognised.

'Of course. Well, I am married as happily as most chaps, have a private income, no particular vices, and I've employed you to find my papyrus for me.'

'Happily married men don't dine with vamps like me, I know nothing about your private income, which might be strained, ditto about your vices which might be curious – I note that you knew a lot about concealing lovers in cupboards – and you might have asked me to help as a way of diverting suspicion,' replied Phryne composedly, lighting a cigarette as the waiter brought coffee.

Professor Bretherton passed a hand over his white hair and laughed.

'All true, my dear young lady,' he said. 'But I'm

afraid that what I said was true and I want that papyrus back very badly.'

'I'll see what I can contrive.' Miss Fisher blew a smoke ring, the picture of an idle flapper. John Bretherton seized her free hand.

'Please, I need that papyrus,' he urged, squeezing her wrist. 'Please.'

There was a slight flurry as Phryne freed herself from this unexpected clasp. Professor Bretherton rubbed his hand, wondering how she had managed to make his fingers open.

'All right, you're in earnest,' said Phryne sharply. 'Now, you will tell me about the papyrus. What is this curse? Is there anything on the document which does not appear in your translation?'

He stared at her, taken aback. Then to Phryne's amazement, he rose and bowed slightly, dropping a banknote on the table.

'I'm afraid I must bid you good evening,' he said quietly, and left.

'Well,' said Phryne to the waiter, handing him the banknote, 'it seems my escort has left me, so you might as well keep the change.'

'Madame will easily find another with better taste,' said the young man, calculating that he had gained almost a week's wages in one tip and wishing to mollify the beautiful lady.

'Without doubt,' replied Phryne, wishing that Lin Chung was with her. This investigation was more difficult than it looked, and she was beginning to wish also that she had stayed home. Sydney was more strange than Paris or London, being both familiar and odd.

'Dot, I've been abandoned,' she announced, sweeping into her suite and flinging her cloche at the hat stand. It hit the peg and hung limply.

'Usually are,' said Dot stoutly. 'That cop reckons he'll search all the hospitals and places for Joan, but he says he thinks she might be Darlo Annie and I don't know what to do.'

'Tell me about your sister,' said Phryne gently, sitting down on the Empire sofa and taking off her shoes. Dot stopped pacing and sat down, ordering her thoughts. Phryne looked at her. Dot was plain, as she never denied, but she was well made and honest and the shadowy, leaf patterned, bark-coloured dress she was wearing made her look like a strong-minded dryad speaking out of her parent tree. Phryne smiled a little at the fancy. She had been reading Ovid recently and he was colouring her imagination.

'Well, Joan, she was the one with culture. Read a lot of books, Joanie did, Mum says she has Pre-tensions. She used to dance like an angel and she was always trying to keep the kids in line, you know, about using a fork to eat peas and tipping the soup plate away to sup the last bit. It was a bit of a surprise that she married Jim Thompson at all, he being a rough sort of bloke. It was all right after she had little Dottie, she seemed happy enough, though the baby came early. She didn't want to go to Sydney, so far away from home, though of course she had to follow her husband's business. He inherited his ironmongery business from his brother. Joan said he was a good provider though he used to get on the booze every Saturday night and I think he used to hit her. But a lot of husbands are like that and their wives don't run away to be ... to be...'

'Dot, don't cry. We don't know that your sister is a lady of light repute, we don't even know if she is Darlo Annie. Dammit, Dot, I am astray in a foreign place! If this was Melbourne I'd know someone who knew someone who could find out for me exactly who Darlo Annie is, and that would solve one problem. Now, take comfort. We've reported your sister's disappearance to the proper authorities and they'll be looking for her too. And if she has taken an unusual path, you think about this, Dorothy Williams. You've got a drunken husband who beats you, you've got two children under five who are crying with hunger, and you're a thousand miles from any help. You can make money by turning whore, or you can watch your children starve, your husband turn into a brute, and all of you thrown out into the street to sleep under the bridge. Moral scruples are one thing, survival is another.'

'Yes, miss.' Dot blew her nose. 'She was always a determined girl, my sister Joan. She might have done it if it meant that the children would be fed – she was fierce about the children. But how could she have left them like that? That's what I can't understand.'

'Neither can I. Now, Joss and Clarence are coming to escort me to Theo's. Did they leave anything for me?'

'Yes, Miss, it's on the table. I'll order some tea, shall I?'

'Tea for you, black coffee for me. And find something showy for me to wear tonight. I want to be noticed. How have you gone with the amulet?'

Dot produced it; she was rather proud of her work. Phryne turned it over in her hands. It was a purple silk pouch embroidered with Solomon's seal in silver thread, suspended from a white silk cord. It crunched slightly in the hand and smelt strongly of herbs. There was something hard in the amulet and Phryne asked, 'What have you added?'

'Well, Miss,' explained Dot earnestly, 'you said it was to protect against magical attack, and I expect that means demons, so I bought a medal of Saint Michael. He was the angel who fought Lucifer and won,' she added kindly, for Phryne's benefit. She was not sure how much Anglicans knew about religion. 'I dipped it in holy water at St Mary's cathedral when I went in to say a prayer for my sister, in case the poor young man really is threatened, not just scared. So that it isn't just a fraud and he can rely on it.'

Phryne kissed Dot, unexpectedly.

'You are a very compassionate young woman,' she told her. 'Thank you. I'm sure that it will be most effective.'

Phryne opened the package on her table. In it was a large book marked 'Not to be removed from the Research Collection'. A slip of paper marked a page.

'The Oxyrrinchus papyrus number 666, translated by Professor John Bretherton of the University of Sydney', she read. A plate showed her an undecorated papyrus with lines of demotic script, not the hieroglyphics she had vaguely expected. Of course, he said they were all in Greek. She could not see any other markings on the paper, apart from the writing which was clear and flowing, arranged like a verse.

The snake be against him on land,
The crocodile against him in water,
He shall be cursed in eating, in drinking
In love-making, in excreting, in urinating,
In laughing and in crying,
In sailing, in walking
In sleeping, in waking.
He shall have no offering
No bread and no beer
No wine and no oil
No earth shall be dug for him
No remembrance carved for him
When he dies,
When he dies.

'One thing about the Egyptians, they were thorough,' she remarked to Dot. 'The person who receives this is cursed in doing absolutely everything, and finally when he dies he will have no tomb. I wonder what behaviour triggered the curse? Do we have any learned notes?'

Dot said, 'I think if you wear the purple silk and the loose patterned jacket which belongs to the black dress, you'll look showy enough, Miss. The colours clash something dreadful. The young gentlemen didn't give me any notes, Miss. Just the parcel.'

Phryne smiled – Dot was definitely distracted – and turned to the beginning of the volume. 'Notes by Professor Bretherton': aha.

This document shows no signs of being posted or affixed to a door or, perhaps, a wall, but the presumption can be made that it was meant to defend either a tomb against robbery or a monument against some defacement. Similar curses, though not as extensive, have been found in the 12th Dynasty tombs and one is carved on the Stele of Hatshepsut (18th Dynasty) at Karnak. It shows a surprising sophistication, which may reveal a Hellenic influence.

Not a lot of use, thought Phryne. But at least she had now seen the curse which the Professor had refused to disclose. A nice, strong-minded, comprehensive curse, thought Phryne as she stretched out on her bed for a small nap before her escorts arrived. Nothing that she could see about it would apply to the modern world, so what had driven Professor Bretherton so unceremoniously away?

She fell asleep wondering about him. Good looking, about sixty, white hair and those disconcerting dark eyes. Shouldn't have any trouble attracting female company if he wanted it.

What was he afraid of?

Seven

The gallows from which he is suspended forms a <u>Tau</u> cross while the figure ... forms a fylfot cross ... it should be noted that 1) the tree of sacrifice is of living wood... 2) that the face expresses deep entrancement, and suffering; 3) that the figure, as a whole, suggests life in suspension, but life and not death. It is a card of profound significance, but that significance is veiled.

A.E. Waite, *The Pictorial Key to the Tarot*

Theo's *was* more interesting late at night, Phryne considered. A promising argument about Symbolism was flaring amongst the poets; the names of Baudelaire and Mallarmé were being freely bandied about. Christopher Brennan was bellowing at a woman in a turban.

'"Mad is the Egyptian race; they are cursed! In war they are not sated. I say what you know. Dark ships, heavily armed; they sailed and they bring an army possessed by anger!" Aeschylus knew what he was talking about, Madame. Why do you bother me with these Egyptians? Nothing good ever came out of Egypt. You need to study the Greeks if you want civilisation.'

'Civilisation is outmoded!' yelled the woman in the turban, flushed with rage. 'We need a new heaven and a new earth.'

124

'Adolescent Nietzscheism,' sneered Brennan.

Two poets dragged the combatants apart. Madame Sosostris sat down to her cards again, muttering, 'Ancient fool!'

Brennan resumed his place amongst the poets, mumbling, 'Ignorant bitch.'

Honours appeared to be about even. Phryne nodded to Chas Nuttall, who called from his argument about Cubism, 'No luck with your lady, Phryne! No one's seen her!' and the bearded poet Jack, suppressing his usual greeting, dropped a Mallarmé quote in mid-sentence to report the same. Darlo Annie, he said, was missing, but no one at Tillie's seemed concerned about her.

Joss and Clarence steered Phryne to a seat against the wall, out of the way of thrown objects, and brought someone to sit next to her. He had brown curly hair and brown eyes, an ordinary young man if one overlooked the fact that he was far too thin and vibrating with nerves.

'I'm Phryne Fisher. Put this on,' she said, holding his gaze with her own green stare. She looped the white cord over his neck and he put up a shaking hand to touch the amulet. She smelt the bracing scent of rosemary and wormwood and hoped he would inhale frequently. Rosemary for courage and wormwood to repel serpents. Also, while he wore it, he would never get moths. She tucked it briskly under his shirt.

'There's a lot of good solid magic in that,' Phryne told him, thinking of Dot and her touching purchase of the St Michael medal.

'But Miss Fisher, this will leave *you* unprotected,' said Adam Harcourt, drawing a deep breath.

'I have power of my own,' said Phryne. 'Don't concern yourself about me, Mr Harcourt. Now, I am trying to extract you out of the soup, dear boy, and I need some information. So Joss and Clarence will go and fetch us a bottle of the good wine, if this place has any, and a few cups, chaps, if you can find some. Then Adam can decide if he wants to confide in me, and if he does, he can do so without anyone else listening.'

At this hint Joss and Clarence removed themselves. Adam Harcourt quavered, 'What about Madame and Marrin?'

'Leave Madame and Marrin to me,' said Phryne with quiet confidence. 'What are they threatening?'

'To suck my soul out of my body,' he whispered. Phryne laid a hand flat against the young man's cheek, feeling his tremors. 'To send an incubus. I am living in Paul's, for the moment, and they know where I am. I have heard it scratching on my window every night, and sooner or later it will get in.'

'In what form?' asked Phryne, familiar with the conventions of this sort of Crowleyite Magick.

'An owl,' Adam shuddered. 'A white owl.'

'Hmm.' Phryne was aware that the white owl meant death in most Celtic cultures. She was also aware that real owls appeared white in moonlight, and hunted the sparrows who lived in the creepers which covered old buildings. She had heard an owl beating the ivy with its wings and the sound could not be called comfortable, especially to a haunted

126

imagination in a cold bed.

'Have you thought of getting a friend to stay with you?' she asked delicately, not being able yet to diagnose the victim's sexual orientation. He was leaning his cheek into her caressing hand and she could feel his cold flesh warming at her touch.

'No, I can't possibly ask someone else to share the danger,' protested Harcourt. 'In any case, the incubus could get me while they slept unaware. Or so they say.'

This young man had been thoroughly bluffed and now was thoroughly terrified. Phryne could smell his fear, a scent as pungent as ammonia. She lit a cigarette to mask it – fear was catching – and asked, 'How did you get involved with Madame and Marrin?'

'She read my cards one night. I don't usually come to Theo's – it's a bit out of my way. I'm not one of these privileged ones, you know, I'm a scholarship boy. My father's a bricklayer. So I haven't any money to spare for Bohemianism, and precious little time. I earn some extra money working in the library and a little more helping poor Mr Sykes with his books, though he has to pay me from his own pocket and he's not too well off, either. But Joss brought me here one night, and Madame read my cards, and she saw right through me, into the fear.'

'Fear?' Phryne offered Harcourt a gasper and lit it for him. His hand trembled and the smoke went up in a wriggling stream, like a snake.

'That someone is going to scream, "What are you doing here? Get back to the brickyard, peasant!" I always feel like that.'

'So did I,' soothed Phryne. 'I come from Collingwood and my father was a wastrel. I know that feeling, Adam. It does, after awhile, almost wear off.'

'It never will.' Adam Harcourt shuddered again. 'Then they asked me to the meetings of the temple. I was fascinated. They showed me some amazing things. I ... became engrossed in it. In magic. I was an initiate. Then they asked me to steal the papyrus and I realised that I was in a terrible situation. I wouldn't steal it – don't think that I did, not in my own mind, I would never do that. But what if they mesmerised me, and I did it in a trance? That's why I haven't been able to defend myself properly. What if I am guilty?'

'I think that very unlikely,' said Phryne.

'Why?' asked Harcourt with the first stirrings of animation, 'because of my moral character? You don't know me, Miss Fisher. You don't know what I've done.'

'I can imagine what you've done. Ritual intercourse with a priestess, even Madame herself, perhaps? Ritual sodomy with Marrin? A little animal sacrifice and a great deal of blasphemy? Denied the Christ, trampled on a crucifix, spat on an icon, and kissed a number of unappetising parts of various images?'

Adam Harcourt blushed as purple as his amulet and buried his face in his hands. 'Some of those things,' he whispered.

'Nothing worse than that, eh? That's not so bad,' soothed Phryne. 'God will forgive you, that's his function. All you have to do is buck up, young

128

man, and defend yourself. And I believe you are not guilty of this burglary for another reason entirely.'

'What?' asked Harcourt, breathlessly.

'If you had been put into trance and told to steal the papyrus, you'd have delivered it, and they would know where it was. They don't. They're still trying to buy it from Professor Bretherton. They might have been intelligent enough to instruct you to steal all of the contents of the safe, and they are certainly nasty enough to instruct you to leave the exam papers where any nosy Professor could find them, so that you would be ruined as a reward for your service to evil. But they haven't got what they wanted, so whatever they tried to do to you didn't work. And it shan't work again.'

'I hadn't thought of that.'

'No. Now, I am going to remove the magical threat. You shall sleep sound tonight or my name's not Phryne Fisher, which, of course, it is. By the Lords of the Sea and the Sky, boy, how could you get involved with black magic without knowing that there is white magic as well?' Phryne used Golden Dawn phrasing quite easily. 'In a Manichean universe, they are equally powerful. Wear the amulet and drink some warm milk before retiring. Ask Joss or Clarence to sleep in your room. Assume that any noises off stage are natural. They will be. Is that clear?'

Adam Harcourt seemed relieved and was looking much healthier. Phryne could feel someone staring at her, but declined to dignify their regard by moving.

'Yes, Miss Fisher.'

'Do you believe that I will do this?' she demanded, holding his eyes with her own. Adam blinked, looked down through long eyelashes, then took a deep breath and met her gaze again.

'Yes, Miss Fisher,' he said firmly.

'Good boy. Now, tell me, in order, the events of Saturday morning. You were in the faculty office, helping Mr Sykes with his ledgers?'

'Yes. We had the whole week laid out carefully and I was collating all the entries to see why we were eleven pounds seven shillings and fourpence out. He'd put an entry into the wrong side of the balance, poor man. If only he'd ask the Dean for some money so that he could employ me to keep the accounts properly, rather than try and fix them after he has made a hash of them, it would be a lot easier. To find that eleven pounds I had to go back to the previous Monday, a boring and laborious task.'

'But you did it.'

'Oh, yes. My field is languages but I'm quite good at figures. We'd finished when the Dean started on Mr Sykes about his inefficiency; he is inefficient but the Dean makes him more so, he bellows at him and flusters him and then he makes silly mistakes. Finally the Dean went away and we stored the ledgers in the safe. Mr Sykes was so upset that he dropped the Book of Hours, and that made Bisset yell at him. Professor Kirkpatrick reproved Bisset for being unmannerly and they nearly quarrelled, too. They don't see eye to eye with each other on Old Norse borrowings, either. It was one of those prickly days. Mr Sykes wanted to get away to his garden club meeting, so we just shoved everything into the safe and went out. I heard the safe clunk shut, so I'm sure it was locked. And Mr Sykes locked the faculty office, too.'

'Have you a good memory for figures as well as a good head for them?' asked Phryne.

'Yes, pretty good,' agreed Harcourt.

'Then you could probably reconstruct the ledger in all essentials,' she continued.

'Yes, but they wouldn't trust me now,' said Harcourt sadly.

'Another point in your favour,' commented Phryne. 'You could have looked at those exam papers at any time. How long had they been in the safe?'

'Oh, they've been there for weeks,' said Harcourt. 'I wouldn't do that. I'm good. I want ... I wanted ... to prove to them all that I'm good.'

'So you shall,' said Phryne. 'Is there anything else you would like to confess? Here come our friends with a bottle.'

'Nothing more. But do be careful, Miss Fisher. These people are dangerous.'

'So am I,' Phryne replied. 'Watch.'

She accepted some of Joss' red wine, took her cup over to Madame Sosostris and sat down uninvited, looking at the array of tarot cards.

'You were trying to attract my attention?' she asked politely. Madame did not speak for a long moment. Phryne sipped her wine – thin, sour and cheap Italian Chianti. She lounged, looking bored and garish in her patterned silk coat and her purple dress. The noise of Chas Nuttall passionately defending kitchen utensils as suitable subjects for the depiction of the Beautiful dominated the room. Phryne glanced at the tarot.

'Interesting,' Phryne commented, as Madame did not seem inclined to speak. 'May I see?'

The dark woman in the turban allowed Phryne to sweep the cards together and look through them. This was another indication that she was not a believer. A real gypsy might be in Theo's reading fortunes, as a real gypsy might be anywhere where there were customers. But a Romany would not allow anyone else to casually handle her cards, believing that thus her own influence would be diluted and her contact with the inchoate future would be lost.

'That young man,' said Phryne, laying down a card.

'The Page of Wands,' said a voice behind Phryne. She did not turn around. She lifted her eyes to a mirror on the wall and saw a perfectly bald man leaning over her shoulder. His front teeth were filed to a point. His fingernails, she noticed as he put one hand flat on the table, were coloured blood red. This must be Marrin.

'He neither has your papyrus nor can he lay hands on it,' she said clearly but softly. 'There is no purpose in tormenting him further. If you do not leave him alone...' She put down another card. On it a young woman forced a lion's mouth closed.

'Strength,' said Marrin.

'...I will be cross,' said Phryne, looking deep into Madame's black eyes. 'And if you were looking for a card for me,' she added, putting one down with a little slap. On a rose-wreathed throne, a crowned woman stared into a pentacle held on her lap.

132

'The Queen of Pentacles,' said Marrin. 'A woman of wealth and power. But equally,' he reached into the pack and drew a card seemingly at random, 'there is me.'

'The Devil,' said Phryne, looking at a pair of naked humans chained at the feet of Baphomet, the alleged God of the Templars, a satyr with female breasts and an inverted pentacle between his eyes.

'And there is Madame.' Another card fluttered to the table.

'Sophia. Wisdom. The High Priestess,' said Phryne. 'Sitting between the pillars of light and dark, holding the scroll of the law on her lap. Do you always award yourselves Major Arcana? Mostly they apply to fates and cosmic events. You should ask Professor Brennan to explain to you about hubris. I'm not impressed and I'm not frightened,' she said flatly. 'Not by the pointy teeth or the nail-polish or the sleight-of-hand.' Marrin moved to stand behind Madame Sosostris. They both stared at her and she neither blinked nor looked away, a Dutch-doll woman with piercing cat's eyes and a mouth set like a lintel.

'You're not,' agreed Madame in a husky, middle-European voice. 'You aren't Hungarian, are you?'

'No.'

The staring match continued. Phryne, who could outstare a gargoyle, was almost bored. Eventually Madame looked away, and a moment later Marrin blinked.

'You're powerful,' he conceded.

'Have I made my point?' asked Phryne.

'You want Harcourt released?'

133

'I do. I don't want to put any damper on your activities – they are none of my business. Find another playmate, there is a wide selection here. But release Harcourt. I want to find out what happened to the contents of that safe. I want to clear his name. And I want to find that papyrus.'

'You want to find it? So do we. For a magical working of great significance.' Marrin sat down and reached for Phryne's cup of wine. She let him take it.

'Scrying doesn't help?' asked Phryne sympathetically. 'A spirit medium is of no use? Surely the original scribe is anxious to tell you where his curse is.'

'No, it's not a re-animation. The scribe is gone and in the Field of Reeds. We want it for another matter entirely,' said Marrin, emptying the cup and setting it down.

'I'm not going to inquire into anything hidden,' said Phryne delicately. 'You can keep your hermetic secrets. But I need to know – is there something on that papyrus which does not appear in the photograph? Is that why you need the original?'

A quick exchange of glances between the two was all that Phryne needed.

'I cannot tell you anything more,' said Madame, portentously.

'But if the papyrus should come into your hands,' said Marrin, 'we might be able to make you an offer.'

'You made an offer to Professor Bretherton, but he hasn't got it either. Nor would he sell it, I fancy.'

'John Bretherton,' said Madame, drawing out the syllables venomously. 'He seeks the same as we do. But we will find it first.'

'Oh, good. I wish you well. And Adam Harcourt?'

'He is of no further use,' agreed Marrin. 'But he is held to us by more than magical bonds. I will release him, but later I will have him in my hand again – you shall see.' He stood up and sketched a sigil in the air with his blood-red nails. Phryne fancied that she could see it glowing. Then he blew it towards Harcourt. Phryne knew that the eyes of Joss, Clarence and Adam were riveted on her meeting with Madame and Marrin and hoped that this gesture might free the young man's mind from doubt.

'He's carrying some defence, what is it?' asked Marrin, surprising her.

'An amulet. Thank you,' she said to Madame, laying a banknote on the tarot, another forbidden act, insolently done. Madame seemed unaware of the conventions.

'Take a card,' she said, fanning them out, face down.

Phryne picked one at random. Madame turned it up and hissed, 'You see?' at Marrin, who grinned like a shark. The card depicted corpses rising from their coffins towards a descending angel.

'Judgment,' said Phryne. She smiled a slight social smile and went back to Harcourt. 'You're free,' she told him. 'Released from all chains and bonds. Your own man entirely.'

'How did you do it?' breathed Harcourt with the expression of a prisoner who has not only been unshackled but invited to tea by the Governor.

'All done by kindness,' said Phryne. Joss and Clarence gave her another cup of sour wine and sighed with relief. Harcourt was recovering before their eyes. His cheeks were pinkening, his eyes had lost the glazed look which had worried them and his whole body appeared to have filled with vitality like a glass filling with water. Joss slapped him on the shoulder in congratulation.

'Told you Miss Fisher could do it,' said Jocelyn. Harcourt smiled at him.

'Magicians are one thing, mysteries another,' said Phryne. 'So temper your transports, if that isn't mixing a metaphor. Still haven't got a great deal further with this puzzle. I haven't found Darlo Annie and no one seems concerned at her disappearance.'

'Oh, those girls come and go,' said Joss airily, making Miss Fisher's fingers itch to box his ears. 'She'll drift back, I expect.'

'You really haven't any idea, have you?' asked Phryne. 'You really don't touch the real world at any point. Where do you come from, Joss?'

'North Shore, of course.' Joss seemed puzzled. 'Dad's in the city and wants me to join his business and I really didn't want to start as a surveyor's mate so I went up to the U. Why? Have I said something wrong?'

'Never mind.' Phryne drank down her wine and held out the cup for more. 'What about you, Clarence?'

'Oh, I'm a third generation medical man, but I can't stand the sight of blood so I chose Arts instead. I'm a black sheep,' said Clarence proudly.

'Perfectly useless.'

Phryne reflected privately on a world in which one could be a black sheep by choosing one university course over another, and contrasted it with the unknown fate of Darlo Annie, who might be Joan Thompson née Williams who had taken a darker road to achieve the status of social outcast. When she reemerged, bearded Jack was mangling another quote from Mallarmé and Phryne decided to enter the conversation.

'No, no, Mallarmé wrote *"La chair est triste, helas! et j'ai lu tour les livres"*. The flesh is sad, alas! And I have read all the books. Myself, I prefer Apollinaire and Jules Laforgue, and you might consider what Verlaine has to say in *Art poétique: "Plus vague et plus soluble dans l'air"*.'

'He pursued the Ideal,' agreed George reluctantly, not willing to try trading quotes with this learned woman but constitutionally unable to see her, being female, as one who would really understand what being a poet was like. 'But he never found it.'

'Only death,' said Marrin, sitting down beside Bill. 'They all sought death most diligently and they all died.'

'A common fate,' said Phryne, watching Harcourt. Marrin had come to make good his boast. Was his hold so strong? Harcourt's thin, inkstained fingers were clutching the amulet under his shirt, but he was breathing evenly and his face was controlled. He had certainly been frightened out of his wits by that unlovely pair, Madame and Marrin, but a measure of backbone appeared to have returned to the young man.

'Immortality,' breathed Marrin. He wore a strange scent. Phryne wrinkled her nose in an effort to identify it. She had smelt it before. In an eastern port somewhere: Port Said? Cairo? Yes, Cairo. Spikenard, the bridegroom's perfume in the 'Song of Solomon'. Phryne had gained an entirely undeserved reputation for piety for reading the Bible in church. In fact she had been beguiling the sermon with that most erotic of ancient love poems. But she did not find Marrin erotic – he was far too cold to be attractive. She considered that it would be like making love to a crocodile. Cold, scaly, and ultimately dangerous.

'The alchemist's quest?' asked Phryne, not allowing herself to smile.

'By another path,' said Marrin.

Yes, and it's a left-hand one, thought Phryne. 'I wish you success,' she said pleasantly. Then, unable to help herself, she added, *'"Et de la corde d'un toise/Sçaura ton col que ton cal poise."'* Naughty, she knew, to quote Villon in such company, and naughtier to misquote his epitaph: and a rope so long/that it will teach your neck the weight of your arse. Marrin laughed hugely, his shark's teeth displayed.

'"La pluye nous a debuez et laves",' he began, capping her Villon quote with another from 'The Ballad of the Hanged Men', a speech delivered by a corpse on a gibbet. *'"Et le soleil dessechiez et noircis/Pies, corbealx, nous ont les yeux cavez..."'*

Harcourt translated as Marrin recited that most macabre of ballads.

'"The rain has rinsed us and washed us,/And the sun has dried us and blackened us/Magpies and

138

crows have made pits of our eyes/Torn away our beards and eyebrows./Never and never can we be still/Swaying here, there as the wind varies/At its pleasure it carries us/Holed by beaks worse than a thimble/Therefore don't be of our brotherhood/ But pray to God that he will absolve us all.'"

Hand on amulet, Harcourt handed Marrin a tarot card.

'Take it back,' he said quietly. 'I will not be one of your brotherhood. *"Mais priez Dieu que tous nous vueille absouldre."'*

His pale face, his black eyes, his cannibal mouth did not react, but the blood-red fingernails bit into the card. Marrin crumpled it and it fluttered past Phryne's hand. She palmed it. Marrin smiled his predator's smile again and drifted away. One of the poets looked away from his argument to sneer, 'Villon? Old-fashioned,' before he returned to the fray.

Phryne inspected the card. A naked corpse suspended by one foot, from a gallows, one leg crossed at the knee into a figure four. The Hanged Man.

'This was your card?' she asked Harcourt. He nodded, still too astounded by his own hardihood to speak. Phryne knew the meaning of the card.

'Spiritual wisdom, gained...'

'At a great price,' whispered Adam Harcourt. 'The price was far too high. More wine,' he said, fumbling in his pocket for his wallet. 'Joss, will you get us another bottle?'

'Adam dear, I'm very proud of you,' said Phryne quietly. She sat down next to Harcourt and he sagged against her. Phryne put an arm around him. He was holding some great emotion in check. She wondered what it was. Fear? Joy? Relief?

Madame and Marrin stood in close converse for a moment in the middle of the floor, turban and shaven head. Phryne would have given a good deal to know what they were talking about. They had lost their hold over the young man; first magically and then socially. She had given Marrin his cue to start quoting the 'Ballad of the Hanged Men', and now she wondered why she had done it; had he dropped that thought into her mind? But even the mention of the Hanged Men had not retrieved Harcourt, and provided he played no more magical games he was probably fairly safe. Holding Harcourt in a close consoling embrace, Phryne saw Marrin bend to kiss Madame's mouth. Her face contracted in pain, and blood glistened on both mouths as Marrin drew away. He licked his lips, relishing the taste.

Cruel and bestial, yet the gesture had been full of raw appetite, and Phryne felt her body react. Marrin turned and gave her a glance so loaded with lust that she wondered how she had ever thought him unattractive. Inadvisable, without doubt, but inadvisable had never been the same as undesirable. She understood the nature of their hold over Harcourt, a young man with no lover, too principled to lie to a good girl, too poor and too fastidious to purchase one of Tillie's women.

'They must be very hard to relinquish,' she murmured. Harcourt clung close to Phryne and rubbed his cheek along her silky shoulder.

'There must be other pleasures,' he whispered.

'In any case, I have left them, and even if I have left my manhood with them at least I'm free.'

'Oh, I don't think you've left your manhood with that disgusting couple,' said Phryne, settling him into her embrace and running a feather light caress along his thigh. She felt the jolt as desire tingled through his body and grounded with a thud in his spine. 'See? Perfectly reliable,' she told him, exploring further and finding a serviceable erection. 'You've got all the manhood with which you reached puberty, Adam. Madame and Marrin have precisely as much power over you as you allow them to have; not one jot or tittle more, do you understand?'

'I understand,' he whispered. 'I understand that you have saved me, that you have put yourself in danger for me.'

'Nonsense. Adam Harcourt, you are very attractive and I'd love to take you home to bed, but I'd be doing you no service. I don't want to replace one form of sexual slavery with another. However, just to set your mind at rest ... Joss, Clarence, sit down on the table, will you, facing the room, and don't turn around until I say.'

They obeyed her without question. The corner was dark. Phryne loosened the front of her dress to allow the young man to touch her breasts and pull up her skirt. She heard him gasp as his questing fingers found no undergarments. Her own hands were busy, undoing buttons until she found what she sought.

He was on a hair-trigger of fear and relief and reached a climax in minutes, his face against her breast, pleasurably smothered in silk and perfume.

141

Conscious that semen was used in some spells, Phryne mopped Harcourt's wet belly with her handkerchief and stowed it safely in her pocket. The young man was lax, faint with release. Phryne was left aroused and shaken, longing for a lover and at a loss where to find one. She could always seduce Joss or Clarence, or perhaps Joss and Clarence together – an entrancing thought – but if they had been shocked by the sight of her stockings, what would they say to such an immoral proposal? Neither struck her as particularly experienced. The night would degenerate into the usual problems with an orgy: where to put what and where and when, and how to find room for one's elbows. She did not feel like overcoming their objections, educating them as to the ways of a female body, and in the end possibly finding herself without the desired satisfaction. They were both, she thought, conventional boys, and it was a pity to debauch them to no purpose.

She kissed Adam, enjoying his taste of relief like salt on her tongue, then re-ordered her garments and watched him attempt to array his buttons. His hands were shaking, and finally she did it for him. Male garments posed no mysteries for Phryne, and she wished passionately that she had not left Lin Chung in Melbourne. He would have recognised her state immediately, and in his caresses her taut nerves would relax into pleasure. With Lin Chung in bed, one needed no other distractions.

She came out of her reverie to find that she was still holding Harcourt close, and he was murmuring thanks into her neck. She patted him gently and sat up straight. Adam Harcourt was charming, intelligent, good-looking and potent, but he was not what she needed.

Neither was Marrin. Phryne had never liked pain. It hurt.

'Turn around, chaps,' she said with forced brightness. 'All's well and I'm going home. You'll stay with Adam tonight, Joss?'

'Yes, and Clarence tomorrow night. We'll be there, old chap,' he assured the elevated Harcourt.

'Good,' said Phryne. 'See you tomorrow?'

'Yes, it's the cricket match,' observed Joss. He was wondering mightily what Miss Fisher had done to Harcourt to make his eyes shine like that, but did not dare to ask. 'The students against the faculty. You promised old Jones that you would be there, you said.'

'So I did. Very well. I'll see you there at ten.'

Phryne left Theo's and was immediately seized by the neck as her foot touched the pavement. A huge man dragged her into an alley.

Eight

Here bowled by Death's unerring ball
A cricketer renowned. By name John Small.

Epitaph on John Small from *Carr's Illustrated Dictionary of Extraordinary Cricketers*, J.L. Carr, Quarter Books London 1983

It was never easy to ambush Phryne, and she was

in such a state of high arousal that she reacted like a cat. She slid through the headlock. How such a small, light sheila had done it Sharkbait Kennedy could never afterwards explain. She put her back against a wall and flicked open her purse.

Sharkbait Kennedy looked into the hollow eye of a small pistol and gulped. Born and bred in the 'Loo, working for a female boss with all the delicacy of a conger eel, he entertained no comfortable illusions about the threats posed by the Weaker Sex. This lady – he hastily redefined her as a lady – was holding her pistol very steadily and he was in trouble.

'I think you should tell me,' said a voice so blackly furious that it stung his ears, 'why you grabbed me. If you are just a common thief I'll let you go. But if you've got anything to do with Madame and Marrin I'm going to shoot you in the belly and it will take you days to die and every moment will be agony. And I think you should talk quickly. I'm not in the mood for word games.'

The last person who had spoken to Sharkbait Kennedy in that tone of voice had been making plans for the deposit of some business rivals at the bottom of the harbour. Sharkbait talked quickly.

'No, lady, I ain't no tea-leaf, and I don't know the parties you said.'

'What do you want with me?' The voice was still level and dangerous.

'You been askin' about Darlo Annie,' said Sharkbait Kennedy, repeating his lesson. 'Tillie don't want yer to ask about 'er no more.'

'Doesn't she?' Sharkbait marvelled that such a lady-like voice could sound so poisonous. 'Well,

144

you tell Tillie this little visit was wet arse and no fish. I'm looking for Joan Thompson, who was born Joan Williams, my companion's sister, last seen getting into one of Tillie's cars. If she's Darlo Annie I'm going to find her and nothing is going to stop me. If she isn't Darlo Annie then I have no interest in the girl, but I am going to find Joan Thompson. Can you remember all that or do I have to put a hole in your unpleasant carcass to clarify your mind?'

'Nah, lady, be nice. Don't!' he urged, as the finger on the trigger took up the slack. 'Don't do yer block. I'll say it nice just like you did. Yer lookin' for Joan Williams, yer want her back, if she's Darlo Annie yer goin' to find 'er, if she ain't yer goin' to find this Joan. I got it,' said Sharkbait hurriedly. 'Dinkum! Don't act the angora, lady! No need for violence!'

'Walk in front of me,' ordered the small, light sheila, and Sharkbait walked into Pitt Street.

'Flag down that taxi,' she ordered, and he stepped out into the road so that the cab was forced to halt, the driver leaning out and requesting in the name of all that was holy that he should speedily explain his impulsive and wrong-headed actions.

'Go and give Tillie my message,' said Phryne, climbing into the car. Sharkbait Kennedy walked away, shaking his head.

'That was Sharkbait Kennedy,' said the driver, nervously.

'Was it?' snapped Phryne.

'He's one of Tillie's standover men,' the driver went on.

'Is he? Hotel Australia,' said Phryne.

The driver, who was about to protest that his innocent cab was no place for a woman who had any dealings with such well known strong-arm bludgers as Sharkbait Kennedy, noticed the gleam of a gun barrel as his passenger shut her purse and decided that, after all, discretion was the better part of valour.

Anyone who could face down Sharkbait Kennedy deserved to ride wherever she liked.

Phryne threw herself down and buried her head in her pillow; she was trembling with rage. Dot, who knew the signs, sat down on the edge of the bed and remarked, 'You know that cop? He telephoned. He said that no one answering the description of Darlo Annie or Joan was dead or in hospital. So that's a relief, sort of. Would you like a bath?' She offered Phryne's usual method of relaxing.

'No. I'd like a drink,' said Phryne savagely. 'The cognac, my notebook, and uninterrupted silence.'

Dot fetched the bottle and the notebook, tiptoed to her own room and shut the door. Quietly.

Phryne tore off her clothes, wrapped herself in a silk dressing gown of great magnificence, and sat down to the table, taking a gulp of cognac from the bottle and choking slightly.

Columns grew under her pencil. She needed to make sense of the players.

Those involved in the theft from the safe. The Dean himself, of course, private income, bad temper, always yelling at poor Sykes for his bad bookkeeping. He might have a reason to steal the

146

books, if he had been diverting some of the bursaries to his own use, but why should he? And his wife had lost her garnets and might be exigent. Sykes. A rabbity man with not a particle of initiative, but he could have been using his perceived inefficiency to cover up his own theft and the loss of the books might preserve him from discovery. Harcourt, in league with Madame and Marrin, might have stolen anything on their orders, but said he hadn't and Phryne was inclined to believe him. Joss the magnate's son and Clarence the Arts black sheep of a medical family, both of whom had got her into this out of their regard for Harcourt? They didn't seem to fit in as thieves or be subtle enough to enact such a double bluff. Professor Bretherton, who wanted that papyrus very badly for something other than the translation. As did Madame and Marrin, who might have had other acolytes apart from Harcourt. What was it about that papyrus? Madame and Marrin wanted it for 'a magical working', but surely Bretherton didn't believe in magic? From the photographic plate, there was nothing else on the face of the papyrus. Was there writing on the back of it? If it had been ancient, surely a good scholar like Bretherton would have translated it also. Until she found the papyrus Phryne did not like her chances of finding out from either party.

Who else? Brazell the anthropologist and Ayers the archaeologist, who wanted different things to be done with the Dean's fund. Ayers wanted to go back to Egypt, Brazell wanted to go back to his desert – Ayers because his tastes inclined towards pretty boys; Brazell, presumably, because his tastes inclined towards sand. Old Professor Jones, who did not seem to have anything to do with any of it. Jeoffry Bisset, who loved beautiful things and grieved for the loss of Juana's Book of Hours.

All of them, with the possible exception of those involved in the papyrus story, appeared harmless. All of them had keys to the faculty office and any of them might have noticed that the safe back could be removed by anyone with a screwdriver and a modicum of strength. Had Bisset taken a lady there on Saturday night to avail himself of the Dean's couch, and improved the shining hour by emptying the safe?

Might be difficult to explain to the lady, of course, unless the lady was hired and very bad company indeed and it was her idea. Phryne's pencil broke and she sat for a moment, contemplating Bisset and watching the curls of wood from her sharpener.

No. Bisset could certainly have robbed the safe and taken the Book of Hours home with him to cherish and protect it, but he could not have put the examination papers in Adam Harcourt's carrel. Bisset was an idealist, and while idealists in Phryne's experience were capable of sacrificing anyone to their ideal – like Chas Nuttall and his art – they were not mean, and the planting of those exam papers had been the act of a fundamentally mean personality.

Which one of her subjects showed that mean streak? Who would want Harcourt to fail? None of them, for all that Phryne could see.

But at least that little encounter in the alley had informed the elusive Tillie Devine of Phryne's intentions, and if Tillie had Joan for some purpose of her own, she might release her to stop Phryne's inquiries into the whereabouts of Darlo Annie, assuming that they were not the same person. She wondered where her own cold fighting ferocity had come from. She had fully intended to gut-shoot the attacker if he had come from the *soi-disant* magicians.

She read through her notes, took a deep gulp of cognac, and steadied her breathing. Should she have taken Harcourt home with her? She had been tempted. A pretty young man, just what she usually chose to beguile the idle hour. But Harcourt would fall in love with her, now that he was free. That would not be a good plan. He was intelligent and nervy, and she did not want to break his heart.

Phryne accepted that, at bottom, she was as promiscuous as a cat, with a cat's honesty, appetite and complete lack of interest in what anyone else thought. She desired a lover at present, but even if Tillie Devine had kept a stable of young men she doubted if she would have bought their attentions. Something would turn up, she thought, pouring some cognac into a glass. One more drink then she would go to bed, dream suitably, and otherwise sublimate her lusts into solving the puzzle and getting back to Lin Chung.

She reflected as she sipped the cognac – shame to gulp such a good brandy – that she had left Lin Chung in the throes of matrimonial negotiation, and she would not have him for much longer. She had made a bargain with his grandmother. Phryne had Lin Chung while he was unmarried, and he reverted to his clan once he was married.

'Heigh-ho,' sighed Phryne, and put herself to bed.

In her dream she did not lie beside the smooth limbs of Lin Chung, but lay unable to move a muscle, splayed under the bulk of Marrin, and his teeth met in her throat. She felt the warm gush of her own blood on her breast and could not even scream.

Morning brought Dot, breakfast, and Professor Bretherton. At a nod, Dot allowed him into the bedchamber, where Phryne was sitting up, eating toast and marmalade and drinking coffee so strong that the scent hung heavy on the air.

'Miss Fisher, where did you get café Hellenico in Sydney?' he asked, inhaling deeply.

'Dot made it for me. Do you want some?' asked Phryne. She was still a little shaky from the dream, which had been so vivid that she had already examined her throat for teeth marks. There were none. The Professor nodded, and Phryne sent Dot to make some more over her travelling spirit stove.

'Heavy night?' he asked sympathetically.

'You are the frozen limit,' said Phryne with admiration. 'The last time I saw you, John Bretherton you were walking out on me at dinner. Have you come to apologise?'

'Abjectly,' he said, taking up her free hand and kissing it. 'Will you ever condescend to forgive me?'

'I'll have to think about it.' Phryne finished her toast and set the tray aside. The strong Greek coffee was clearing her head of the remnants of the dream. What had happened? Psychic rape, or the actions of her own imagination? Perhaps she might ask Dot for a holy medal – Phryne was not usually given to nightmares.

On the wings of her thought, Professor Bretherton reached into his pocket and produced a small stone which he dropped into her hand.

'I understand from Harcourt that you rescued him from Madame and Marrin, a remarkable feat,' he said. 'More than I was able to do.'

'Yes?' Phryne encouraged. Dot handed Bretherton a small cup of the concentrated coffee and he sipped slowly. Phryne turned the pebble over. It seemed to have some carving on the smooth side, but she could not read it. It was evidently very old. It felt strangely warm, as though it had lain in the sun, and strangely natural, as though she was holding a cicada or a deep-sea shell, not an artifact.

'I couldn't get finer coffee in Athens,' Bretherton said to Dot, who smiled and took the cup. Bretherton waited until the door shut after Dot before he began. 'Madame and Marrin are devotees of Crowley and he is a devotee of Egyptian magic, or what he thinks is Egyptian magic. So are the Golden Dawn and you seem to have had some acquaintance with them, so possibly you have your own defences.'

Phryne scanned his face. He still looked like a respectable middle-aged Professor of Greek. White hair, still thick. Intelligent grey eyes. A strong face with the slightly pointed ears of the Celt; a Juvenalian who reliably found that the worst should be expected of human nature. This mysticism was unexpected.

'But...' she prompted.

'You must have a great deal of natural force or you could not have out-faced that bounder Marrin. He had poor Harcourt firmly in his clutches and nothing I could say would convince the poor young idiot that it was all nonsense. Indeed, belief is a power all by itself. All the ancients agree, even Lucretius, who strove to convince men that they had nothing to fear from death because death was the end of all consciousness.'

'I see,' murmured Phryne, deciding that the Professor was wittering. 'Tell me about this pebble.'

'It came from a dig near Luxor,' said Bretherton. 'It's very old. Stone Age for Egypt was five thousand years ago. I bought it from a fellow on my staircase at Oxford who'd gone all Muscular Christian. An amulet to preserve the soul in the body, Miss Fisher. You might find it of use.'

'But you don't believe in magic,' murmured Phryne.

'But I do believe in belief,' he answered. 'And I would not like you to be, er, frightened off before you find my papyrus.'

'Or injured?

'Marrin may well be capable of that, also.'

'I hope it works on standover men.' Phryne remembered her nightmare and shuddered slightly. 'Thank you. Now, are you going to tell me what else is on that papyrus, and why you and the Crowleyites want to find it?'

'No,' he said slowly.

Phryne took his hand. 'I really need to know,' she told him. On impulse, she drew him to lie

152

down beside her. 'But I'm not trying to seduce the answer out of you,' she added. 'I'd like to be hugged. I had a bad dream.'

'I thought you might have,' he replied. Phryne slid her arms under his coat and laid her head against his chest. He smelt agreeably of coffee and pipe tobacco. After a moment's hesitation, he embraced her with comforting warmth.

'What did Marrin do to you?' she asked, her voice rising from his third shirt button.

'He told my wife – he allowed my wife to infer, rather, that I had been involved with Madame.'

'Was it true?'

'Yes. Marrin obviously thought that Madame could, er, seduce the papyrus out of me. Well, she could seduce me easily enough, that wasn't difficult at all. There may be upright, noble chaps out there who are proof against those Hungarian wiles, but I'm not one of them.'

'You didn't have a snowflake's of avoiding it,' said Phryne sleepily. His arms were strong and she had not slept again after waking with Marrin's snarl in her ears. 'She did a tarot reading for you. She gave you ... The Chariot? The Emperor? The High Priest? as your significator. She told you that you were a strong man, a man before whom weak womanhood could only pay its devotions on its knees. Then she fell to *her* knees and started on your buttons. Don't feel guilty. That method would work on anyone except John Knox and even John Knox would have had to beat his erection down with a stick.' She felt him flinch, then subside, and knew that her guess had been correct. 'But you didn't give them what they

153

wanted, even when you had been so comprehens-ively seduced? That indicates a strong will. She might have been right about your card after all. Which one was it?'

'The Chariot.' His voice quavered a little. Phryne realised he was on the edge of laughter.

'Domination,' said Phryne. 'Strong over weak. Male over female. So then Marrin tried black-mail? Usually a reliable method.'

'I've been married for twenty years,' said Bretherton. 'My wife knows me and my nature. She knows that I love her. It didn't work, though there was the deuce of a row. But in the end she agreed that Hungarians can happen to anyone and forgave me. Then the papyrus went missing and I was sure that Marrin had it until he came sliming up my stairs to make me another offer to buy it. Now, I don't know where the thing is. I can't tell you any more about the papyrus, Phryne, I gave my word, my solemn oath, and I cannot break it. The only other person who knows about it is Ayers. You might talk to him. Are you feeling better now? You know, I used to hold my daughter Alice like this, when she had nightmares.'

'Your daughter was fortunate,' said Phryne, sit-ting up. 'Thank you, I feel much better. Now, I'd better get dressed. Are you going to the cricket match?'

'Even better, I'm playing in the cricket match,' replied Professor Bretherton, withdrawing to the parlour.

As Phryne dressed in her cricket-going clothes, she handed the pebble to Dot.

'Do me a favour, old thing,' she said. 'Sew this

into that hankie I had last night – yes, I know that it is stained – and sling it on the rest of that white cord. I've been making amulets for other people, it might be time I made one for myself.'

The combination of the ancient Egyptian belief in the *ba* soul and Phryne's own present belief in the flesh (represented by a semen-soaked cloth) might well, she thought, prove powerful. Dot did as requested and Phryne slung the amulet around her neck under the heliotrope cotton blouse. The little bundle nestled between her breasts and felt, still, oddly warm. It was an animal heat, like that generated by holding a sleeping dormouse in the hand. She clapped on her panama and joined Professor Bretherton at the door.

'Back by five,' she called to Dot, and went out.

Sydney was hot and grimy, and the green gardens of the University were a relief to the eye and the nose. Someone had laboriously watered and rolled the pitch, and even the outfield was green. Phryne took her seat with the aged Professor Jones in a small wooden pavilion.

'Nice day,' he commented. 'What a fortunate old crock I am! Cricket match to watch and beautiful lady to watch it with. Here's your score card,' he said, giving Phryne a folded sheet of cardboard with two lists of names, 'and there's Bretherton and young Joss Hart going out. Toss of the coin and – yes, Bretherton has won and decided to send the students in. Hope he wasn't using that lucky Roman coin of his. The students have got a fine opening pair, too. Harcourt and Ottery. Of course, young Harcourt's in disgrace, but I told Waterhouse to his face, I told him, Waterhouse, I said, that young fellow's a fine bat and I don't believe a word of the charges against him. And if the Senate has any sense they won't send down a chap with such a beautiful cover drive. Quite a competent spinner and an excellent fielder, too. Such a good sportsman would never cheat! Preposterous, and so I told him. Wonderful thing about being retired: I can speak my mind for the first time in my whole academic life.'

Phryne smiled at the Emeritus professor. He patted her knee.

'They told me you're looking into it, m'dear. Kind of you. They tell me you're an investigator. About time they had women investigators. That's what women have always been good at. Never miss a thing, women. Recall m'own mother looking at me for only a moment before she knew that I'd been eating green apricots, and me protesting all the time that I hadn't been near the tree. Knew from the green stains on m'shirt. Very acute, mothers. Well, stands to reason. No one tells them the truth about their misdeeds, and what difference is there between me and my stout denial about the apricots – I thought I was dashed convincing, too – and some murderer protesting that he didn't kill his wife? None at all, as far as I can see. They tell me you're brilliant, well, I could see that for myself as soon as I heard you talk about Tennyson. So you get to the bottom of this theft, m'dear. We can't afford to lose an opening bat like Harcourt.'

'I'll do my best,' said Phryne.

The old man continued, his eyes on the field. 'And of course Ottery's good enough to play for

New South Wales except he don't want to – can you imagine that? A possible Test place eventually and he don't want it because he's pursuing his studies!'

Professor Jones paused to snort. Phryne, a little overwhelmed by this academic vote of confidence, wondered how he had viewed such matters before he was Emeritus and decided that he would have been just the same. She began to feel that she might have enjoyed university.

The ground looked like a painting. The bulk of the University buildings shone with a ruddy glow on the right. The expanse of meadow sizzling gently with gnats in the warming sun. A few passing seagulls. The white-clad fielders spreading out across the green grass. The umpires settling down beside the wicket and at square leg. The captain and the bowler having the first argument of the day about field placings. Professor Jones observed this and chuckled.

'You know what S.F. Barnes used to say? "When I'm bowling, there's only one captain, me!" That's Kirkpatrick. Slow left arm Chinaman. Odd thing for a Scotsman to bowl, but he's effective. Though I don't think he'll get too far against Ottery and Harcourt.'

The captain waved an arm and some fielders moved. Then Kirkpatrick waved, and they moved back. Phryne saw Bretherton shrug and walk to his own position at mid on, where he could see the game and not be surprised by any fast deliveries.

'Never argue with a Glasgow man,' chuckled Professor Jones.

'Play,' called the umpire. The batsmen, who

157

had been patiently leaning on their bats awaiting the outcome of the argument, straightened. Ottery took block.

The ball looped in, quite slowly, and after examining it for deviant tendencies, Ottery stepped out confidently and drove it to the boundary.

'Pretty style he has, don't you think?' asked Professor Jones.

'Very stylish,' agreed Phryne. It was extremely pleasant to just sit in the shade and watch a cricket match. The word predictable didn't really describe cricket, prone as it was to sudden changes and shocks, but the ritual of the game was as familiar and soothing as cream.

Kirkpatrick's next ball seemed to be exactly the same. Ottery had taken a pace forward before he realised that the ball was turning, and managed only a flat batted swat which drove it into the ground. 'That Kirkpatrick isn't as innocuous as he seems,' she commented, as the batsmen crossed.

'Watch the next one,' said Professor Jones.

Harcourt faced Kirkpatrick. The ball left the bowler's hand and slipped through the air, hit and turned on a right angle which Harcourt tried and entirely failed to keep out of his stumps.

'Very pretty,' approved Professor Jones. At one wicket for five runs, Harcourt trudged back to the pavilion, noticeably cast down. There was a pause before Joss Hart emerged, limping a little. 'Hart's their best bat,' Professor Jones told Phryne, 'But Kirkpatrick's motto is, "If you can't blast 'em out, niggle 'em out." If we had him in the Test team we wouldn't have had to watch England make six hundred-odd. He might even make headway against Hammond. And we've got Bisset's fast bowling to supply the blasting. But it's a long way to the end of a cricket match, m'dear.'

'So it is,' said Phryne. 'Three balls to go.'

Kirkpatrick retreated behind the crease, took two steps and the ball flew again. Joss Hart had watched the fall of Harcourt and was not going to take any risks. He waited until the ball reached him and struck it along the ground. The batsmen began to run. The ageing fielders raced after the ball. Phryne saw Joss Hart reach the other end, turn, then halfway down the wicket he suddenly winced, staggered a few steps and fell. Bisset threw in the ball and the bails were knocked off with a triumphant cry.

'What's wrong with the young chap?' asked Professor Jones, getting arthritically to his feet.

'Something very wrong,' said Phryne, leaping from her bench. Joss Hart had gone down as though he had been shot and now lay unmoving on the pitch. Phryne ran out of the pavilion and onto the ground as the players gathered around. Bisset, who was kneeling beside Joss, gathered him up into his arms and Bretherton and two others lifted the young man.

His face was congested, Phryne saw. He was vainly struggling for breath. She had a sudden intuition. Why had he been limping? She grabbed at his foot and unlaced the cricket shoe, dragging off the sock. Bretherton, who had been about to demand what she thought she was about, almost dropped the body he was holding.

'How could that have happened?' asked Bisset. 'Bring him into the shade. I've got a kit here in the gear, but I never saw one! Quick, Ottery, run back to the telephone and ring the infirmary. Tell them what's wrong. I'll do the first aid. Give me your knife, Kirkpatrick.'

He grabbed a bottle of lemonade from a lady spectator and drenched Joss's skin, then cut deeply into the two punctures on the side of his foot. Joss Hart moaned.

'"The snake be against him on land",' quoted Phryne to Professor Bretherton, who had gone as white as his hair. 'Are you sure you haven't any more to tell me?'

'We'll take care of this poor fellow,' he said. 'There's Ayers, Miss Fisher. Take him away and make him tell you. I still can't.'

'Will Joss die?' asked Phryne.

'I don't know. I don't even know what sort of snake it was. No one's seen one.'

Phryne picked up the shoe and, carrying it by the laces, homed in on Professor Ayers like a ranged five pounder. Behind her she heard Harcourt protesting, 'But he wore my shoes, my bloody cheap shoes! They must have been thin enough for a snake to bite through! Oh, Joss, don't die or I'll never forgive myself.'

'Professor Ayers?' called Phryne to a slim man contemplating infinity at deep square leg. 'A word.'

He saw her coming and ran.

Nine

Ainsi m'ont Amour abusé
Et pourmené de l'uys au pestle,
Je croy qu'homme n'est so rusé
Just fin comme argent de coepelle
Qui n'y laissant linge, drapelle
Mais qu'il fust ainsi manyé
Comme moy, qui parout m'apelle
L'amant remys et regnyé.

Just so love misused me
Drew me out and locked the door
And no man exists clever enough
Even if he was subtle as silver
Who wouldn't have lost his lingerie
If he'd been befooled like me.
And now everyone calls me
The duped and rejected lover.

Francois Villon, The Testament

Phryne took off after him like a gazelle, thanking the powers that she had worn a loose skirt and flat-heeled shoes.

Away from the cricket field, toward the main buildings of the university, Ayers ran and Phryne followed. He had longer legs, but she had the advantage of at least twenty years and she was betting on him not having taken any violent exercise recently. Up the hill, up the stairs, past the lions and the Roman Senator, through another door, their footsteps hollow and echoing.

By the time they reached the Quad, the professor a short half-head in the lead, Phryne was recalling that neither had she and wishing that she hadn't smoked so many Gitanes while she had been compiling her list the previous night. Ayers was, however, slowing and gasping and Phryne decided that she had run enough for one day. Grabbing for his belt, she tripped up his heels and sat on him as he fell, so that the tableau confronting the amused student body in the Quad was one recumbent professor, prone, and one fashionably dressed young woman, with panama hat, sitting on his back, both parties as devoid of breath as propriety.

'But what are you going to do with him, now you've got him?' asked a fascinated spectator.

'I'll think of something,' said Phryne and grinned lasciviously, startling the student so much that he walked away, wondering what modern young women were coming to and mulling over an article to that effect which *Hermes* might publish.

'If I let you up,' panted Phryne, 'will you run away again?'

'No,' panted Ayers. 'By God, you're fast!'

'So is retribution, and it is approaching at a rate of knots. Come along, Professor.' She stood up and offered him her hand, ready to react if the skittish archaeologist showed signs of flight.

'There goes my reputation,' sighed Ayers as he rose to his feet and slapped at his whites. A cloud of dust arose.

'Deny everything and no one will believe what

they saw,' advised Phryne. 'Do you have an office here? Good. Let's go there.'

To forestall any sudden moves, Phryne tucked her arm into the Professor's and they walked across the green like lovers.

Phryne kept a tight hold on Ayers until they reached his office and she could shut the door and lock it. The window in the door was provided with a small curtain, and she drew it.

'People will think that...' Ayers began.

'Well, that may prove useful to you,' said Phryne. 'When I said I was retribution,' she added, sitting down on the edge of the desk, 'I was not overstating the matter. This is no longer a potty little academic quarrel, carried on by people who are far too intelligent and have far too little occupation. That's a real boy out there and that's real venom in his veins and he might die. He may be dead, even now. And some of that is down to you.'

'I can tell you nothing,' said Ayers. He was a tall, slim man, very good looking in a fine-drawn, English way. The weathering which much standing around in Egyptian sun bestows on the skin made it difficult for him to pale, but a tic had begun below his left eye and he was biting his lip.

'What is this all about?' asked Phryne. 'I began to investigate it at the instance of two young men anxious to clear their friend's name. Now I'm up to my elbows in black magicians, tarot cards, foretellings and secrets, and I'm beginning to get quite cross. I am loath to threaten you with actual physical harm, Dr Ayers, but I will if I have to.'

'Miss Fisher, it doesn't matter what you threaten me with,' said Ayers with an appearance of frankness. 'I will tell you nothing.'

'About the papyrus?'

'Nothing.'

'Why won't you tell me?' asked Phryne.

'I can't tell you that, either.'

Phryne considered him. He was speaking, though not freely, and the best thing to do would be to keep him speaking. Perhaps she could get at the truth another way.

'Dr Ayers, why did you run?'

'I was startled.'

'What startled you?'

'Joss's injury.'

'The nature of his injury?'

'Yes,' said the professor.

'"The snake be against him on land",' Phryne quoted. 'Easier, perhaps, than trying to find a crocodile in the middle of Sydney. The closest I've seen to a crocodile is that bounder Marrin.'

At the mention of Marrin's name, Ayers flushed red.

'That scoundrel,' he snarled.

'Indeed. You have had dealings with Marrin?'

'He wanted to buy the papyrus from Bretherton, as if it was his to sell. I'd burn it myself rather than let Marrin get his filthy hands on it for his disgusting magic.'

'You think that Marrin brought this snake bite about?'

'Who else could? I saw no snake.'

'Do you believe in magic?'

'No one who has any acquaintance with the East disbelieves in magic, Miss Fisher.'

'Have you got the papyrus?'

164

'No,' said Professor Ayers.

'Do you know where it is?' asked Phryne. Ayers leaned forward and grabbed her by the shoulder, shouting into her face.

'If I knew where the bloody thing was, would I be so worried? Would I be asking Bretherton to ask you to find it? Use your bloody brains, Miss Fisher!'

'Take your bloody hands off me or I'll break your bloody arm,' said Phryne with calculated violence, and he released her immediately with an expression of loathing, as though he had found himself clutching a snake.

'Yes, you don't like women, do you? In the parlance of my own milieu, Dr Ayers, I'd say you were stone butch.'

He staggered to his chair and sat down again, putting his head in his hands.

'You bitch,' he muttered.

'The original bitch,' said Phryne with some pride. 'But I'm not out to get you, if you didn't poison Joss. Nor am I interested in blackmail. You are clearly being blackmailed by someone who knows about your proclivities. Who has you over – excuse the metaphor – a barrel, Dr Ayers?'

'I can't tell you,' he groaned. 'I really can't.'

'Will you let Bretherton tell me, then? You can release him from his word,' insinuated Phryne. Ayers removed his hands and stared at her.

'Bretherton hasn't told you about the papyrus?' he asked, wonderingly.

'No, he's a man of his word and he's keeping it, which is very inconvenient.'

'He's a good chap, Bretherton,' said Ayers.

'I gather from that question that even if Bretherton *had* told me what he knows, there would still
be more to know,' commented Phryne, watching
Dr Ayers like a hawk. He nodded almost imper-
ceptibly. This might be a way of extracting information.

'You're sworn not to tell, aren't you?'

'Yes.'

'But you can nod. Indicate whether I am on the
right track. Shake of the head for no, and hold
out your right hand for don't know. Agreed?'

'All right,' he said. The tic beat beneath his eye.

'Is there something else written on the papyrus?'

He nodded.

'On the back?'

He nodded.

'Ancient writing?'

He shook his head.

'Modern writing?'

He nodded.

'This is what Marrin wants as well?'

Nod. Phryne swung around on the desk so that
she was facing Dr Ayers. She did not want to
miss any nuance of his expression.

'Does this writing relate to the curse, I mean
the magical effect of the curse?'

Shake of the head.

'Has anyone else got a copy of it?'

Shake of the head.

'Have you got a copy of it?'

Another very sad shake.

'Have you read it?'

Nod. Then he extended his right hand and
turned it from one side to another. There was

more to be found out but Phryne did not have the right questions.

'Is it in English?' Ayers nodded and waved the hand again. Phryne sensed that under the fear he wanted to help her, but he could not risk breaking his word because the consequences would be dire. Who would be writing English words on the back of an ancient papyrus?

'Is it a note made by an archaeologist?' she hazarded. He nodded. 'The discoverer?' He nodded again. What would be there, apart from a few numbers which would identify where the papyrus was found, when and by whom? Presumably it was Oxyrrinchus 666, the identifying number on the translation. That number rang a bell with Phryne. Something to do with church. She filed it to think about later.

'A cross reference?' she guessed. Ayers shook his head. There could be anything on the back of it, thought Phryne angrily. A shopping list, a sudden insight into the placement of a particular temple, a recipe for goat soup... She could not think of the right question to ask, and fairly soon Ayers would get restive. She was never, purely on principle, going to blackmail him with being homosexual in order to make him tell her. Nothing wrong with a little light blackmail – she had always found it worked well in most circumstances – but not sexual preference. Inverts had enough troubles, Phryne knew, without her adding to them.

She would have preferred to just beat him to a pulp, which seemed to her more honest, and would have done it if it seemed likely to be effective.

'Can it be found in any other place?' she asked, and Ayers shook his head again. 'Drat,' said Phryne. 'I've run out of questions. Can't you give me a hint?'

'You know I can't,' said Ayers.

'The nature of the threat,' she asked. 'Is it blackmail over your preferences, or is it a fear that you'll find out-of-season scorpions in your slippers?'

'Both,' Ayers sighed.

'Professor, just at this moment,' Phryne produced the gun from her purse and pointed it at his head, taking up the slack of the trigger, 'who are you more afraid of – your blackmailer or me?'

'Him,' said Ayers. 'You've got principles and you probably aren't insane. Therefore you probably won't shoot me, though there's always a chance that you will; you have the reputation of being very dangerous. I've looked down my share of brigand gun barrels in my time in the desert. I can't say that I like the experience and I am not enjoying this. But he is quite determined and cares nothing for consequences. He's got the goods on me, and he would ruin me on a whim.'

'In which case you might as well tell me, because I might be able to protect you, and he'll find out that we were closeted in your room with the door locked and assume that you have told me anyway.'

'Oh, sweet Christ,' whispered Ayers. 'Sweet suffering Jesus.'

'Quite.'

'You couldn't protect Joss,' he said, the tic beating metronome-steady under his eye.

'I didn't know that Joss needed protection. Indeed, it may not have been aimed at Joss, but at

Adam Harcourt. I'll know if you have a pocket knife.'

Phryne put the shoe she was still carrying down on the desk. Ayers rummaged in a drawer and produced a knife. He watched fascinated as Phryne cut the cheap white shoe in half, revealing a cross section of sole and upper, and then folded down the leather flap with the point of the knife.

'Not magic,' she said. 'Machinery. Don't touch, Professor, unless you want to join Joss Hart. See? A pair of hollow needles, a rubber top from an eye-dropper, buried in the sole. A clever little booby trap. They would have taken a while to work their way through into the actual foot. Harcourt's shoes. He was meant to die. But he was bowled by the remarkable Glasgow spin of Professor Kirkpatrick and he lent his shoes to Joss. Thus a snake bite, a fulfilment of a prophecy, and more terror for the others in the know. Would you like to tell me who is blackmailing you?'

'No. Magic or machinery, this could still kill me, and there is something I need to do first.'

'Dammit, Tom Ayers, if you don't tell me immediately, I'll kill you myself!' Phryne seized the shoe and leapt off the desk. For some reason Ayers fell to pieces all at once and began to talk. Phryne was not sure what had convinced him.

'All right, all right, I'll tell you, get that infernal thing away from me. On the back of the papyrus is a note written by the original cataloguer which reveals the location of the tomb of Khufu, that we call Cheops.'

'The great pyramid Cheops?'

'Him. It seems unlikely that he was buried in the

pyramid. Everyone assumes that there was a tomb there and it was looted in antiquity, but I don't think so, and neither did Graham, who was at the original dig at Oxyrrinchus and catalogued the entire find. He left no memorial otherwise. No one has ever found his notebooks. He was ambushed and murdered, presumably by wandering Bedouin, only a few months later. I must find that tomb. It would be as famous as the tomb of Tut Ankh Amen. If I had the note I could convince the Dean to fund the dig. It would shed a glow on Australian universities and attract more scholarships – he would have to give it to me.'

'How did you come to find this scrawl?'

'I heard the rumour that Graham had located Khufu years ago, and I was fascinated. I talked to all the chaps, but they didn't know anything. Graham was an odd, crotchety man, given to claiming that he'd discovered things – he also claimed to have found Tanis and we're still not sure where that was. Also that the Tablets of the Law were in Ethiopia. I gave up searching for his notebooks; they've probably been firelighters for twenty years. Then I wondered if there was another way to approach it, and so I asked Bretherton if he had looked at all his manuscripts, and he said the only one with anything on it was the 666. You know that's why Marrin wants it? The number of the Beast is 666 from the Revelations of St John the Divine. He thinks that there is a magical golden box in the tomb which contains a spell will make him immortal.'

'I knew that 666 rang a bell – a church bell, in fact,' commented Phryne. 'What did Bretherton tell you about the note?'

'It's in pencil and very hard to read. All I could make out was the name Khufu and some cursive Egyptian which I would have to photograph through a filter to have a chance of reading. Then there's several lines in Greek and Bretherton was going to help with those. And then someone stole it, and my world fell in on me. Please help me.' Ayers took Phryne's hand.

'I'll try, I already promised that I would try,' she replied, thinking hard. 'Now, we need to secure your safety. Where do you live? In College?'

'Yes, in John's.'

'Don't go back there,' she ordered. 'Walk out of the University and take a bus into the city to the Hotel Australia. I'll telephone for a room – at my expense. Your name is...' She scribbled on a piece of paper and Ayers gave a slight hiccup which might have been a laugh. 'Wait for me. I'll speak to you this afternoon. If you tell me who's black-mailing you, I can go and do him an injury,' she added hopefully.

Ayers shook his head. 'I might retain a faint chance of living if I don't tell you,' he said. 'Oh, and tell Bretherton he is relieved of his oath, and that I honour him for keeping it under what must have been great pressure.'

'I'll tell him. Off you go. Send out for a news-paper. When I call you, I'll ask for a cricket score. If you can't tell me, then I'll know something's wrong. Clear?'

'Clear,' agreed Professor Ayers.

He left. Phryne sat on the desk for some time, pondering the power of blackmail, and wondering how she could properly apply it to work out who had tried to kill Adam Harcourt and might have killed Joss Hart.

First thing to do was to find out if Hart was dead, and she returned to the field, where she met Professor Bretherton.

'Terrible thing,' he said, shaking his head. 'They've taken him to the infirmary. I doubt that we can do much. Bisset's put a tourniquet around the leg and washed out the bite. We've got the gardeners beating the grass for the snake. Oh, and the game's been called off – we'll replay it next week.'

'Poor Joss,' said Phryne.

'Yes, well, we'd arranged a lunch and we might as well go to it. Will you come? We've telephoned Mr Hart – the only family the boy's got is his father – and told him. Nothing more we can do for the present.'

'I'll walk with you. By the way, I caught Ayers, and he told me to tell you that you may tell me all about the papyrus.'

'Ayers has told you? That's a relief. What has he told you?'

'That the papyrus had a pencil note on the back which relates to the site of a tomb, that it is the only clue because the man who wrote it was murdered and his papers lost, and he needs it to convince the Dean to pay for his next dig.'

'Ah, well, those are the main points.' Professor Bretherton looked relieved. 'Do you know who's blackmailing him and for what?'

'No, he wouldn't tell me. I can only assume it's for the papyrus and the blackmailer is that Marrin fellow. Frightful bounder. He may know something about Ayers; they move in the same circles. However, about the papyrus. You really know all that I do. I looked at the Greek, it's ancient demotic. Graham used it for shorthand. It's unlikely that any of his Arabic labourers would understand it. It just says, "To the north, beside the foot of the old wall, at the end of the avenue of sphinxes", and then there's a bit in Egyptian which I can't read and neither could Ayers, plus a note in English out of which I could only pick a few words, but one of them was Khufu, that is, Cheops. Trouble is, there are hundreds of avenues of sphinxes, apparently. First thing any pharaoh worth the name did when he was planning his mausoleum – you know that that is a Greek word, from the tomb of Mausolos? – was to order an avenue of sphinxes. The most famous is at Karnak, of course. They've got ram's heads, rather decorative. Ayers assumed that the rest of the note explained which avenue, and I was going to have the papyrus photographed with different filters, which might have brought up the writing. They're doing rather clever things now with ultraviolet light. I even had a photographer lined up to take the pictures, he said it would be such a change from doing wedding portraits, but it's too late now.'

'It may not be. We just have to find the papyrus and all will be well, assuming that Graham wasn't an absolute dingbat.'

'There is that,' agreed Professor Bretherton. 'He was undeniably eccentric.'

'Now, what I have to do is go back to first principles,' said Phryne. 'This is an attempted murder investigation now. I need to know about that burglary, and the first thing I need to know is, where were you on Saturday and Sunday of last week?'

'Eliminate the suspects, eh? I went to the faculty office in the morning to pick up some papers. Then I went home. I spent the afternoon reading and marking essays. Then I took my wife and daughters to the cinema to see the new Douglas Fairbanks, came home and went to bed. Sunday – what did I do on Sunday? Oh, yes, Sunday was very hot, so I took the girls to Taronga Park to feed the elephant, then we came home and had tea, then more essays of unusual idiocy, then dinner and bed. And then I arrived on Monday morning to find everyone screaming.'

'Who was in the office when you arrived?'

'Harcourt, Sykes, the Dean, Kirkpatrick and the secretary – what is the girl's name? Dora.'

'Thank you,' said Phryne. Bretherton was looking at her with a crease between his eyebrows.

'You said an attempted murder,' he said. 'Did you mean Joss Hart?'

'Or Adam Harcourt,' said Phryne. 'I have to get some authority to ask questions,' she added. 'This is no longer just a question of the burglary. Should I see the Vice Chancellor?'

'No,' said Bretherton hastily. 'There was never a chap for getting the wrong end of the stick like old Chas Waterhouse. We'll all be at lunch. Put it to the meeting. If it's a choice of you or the police, I know which way it will go. But let them get the main course down before you start talking.'

'A good plan,' said Phryne, and allowed him to show her into the small faculty dining room.

After absorbing a good clear soup, a chicken

174

salad and a glass of champagne, she watched the faculty push back their plates, fill their glasses and light cigars. She rose to her feet.

'Gentlemen, I have something to report,' she said, putting the parcel she had hastily wrapped in Ayer's office on the table beside her. 'You have a murderer amongst you.'

'Surely, Miss Fisher,' objected the Bursar, 'the injury to Hart was an accident.'

'No, it wasn't.' She scanned the faces. Not a flicker. The practice of University politics clearly required a straight face. She would not have liked to play poker with any of them. She could detect some lurking doubt in several countenances. Was this a disturbed woman? It was well known that the Fair Sex were flighty.

'I would ask you to look at this,' she said, exhibiting the shoe and explaining the mechanism. It was passed from hand to hand around the table.

'But this is ... diabolical,' said Kirkpatrick.

'Certainly is. We should call the police.'

There was a loud murmur of disagreement.

'Then the whole matter of the safe will come out,' objected Bisset. 'There will be a most filthy row!'

'So there should be, if one of your number is willing to go to these lengths to get what he wants. We should summon the police immediately.'

'God, the scandal,' whispered Sykes. He was echoed by Bretherton, who said, 'Can't you find out who did it, Miss Fisher? Then we can just hand him over as a nice neat package and all this other stuff needn't concern anyone.'

'Very improper,' reproved Phryne. 'But I'm

willing to have a try, because otherwise I believe that this may go unpunished. It's a bit out of the way for your ordinary cop. If you want me to look into it, gentlemen, then I will. One condition.' She raised a hand to still their thanks. 'I need your authority to ask any questions which I see fit, and I want you to answer them. This will be boring and perhaps embarrassing but you can see that it must be so. I am discreet and will not disclose anything I don't have to disclose. Do we have an agreement? I'll step outside while you talk about it. And do be careful with that shoe, Dean!' she said sharply, taking it out of his grasp. 'One snake bite victim is enough for today.'

She walked out of the wood-lined room and closed the door on the rising buzz of voices.

After a moment, Bretherton came out to her in the Quad.

'I've made my position clear,' he said. 'I'm voting for you. But – and this is the important question, Miss Fisher – do you think you can solve it?'

'Given a little co-operation, I think so,' she replied, lighting a cigarette. He surveyed her a moment as she stood in the shade of the jacaranda tree. Light was dappled across her concentrated, intelligent face.

'I believe that you have a better chance than anyone else,' he said quietly. 'I wish I had met you, Miss Fisher, when I was much younger.'

'Thank you,' said Phryne.

An hour later, Phryne was in the faculty office, interviewing suspects. This was not improving her temper. For one thing, all of the interviewees were nervous. For another, she was coming to the conclusion that academic life was so routine that no one should be forced to live it.

Jeoffry Bisset advised that he had been in the office on Saturday morning when he had reproved Sykes for dropping the Book of Hours, then had gone to his digs for lunch and gone fishing. Then he had attended the ball at eight, held in the Great Hall, and had got rather sozzled. Not wishing to present himself to his College in that condition, he had dossed down on his own office floor and woken with rather a headache on Sunday morning, gone home, gone to church, and spent the rest of the day and night marking essays.

The Dean had lunched with some patrons of the university, slept away the afternoon, gone out with his wife to the same ball, and spent Sunday blamelessly, in company, in divine service and more napping. He had not come near the University until Monday morning.

Kirkpatrick told Miss Fisher that he had had a meeting of the Band of Hope on Saturday night, and had naturally spent Sunday at the Wee Free Kirk and in meditation and prayer.

Sykes had gone to his Garden Club and had spent Saturday night reading books on azaleas and Sunday working in the garden with his wife.

Professor Brazell the anthropologist was not available for interview, because he had been called away to attend to some new discovery in Queensland. She could lay hands on Professor Ayers at the hotel that evening, under the name of Sanders.

Everything she had so far, Phryne observed to herself, amounted to less than nothing.

She decided to talk to Dora, the secretary.

'Dora?' the Dean snarled. 'She's working in the faculty office now. Trying to catch up with the correspondence which the Bursar has been too distracted to deal with. We have to account for our time as well as our money, Miss Fisher, as some of my staff may have forgotten.'

He really was a poisonous man, thought Phryne. Not a word of sympathy for Joss Hart, who might be dead. And even when conveying some harmless information he just had to get in another dig at the poor Bursar. She began to wonder how the Dean would look with an axe in his head, took her leave, and went to find Dora.

She heard a typewriter clacking, used by someone who was fast, skilled, and in a very bad temper, to judge by the way the carriage was slammed back until its little bell rang in protest. When Phryne opened the door, the girl snapped, 'The office is closed. Come back on Monday.'

'That might be too late,' said Phryne, and Dora turned in her swivel chair and swept a load of paper off her desk.

'Drat,' muttered the girl, dropping to her knees to gather it up. 'No, don't trouble, Miss, I'm just clumsy today.'

'And not pleased to be here,' said Phryne, sitting down on the edge of the desk.

'Who would be, a nice day like this? He's told me to finish all of this before I can knock off. At this rate, by the time I get home the shops will be shut and I've got my eye on a silk dress in the Strand Arcade, marked down from ten pounds. Someone else will get it,' said Dora. 'And I've been watching that price come down for weeks. Heavy silk, too, none of this artificial stuff.'

'I've got executive powers,' said Phryne, assuming them. 'Talk to me now and I'll send you home,' she said, and Dora looked at her like a dog offered not just a bone, but a mastodon bone.

'Yes, Miss? What can I tell you?'

'Your unvarnished account of the events of last week, omitting no incident and not sparing any personalities.'

'I got in and everyone was as usual, Professor Kirkpatrick disapproving of the length of my skirt and Professor Bretherton trying to look up it,' said Dora frankly. 'No, he came in later. But he always does.'

'Do you mind?'

'I'd mind if it was Mr Gorman,' said Dora. 'But the Professor just likes to look and there's no harm in that. A girl likes to be appreciated.' She tucked back a wisp of hair and smiled complacently. She was a trim little package, no taller than Phryne, with elaborately dressed hair of a suspiciously bright shade on which she used Koko-for-the-hair. She had blue eyes and wore rather too much lipstick. But her clothes were tidy and her fingernails were short and well kept. A working woman, occupying the time between school and marriage as agreeably as possible.

'Go on,' encouraged Phryne. 'Begin with Saturday.'

'You want the whole thing? Well, I came in first, like I always do, took off my hat, made the tea – there's a little tea-room just along the passage – laid out the biscuits on a plate. They were ginger.

Then I took the cover off my typewriter, opened the letters, sorted them, and then while I was doing that Mr Sykes came in. Poor Mr Sykes. Saturday's a half holiday and he always wants to get to his garden club. Lovely flowers he grows. Then the Dean started on him, like he always does, about the books. Mr Sykes got flustered and dropped the ledgers. Then he got more flustered and dropped the Book of Hours of Juana, and Professor Bisset was upset. Then the Scotch professor had an argument with Mr Bisset about being annoyed with Mr Sykes. It wasn't a nice day and everyone was cross. Finally Mr Sykes and Adam Harcourt shovelled everything into the safe, I closed up, and we went out.'

'And you didn't come back to the university until Monday?'

'Why should I do that?' demanded Dora. 'I spend enough time here as it is. On Monday I got in as usual, laid out the biscuits and made the tea, when I heard shouting. I thought it was just the Dean ear-bashing Mr Sykes, but when I came back the money was gone and all the other things, jewellery and that. Terrible. Can I go now, Miss? The shops shut soon.'

'Who do you think did it? I promise not to breathe a word,' said Phryne.

Dora's blue eyes flashed. 'It can't be any of our professors,' she said firmly. 'Mr Kirkpatrick's real religious. Professor Bretherton wouldn't steal anything but a kiss. Mr Sykes wouldn't dare. Mr Brazell's a nicely spoken chap. Mr Ayers never says boo to a goose. But the Dean's a beast, I really hate him. It'd be bonzer if you could make it him,' said Dora.

She drew the cover over the typewriter, grabbed a straw hat, preceded Phryne out of the office, locked the door and dived down the stairs.

Never stand between a lioness and her prey, a bear and her cubs, or a woman and a bargain, re-lected Phryne. I believe that I may have a talent for aphorism. What a thoroughly unhelpful young woman! Dora had told Phryne everything she already knew.

Now to see whether she was investigating a murder, to find out if Joss Hart was alive or dead.

Ten

Everyone but narks, dogs, phiz-gigs and jacks

'Guest List for Tillie Devine's Birthday', quoted
in Butel and Thompson, *Kings Cross Album*

Love is universal. It happens just the same in Darlinghurst as in Oodnadatta, only in Darlinghurst it happens at shorter intervals.

'Nothing Like Love' in Lennie Lower,
Here's Lower

The infirmary was a rather severe building, con-structed when all illness was considered to be tantamount to sin and thus to be seriously discouraged among the student body. Phryne's shoes slid on a floor polished to within an inch of extinction and a white-clad nurse materialised at her elbow.

'Yes?' she asked, with the unshakeable superiority which is given to one who knows the worst of human nature.

'I want to see Joss Hart,' said Phryne.

The nurse seemed about to argue. She stood for a moment and analysed Phryne: her clothes, her assurance, and probably her bank balance and the name of her hairdresser, then turned and bustled away. She stopped outside a half-open door.

'His father is with him,' said the starched figure. 'Doctor will be back in an hour.'

'What's his condition?'

'We've done all we can for the moment. He's a strong young man. We shall have to see,' said the nurse, and walked away.

That sounded bad, Phryne thought, sitting down on the one iron chair in the corridor. Voices came to her and she listened.

'Joss, Jocelyn, I'm so sorry,' mourned a deep male voice. 'I'm so sorry, son.'

Phryne could hear no reply. Interesting. Why was Mr Hart apologising to Joss? How could Joss's snake bite have had anything to do with his father? She heard the noise of a chair being pushed back and the elder Hart said, 'I'll be back in an hour, son, I have to arrange something.'

Phryne watched a large man in an exquisite suit plod slowly away, as though he was carrying a heavy weight. Harcourt and Clarence passed him and rushed to Phryne.

'We had to leave for a moment,' said Clarence. 'How is he?'

'I don't know,' said Phryne. 'Come and see.'

Joss Hart was lying in a white bed. His leg was elevated and the tourniquet had been replaced with a tight bandage. His foot had swollen like a balloon of tightly stretched, purple skin. He was moaning very quietly, a terrible sound full of despair which set Phryne's teeth on edge.

'Joss,' breathed Harcourt.

'Joss,' said Clarence, horrified.

'Listen,' said Joss, and they both fell silent. Hart did not speak again for some time. Phryne took his hand and sat down on the edge of the bed, a surface as hard as a porcelain bath. The hand was slack and cold.

'What did you want to say, old chap?' ventured Harcourt. 'We're here, both of us and Miss Fisher, you know.'

'Phryne,' said Joss. The cold hand flexed a little. Phryne leaned forward until her ear almost touched Joss' lips. He breathed a phrase, choked, and spoke again.

'Yes, of course,' said Phryne clearly. 'I'll do as you say. It's all right, Joss. Now all you have to do is get better,' she said bracingly, not allowing any of the fear she felt ooze into her voice. She racked her brains for what she knew of snake venom, assuming it was snake venom in that diabolical machine. Presumably it was. She was striving not to remember the death of a small companion at a Sunday School picnic, bitten by a tiger snake in the long grass. That had been the same. The slow paralysis, the symptoms of suffocation, convul-

183

sions and then death.

The return of the doctor coincided with Mr Hart, and Phryne took both boys out into the corridor. When the doctor emerged alone, she tackled him. He was a man of good age with a competent air. Phryne judged him to be a man with a short way with hysterics but a basically compassionate nature, which by now ought to be immune to surprise.

'Phryne Fisher.' She held out a hand and the doctor took it. 'I haven't any standing at all in this matter and I want a brief lecture on snake venom.'

The doctor was on the point of dismissing this importunate female when he looked into Phryne's eyes and decided not to. She was in deadly earnest.

'Australian snakes have a colubrine type of venom, that is, akin to a cobra,' he answered. 'It's a neurotoxin. It works by paralysis, eventually slowing down and stopping the heart and suppressing respiration. The victim gets cold and can't breathe,' he added, translating. 'But I've injected 100 cc of Calmette's Solution. It doesn't seem to have been a huge dose, he's still alive, and we shall see what we shall see. Don't give up hope, Miss Fisher. Still a chance. If we knew what sort of snake bit him it would be a great help, but the gardeners can't find it.'

'I can provide you with a sample of venom; would that help?' asked Phryne.

'Yes,' said the doctor, shelving a large number of questions, beginning with how, why, and what in the name of Moses?

'I'll send it along directly,' said Phryne. 'Come

along, gentlemen. I need to talk to you. But I'll just have a word with the chemist first.'

Phryne walked into the pharmacist's room, leaving her escorts in the Quad. There she demanded a syringe, a clean phial, and a witness. The dispenser watched as she carefully inserted the needle into the rubber stopper in a partially dissected cricket shoe and extracted a clear fluid which looked like sugar syrup. She squirted it into the phial and dropped the syringe into the sink.

'Snake venom,' she told the white-coated woman. 'Be careful of that syringe. Can you give this to the doctor who is looking after Joss Hart?'

'You wouldn't like to tell me what this is about, would you?' asked the woman, fascinated. Phryne smiled at her and wrapped the damaged shoe.

'No,' she said sweetly, and went out.

'Now, chaps, your undivided attention if you please,' she observed to Clarence and Harcourt. 'This is now an attempted murder and all bets are off, and that includes any delicacy you might have about telling on anyone else.'

'Attempted murder?' demanded Harcourt. 'You mean Joss? Someone tried to kill him with a specially trained snake? That isn't funny, Miss Fisher.'

'No, wait.' Clarence was watching Miss Fisher and she did not appear to be amused. Painfully learned sensitivity to female voices was causing all his alarm signals to go off. 'You mean it, don't you? This is an attempted murder. Someone did try to kill Joss. But why?'

'That is what I am trying to ascertain, and you are going to help me, aren't you?

They both nodded, looking scared. Phryne glanced from face to face as she talked. Harcourt, chewing his thumbnail, was as white as a sheet. His curly hair was the most robust thing about him. Clarence was sleek, as always, but his mouth was set and he was, for perhaps the first time in his life, unconscious of his own beauty. He gave the appearance of someone who was thinking hard.

'Where were you on the weekend? Start with Saturday morning. Clarence?'

'I was at the University, looking for old Bisset, to ask him about the damnable mark he gave me for my French essay,' said Clarence. 'I went up to his office but he wasn't there. I heard him in the faculty office yelling at Sykes, and he seemed to be in a wax so I didn't want to approach him in that mood. I went away to find Joss and we went to collect Harcourt. We spent the afternoon wandering along the shoreline at Glebe and talking to the old fishermen. It was interesting,' said Clarence dutifully. Phryne could not see the dapper and polished Clarence enjoying such an excursion, but was prepared to believe it. 'Joss is really keen on the history of Sydney. He thinks there's a treasure ship wrecked off Glebe Point. I suppose it's possible.'

'No, old chap, you've left out a bit,' said Harcourt helpfully. 'Joss went off on his own for a couple of hours and left us in the pub, remember?'

Clarence nodded. 'Yes, that's right, he did. Then we toddled off to dinner at a little Italian place and went to the ball, and there we stayed until it sort of died at about two o'clock. Bisset was there but he was having such a good time that I didn't like to approach him about my French essay. I clicked immediately with a very pretty piece and rather lost the others but I found them again later. We sloped off at three or so and walked back to Harcourt's room in John's, and talked the rest of the night. Then on Sunday we slept in and went to lunch at the Coll. and I did my Anglo-Saxon essay. Sunday night I went back to my lodgings to have a wash and pick up a clean collar and we went to Theo's. That's about all, really.'

'Adam, does that agree with your recollection?'

'Yes, that's it. I didn't click with any pretty pieces, though. I spent some of the ball with Bisset – he was drinking like a fish and I was a bit worried about him. The punch wasn't strong, but anything will have an effect if you drink three gallons of it. Christopher Brennan was there with his disciples, roaring drunk, and Anderson as well with the Andersonians. They had an awful argument about free will and the porters heaved them out at about eleven-thirty. Then ... I can't really remember what I did, Miss Fisher, but I was at the ball. Clarry and Joss and I went back to my room in John's and talked, and then spent the Sunday as he says. Except I did my Theocritus and Joss did his Catullus. Theo's was rather full and a bit sordid with all the girls from Tillie's talking about the raid.'

'Was Darlo Annie there?' asked Phryne.

'I don't remember. Then we went to our several homes and woke up to the Monday, which shall always be marked with a black stone. That's when my world all fell to bits around me. I'm facing a

Senate hearing on Monday and they'll expel me,' said Harcourt, starting on another fingernail.

'Never mind, old chap, don't take it like that, you can find a job, chap with your skills.' Clarence tried to console him.

Adam Harcourt's thin face flushed with rage. 'Second best, all my life I'll be second best to what I could have been!' he said with ferocious intensity. 'Certainly I can find a job, Joss' father might even give me one as he promised, but this is where I want to be, where I have always wanted to be. This–' he waved a hand at the green lawns, the strolling scholars, the massive bulk of the buildings – 'this is what I want. More than anything. And if they throw me out, it'll break my heart,' he said, and Phryne did not think that he was exaggerating at all. He meant exactly what he said. Jude the Obscure had the same outlook. Adam Harcourt's spiritual home was the University.

For a moment she envied anyone who had found exactly what they wanted, had located exactly where they wanted to be until they died. Phryne was a wanderer. Like Kipling's cat, all places were alike to her. As long as they were weatherproof, well-decorated and supplied with suitable furniture and adequate food and drink, of course.

'What about you, Clarence? What do you want to do?'

'Oh, nothing,' drawled Clarence. 'I mean just that. I have such a good time, just floating about, a few lectures here, Theo's at night, going to a show or perhaps a little row on the river, that I don't want an occupation. I just want to exist beautifully, as Walter Pater said, "To burn with a

188

hard, gem-like flame", if that didn't sound far too energetic. That Joss, now, he always wanted to do well and impress his father, terrible hard the old man was on Joss. Called him effeminate, imagine, because he wasn't doing hearty things with rocks. Mr Hart's something of a mining magnate. Head of a big corporation. Not precisely born to the purple, between ourselves. Old man Hart worked his way up from being a simple mining engineer to head of Hart and Co., and *his* father was a prospector, I believe. Joss never gets a chance to forget that.'

'No, his father nagged him all the time,' agreed Harcourt. 'Joss was always sure that his father despised him, but he looks pretty overcome now.'

'What happened to Joss' mother?' asked Phryne, identifying an absence at Joss' bedside.

'She's dead,' said Harcourt. 'Died when he was a little boy. It's a sad story.'

'Well,' said Phryne, standing up and brushing off her skirt. 'Entrancing as it is to lie on the grass with you, gentlemen, I must be getting on. The afternoon's wearing away. What are your plans for the moment?'

'We're going back to the infirmary,' said Harcourt, a little surprised that she should need to ask. 'To sit with Joss.'

'Indeed,' agreed Clarence, perhaps a shade reluctantly.

'Then I will bid you farewell,' said Phryne, and did so.

It was a puzzle, she thought as she walked through the gardens. Why kill Joss – or Harcourt? To cover up something they knew, to remove

189

them from the scene, to prevent them from telling – what? What did these two harmless young men know? Could be anything. And the field was wide open in relation to the burglary. All of the boys had been out of touch with each other on Saturday night, which was when Phryne suspected the burglary had taken place for no reason other than intuition. Most of the academic staff had been on or near the premises as well, though she excepted Kirkpatrick. The Wee Frees were of such rigid rectitude that he would literally have rather been burned at the stake than have taken part in a magical ritual, and magic was at the heart of the burglary.

And what about Ayers? That blackmailer had him firmly in his or her grip. Ayers had impressed Phryne. Ordinary violence would not work on him. It needed a combination of magic and terror to keep him silent. He said he did not know where the papyrus was, and she believed him. Equally he desperately desired to make a great find, and Khufu's tomb would certainly be that. Bretherton had been helping him, did not appear susceptible to ordinary blackmail, and had kept his word to Ayers with commendable, if inconvenient, probity.

Where was the elusive Brazell? He had an excellent motive for suppressing that papyrus. He wanted the archaeology money spent in Australia, not overseas. He knew that the notes on the papyrus, once the inherent possibilities were carefully explained to the Dean, would ensure that Ayers was funded and Brazell was not.

So. Brazell had an excellent reason for stealing the papyrus and suppressing it, if not forever. All he really needed to do was to mislay it until after the Dean had made his decision. Then Ayers would have to wait a year for funds. Further study of the strange, miscellaneous notes might reveal that they were useless, there being, as Bretherton said, a lot of avenues of sphinxes in Egypt. Ayers needed the papyrus now, before long study could ruin the first fine careless rapture of discovery. Had Brazell stolen it?

Interesting but hardly evidence, Phryne thought. If he had stolen it, what had he done with the other things, and who had planted those examination papers in Harcourt's desk? Her memory of Brazell was clear, if brief. Bright eyes and a charming manner. But that could cloak all sorts of things. Handsome is was certainly not as handsome does in Sydney in 1928.

What, then, was she to make of Joss Hart's fading whisper, 'Stop Dad. Forgive me'? Forgive him for what? The burglary? Why would Joss steal the papyrus? Which brought Phryne to consider Marrin and Madame. She did not think that Marrin would pause for more than half a second if he saw a chance to rob the safe and cast the blame on Harcourt, who had laughed at him. The problem was access. Marrin could not just walk into the university, he did not have keys to the various doors, and any porter who met a man with a shaven head and teeth like a crocodile wandering around the main building would have screamed police – fire – murder at first sight, even if he had then run like blazes.

And the papyrus was not in Marrin's possession, or he would not have tried to buy it from

Professor Bretherton, a fact confirmed by Ayers. Madame had seduced Bretherton – in Phryne's experience men were fatally easy to seduce – but that had not gained anyone anything. Marrin had told on Bretherton and Bretherton had confessed all and his wife had forgiven him.

Phryne realised that she was out in George Street West and was wandering towards the city. Walking suited her humour, so instead of waiting for a bus she kept on. The rain of the previous night had washed the pavements clean and the air was sparkling with life. Even the sad trees in tubs outside depressed Glebe houses appeared refreshingly green.

As she approached the corner of a long street, a big car drew up beside her. Phryne stopped. An attack? A woman in a Fuji dress of the startling pink called 'baby's bottom' leapt out and called, 'Miss Fisher? Are you Miss Fisher?'

'And if I am?' asked Phryne, keeping her back to a rusty iron fence.

'Oh, please.' The woman came closer and Phryne saw that her cheeks were streaked with tears, cracking her maquillage. 'Miss Fisher, is it?'

'Yes,' said Phryne, still unsure.

'Let me talk to you,' pleaded the woman. 'It's about my son. My little boy. Hart, you know. Joss Hart.'

It was a tea-shop which mainly served labourers from the bridge and Phryne bought two cups of tea like tar, served in thick cracked cups. There were three tables with splintery wooden benches. The one window wept grease. Phryne gave up hope for her stockings and sat down next to the bright pink shimmering dress and the desperate face under the curled blonde hair. Mrs Hart dabbed at her eyes.

'I haven't seen him since I ran away,' she whispered. 'His father was rough. Big bruiser of a man and he took it out on me, but not on Joss. Never on Joss. He loved Joss. So I left Joss when I ran, when he put me out on the street in my nightgown for the last time. And where could I go but on the game? Never trained for anything. Not a penny in my pocket. Nowhere to go. Tillie took me in. Looked after me. When the bruises healed I started to work for her.'

'How long ago?' asked Phryne.

'Ten years. I used to send little presents to Joss, letters, too. But they always came back unopened. His father was very angry with me. Still is, I expect. No one ever defied him before. But I did,' said Mrs Hart with a trace of pride. 'And, you know? Life as a tart is a good deal easier than life with Vivian Hart. Silly name. A girl's name, but I never told him so. I didn't want him to call the boy Jocelyn because I thought it would be difficult for him at school, and it was, but he did it anyway. Never listened to me,' she sighed. 'But every working girl's got a story,' she said. 'I went looking for you at the University but they said you'd left. Professor Bretherton told me, he's one of my regulars. Nice bloke. Real gentleman. Told me Joss was injured and told me you could smuggle me in somehow if anyone could. Then I saw you in the street and I thought it must be you. Green eyes are rare with black hair.'

'Why don't you go and see Joss?' asked Phryne. 'The infirmary would let you in, you're his mother.'

'I can't, Viv's there and he told me he'd kill me if he saw me again. He means it. Came looking for me several times. The last time he took on Shark-bait Kennedy and got a real larruping. Tillie looks after the girls.'

'Until they are of no further use,' said Phryne. 'I have no moral objections to your profession, Mrs Hart, but in another few years, perhaps, you will run out of customers, and then...'

The shrewd, blotched, painted face turned up to Phryne's. 'Call me Dolly, do. Same thing with athletes and movie actresses: they're out when they get older. By the time I retire I'll have saved enough for a nice little house and an annuity. It's a profession like any other,' said Dolly Hart, and Phryne began to like her. 'And I never had to do anything for it which Viv Hart didn't do to me, against my will.'

'What do you want with me?' asked Phryne.

'Tell me about Joss.' Mrs Hart began to cry again. 'What happened to him?'

'He was bitten by a snake,' said Phryne. 'He is very ill. I really think you ought to see him.'

'I dursn't,' said Mrs Hart, sobbing into her handkerchief.

'You durst,' said Phryne gently. 'Come back with me and we'll get you some clothes and we can carry this off. I'd disguise you as a nurse but I can't see Florence Nightingale of the infirmary co-operating. You look about my companion's size,' she added. 'And if you can tell her what happened to her sister Joan...'

'Joan? Joanie Williams? Do you really think you can do this, Miss Fisher?'

'Yes,' said Phryne.

'Tillie sent me out with a message to deliver, and gave me leave to be away if I could get in to see Joss. She trusts me not to run away. I won't, reason being, I don't have anywhere to run and in any case...'

'She was good to you and you're saving up for your retirement,' concluded Phryne. 'Is the car still there?'

'Yes, Sharkbait's waiting for us.'

'He isn't going to be pleased to see me again,' said Phryne.

'Of course, you're the "little light sheila" who slipped out of his headlock,' chuckled Dolly Hart. 'No one's ever done that to him before. I think he likes you. Come on.' She clapped down her cup and escorted Phryne to the Bentley.

The back door opened and Phryne got in. Dolly said, 'Hotel Australia' to Bluey 'Sharkbait' Kennedy, who smiled at Miss Fisher in a manner which suggested that he was unaccustomed to the exercise. She smiled cautiously back.

'You have to understand that Tillie's the Queen of Vice in Sydney,' Mrs Hart began, evidently in the throes of an explanation. 'She's got the game stitched up and no one dares to cross her. Just lately she's been worried that her girls are too rough. Like, gentlemen who want a pretty girl on their arm for a night at the theatre and the ballet and all that don't want some slut from Darlo who's never bathed in her life and who thinks a pie and gravy is haute cuisine. Likewise he don't want a tart who looks like a tart – gentlemen are peculiar like that. They want some girl who's never heard the word "sin" and will do any filthy act he has a yen for, but he wants her to act like a lady the rest of the time and not grope the bellboy or throw up in the lift. Follow?'

'Certainly,' said Phryne. Mrs Hart still retained most of her genteel vocabulary, though it was overlaid with rougher street idioms.

'So there was this woman, see, one of Tillie's look-see men saw her standing on the street corner, saw her take several men into an alley. Tillie don't like amateurs. She says they ruin the trade. Sharkbait there put the frighteners on her and she ran away, but the dog said he saw her back in the same place a couple of nights later, playing the same game, and they took her to see Tillie. Tillie says to her, it's dangerous out on the street, you never know who's out there, you could get hurt, even killed, why not work in a house where you're safe? Implying, you see, that even if she had been safe before she wasn't going to be safe now. Drive around, Bluey. I got to finish this story before we get where we're going.'

Bluey grinned and swung the car around to circle Hyde Park.

'So Miss Williams, it was, she says that she never wanted to be a tart and she was married with children, and they were desperate, about to be put out on the street and her husband's business failing and her children hungry. Well, Tillie's heard that story before, we all have a story, but she believed Joanie because she was telling the truth.

196

Tillie hardly ever gets people wrong. That's one reason why I stay with her.'

Phryne thought about Joan Williams, so destitute that she serviced strangers in alleys. That was by any measure desperation indeed, and she could also imagine how disgusted the fastidious, refined girl whom Dot described would have been at being reduced to such an extremity. Tillie's establishments, however dire, would have to be an improvement.

'So Tillie heard Joan's voice and looked at her clothes and asked her if she could dance, and did she know all about table manners and that, and Joanie said she did, and proved it – you'd never think that anyone could dance with Sharkbait there, would you? But Joanie managed it.'

'She's a bonzer dancer,' commented Sharkbait. 'Only tart I've ever known who'd dance with me.' He grinned into the rearview mirror. Phryne examined her imagination. It boggled. Mrs Hart continued, speaking quickly.

'So Tillie said she was far too soft-hearted to be a tart and she'd better take a job teaching all the girls to dress and how to act like ladies, and Joan accepted it. Tillie's right. Joanie wouldn't make a good tart. She hated it, really hated it, and men can tell. Well, some men can tell. And some of them care. They're buying a girl who can seem to want them. Joan's been really nice to have around. The girls like her too, only the roughest ones complain about too much washing and not laughing too loud and they never last too long, anyway. Get on the gin and that's the end of them. But Joanie don't drink. And she can dance like a dream. Until she came I hadn't danced for years. Tillie's even planning to have dance parties.'

This was much better news than Phryne had been expecting. Leaving aside the unfortunate beginning to the story, which Phryne was intending to suppress completely, Joan had not actually committed any discoverable sins for which her family might have to forgive her. Dot would be very relieved.

'But where is she?' asked Phryne. 'I've been looking for her, and possibly Darlo Annie, for days and no one's seen them.'

Mrs Hart's plump hand closed on Phryne's wrist.

'I can see how you confused 'em,' she whispered. 'Darlo Annie's the same build as Joanie, the same blonde hair and blue eyes. You been asking at Theo's and those places, and they never look at a girl well, only see the colouring and maybe the body. A girl's not a person to Theo's, just a collection of arms and legs. I can see how they got it wrong, they might not have been trying to mislead you. But Darlo Annie's dead, took laudanum last week after her steady chap went and got married. She thought he was her ticket out, did Annie, poor girl. That's why Tillie didn't want you looking into her death, it was natural but Tillie don't want to attract police attention, because there was a police raid on Palmer Street on Saturday night last, and Joanie's...'

'In jail,' said Phryne.

Eleven

...the eyes, legs and hands of the middle wicket are never occupied. This situation will furnish lively employment for an active young gentleman.

John Nyren, *The Young Cricketer's Tutor*

Dot had been staring out of the window at the harbour and Phryne suspected that she had been crying, but she rose briskly as Phryne and her visitor came in.

'No word from the cops, Miss,' she told Phryne. 'No news is good news.'

'Your mind is about to be relieved. Dot, this is Mrs Hart, who needs to deliver a message to you,' said Phryne, kicking off her shoes.

'You look like your sister,' said Dolly Hart. 'Joanie gave me this for you.'

Dot took the folded piece of paper. The outside was grubby but it opened cleanly. She stared at it, then handed it to Phryne. In clear copybook script Phryne read, 'Dot, dear, it's not what you think. Look after the little ones for me. I'll explain later, your loving sister Joan.'

'What does it mean?' asked Dot, immensely relieved at knowing that her sister was alive. It didn't matter what Joan had done, that could all be adjusted, she was alive. Dot fought back tears. Phryne gave her a quick hug.

'Put some nice clothes on Dot, hospital-going clothes, you're accompanying Mrs Hart to the University. There you will find Professor Bretherton and ask him to sit with you and Mrs Hart in case Mr Hart cuts up rough. Now, we have to bluff a very unpleasant deceived husband. Mrs Hart needs to look respectable. It'll put him on the back foot. None of my clothes will fit Mrs Hart, so can you lend her your linen coat and skirt? And perhaps that oatmeal coloured shirt and the small straw hat. She has to look right or this will not work.'

Dot sized Mrs Hart in her mind's eye, nodded, and drew her into her room to change. Events were moving with their usual speed around Miss Fisher; she had found Joan and Joan was all right, and for that Dot would have given her whole wardrobe to this ageing tart if Phryne required it.

Stripped of the unbecoming dress, her face scrubbed, her hair drawn back into a French pleat and Dot's exceptionally respectable clothes assumed, Mrs Hart could hardly be recognised. She looked at herself in the mirror, marvelling.

'Well, will you look at that,' she observed. 'Might be anyone's mother.'

'You're Joss Hart's mother,' said Phryne. 'And you had better get back to him quickly. Dot, dear, I'm sure that Mrs Hart will explain about Joan on the way, but a brief précis is this: your sister hasn't done anything which might cause a blush on a priest's cheek. She's been teaching deportment to Tillie's girls, because Tillie wants them refined. That's all, eh, Mrs Hart?'

Mrs Hart recalled a ladylike smile from her

200

past and said, 'That's all. But the cops raided Tillie's on Saturday, and swept her up. And now she's doing fourteen days without the option. But it won't be on her record. She's there under a bodgy name. Once she gets out she can go home to her husband and children.'

'If she wants to,' snapped Dot. Outrage at Joan's husband's reaction was growing in her bosom. 'Jim Thompson doesn't deserve to get her back if he doesn't change his tune quick smart. Assume my sister is a slut, will he? Assume that I'm one too! I knew she couldn't have taken the bad path. I'll go and see her and tell her that the children are being cared for. But there's nothing wrong with teaching deportment,' declared Dot. 'Whoever you teach it to.'

'That's the spirit.' Mrs Hart smiled again. Phryne was full of admiration. 'Now, dear, can we go?' Mrs Hart's smile cracked. 'That's my son, dearie, lying in that hospital. I haven't seen him since he was eight, and I might never see him again if we don't get a move on.'

'Right away. Miss, a Mr Sanders left a message that he's in room 64,' said Dot, grabbing for a light summer coat, her hat and her bag. 'And there's the telephone messages on the little table,'

A brief flurry and Dot and Mrs Hart were gone. Phryne was pleased that Mr Sanders had made his way to the hotel. She was banking on his having read an entrancing book by A.A. Milne which had just been published. It concerned the adventures of a group of toys and one of them, Piglet, lived under the name of Sanders. The telephone messages were not interesting – except for the last,

201

a block-printed, hand-delivered sheet of paper.

'Come to the jacaranda tree at seven o'clock and you will hear something to your advantage. Destroy this note.'

No signature, no clue to the identity. Just what sort of heroine do you think I am? Phryne asked the air. Only a Gothic novel protagonist would receive that and say, 'Goodness, let me just slip into a low-cut white nightie and put on the highest heeled shoes I can find,' and, pausing only to burn the note, slip out of the hotel by a back exit and go forth to meet her doom in the den of the monster – to be rescued in the nick of time by the strong-jawed, young hero (he of the Byronic profile and the muscles rippling beneath the torn shirt). 'Oh, my dear,' Phryne spoke aloud as if to the letter-writer. 'You don't know a lot about me, do you?'

Phryne's preparations were more elaborate (and, in any case, she did not wear white or high heels). After their completion, she picked up the house telephone.

'Mr Sanders?' she asked.

A voice replied, 'All out for 253 and Hobbs and Sutcliffe are still in.'

'How about dinner? I can have some sent up,' she offered.

'I'd rather be on my own, if you don't mind,' said the voice politely. 'I've got rather a lot to think about.'

'If you are being constrained, all you have to say next is, bandersnatch,' said Phryne.

'Not even a Jabberwock,' chuckled Ayers. 'I just feel the need of some silent meditation.'

'Fine. Comfortable?'

'Lovely,' he affirmed.

Phryne rang off. She felt like some company but none of the available persons pleased her. She shook herself, ordered a steak from room service and took a long, thorough bath.

When she went out at half-past six, she had left a note for Dot in the room, a letter at reception, and had stowed her notes on the case in the hotel safe.

The journey to the University was quick. She would be on time for her appointment. It was getting dark and the campus seemed deserted. She stepped lightly, listening for footsteps.

Phryne believed in precautions. She was not prepared, however, when a blanket was thrown over her head, her feet were kicked from under her, and she was rushed through what sounded like stone corridors and down stone stairs before she could scream.

Then she heard a terrible ringing scrape, and she was falling. She fell into the dark, feet first, not knowing how far she had to fall.

Dancers, acrobats and fighters learn to fall. Phryne concentrated, shelving all other emotions, and collapsed gracefully as she hit the ground, rolling with the impact, so instead of breaking both ankles she was lightly bruised all over. A reasonable exchange, she thought, gathering her wits. She estimated that she had fallen ten, perhaps fifteen feet.

Onto what? The ground was hard and slick with moisture. Stone. Paving stone, she decided, feeling the straight joins. So. Ten to fifteen feet down onto a stone floor. She stood up uncertainly in the darkness. Where was she?

The journey had been bumpy and she had been muffled in a blanket which had come down with her. She gathered it up and walked with one hand extended until she came up against a wall. More cold damp stone, curving under her touch. Phryne began to shiver. Was this a well? Is that why it was wet? And did her kidnappers expect her to die here, drowning slowly as the water rose?

The darkness pressed close. She strained her eyes to see, inducing light-spot illusions. She shut her eyes, abandoning the sense as unreliable, and began to feel her way along the wall, stepping carefully. Her sliding feet impacted on something soft after only a few paces and she crouched next to it, hoping that it was, firstly, not dangerous and, secondly, useful. A rope ladder would be a favourite, or some means of making light.

Her fingers touched cloth. A jacket. Tweed. She felt further down and found trousers, then further up and found a face. The clothes were inhabited by a man; she touched a beard. A corpse? Not pleasant company, she reflected, though he was unlikely to offend her for long if this really was a well. Dead? She leaned down and listened for a breath, her hand on the tweed-clad chest. Alive. The jacket rose and fell. Warm breath gusted past her cheek. Alive was good, though he was not precisely kicking. What was wrong with him? Drugged? If he had been dropped down as she had, he might have hit his head. Her theory was confirmed when she laid her hand on the unknown man's hair and felt it was matted and sticky.

Feeling better now that she knew that she was not entirely alone in the dark, Phryne sat down on her blanket and considered herself. She had been snatched off the Quad and her handbag had gone, but she had been wearing a skirt with an old-fashioned pocket. In that pocket...

Hardly daring to breathe, she rummaged, and gave a cry of triumph which echoed oddly in the confined space. A packet of Gauloise Gitanes. A comb. A handkerchief. A box of matches.

Phryne Fisher ritually blessed the names of both Bryant and May, extracted a cigarette by feel and lit it. In the first flare she saw that she and the unknown man were in a circular chamber which seemed to have no exit except from above. The cigarette glow did not extend high enough to see the roof, but the walls seemed unbroken by any door. Phryne counted her matches.

She had eight left. Eight matches were not going to last long. Drawing grateful draughts of smoke into her lungs to keep the gasper alight, she began to work on the edge of the blanket with the comb. It wasn't going to work, of course, she realised after a moment: the blanket was wool and wool did not burn. What was she wearing which might?

Mr Edmund Brazell, Professor of Anthropology, opened his eyes, feeling like death, and saw a beautiful woman stripping off her garments. A chemise dropped onto his face, followed by a bust-band and French camiknickers. It was obvious, he decided, that he had died and gone to Heaven, which was a distinctly more interesting place than he had been led to believe.

Phryne rolled the knickers, applied the cigarette

end, and blew gently. A small flame sprang up.

'Silk,' she said with satisfaction. Carrying the improvised torch, she stood up and began to carry out a circuit of the walls, looking for cracks.

Mr Brazell propped himself on one elbow. He believed that the Mohammedan paradise did rather feature naked and beautiful women, but they were unlikely to be clad in stockings, shoes and a blanket, smoking what his nose told him was a French gasper, and he decided that he had not died after all.

Still, his immediate future looked distinctly interesting.

'Excuse me,' he began, touching his aching head with tentative fingertips and instantly regretting it. 'Ouch!'

'Oh, you're awake. Stay still, that's my advice. You've a nasty bang on the head.'

'S-So I discover,' he agreed, watching her progress with fascination. She seemed perfectly unconcerned at her near-nakedness. She was small, straight-backed and as slim as a nymph, her cap of black hair swinging forward as she moved. He watched through watering eyes as she completed her inspection of the walls and came back to him. She knelt down, looking concerned.

'Let's have a look at that bump. I don't think my torch is going to last much longer.' He leaned forward and she touched the wound gently. Her fingers were very sure.

'I don't think they've cracked your skull, just split your scalp. I'll put my hankie on it. Can you sit up?'

'I think s-so,' gasped Brazell. She helped him sit

206

up with his back against the wall and he held the torch as she reassumed her skirt and blouse.

'Now, we've got a blanket and some cigarettes and the rest of my underwear in reserve, though I've only got seven matches. But I've set out on picnics with less. What have you got in your pockets?'

'Madam,' said Edmund Brazell, 'who are you?'

She grinned a gamine grin, which lit up her face and set her green eyes alight. 'I'm Phryne Fisher, who are you?'

'Edmund Brazell. Of course, we've met. At that frightful faculty do. What are we doing here?'

'There you have me. I haven't the faintest. Though if I ever get out of here I shall find whoever did this and rivet their genitalia to a Bondi tram, laughing merrily the while and probably selling tickets. We'll have time to talk, Edmund dear, but just now I need to know if you have anything inflammable in your pockets?'

'Papers,' he gasped, gesturing to her to search his right-hand side while he went through the left.

Phryne wondered why men made jokes about women's handbags. Edmund Brazell was carrying his own weight in rubbish – fortunately. She managed to catch the last flicker from her charred knickers on an old bus ticket and transferred it to a tightly folded playbill for The Sydney Follies.

'Those Sydney Follies were obviously hot stuff,' she observed. Brazell laughed. Phryne looked up from folding an advertisement for a new translation of Homer's *Iliad* and considered him.

Not a very young man, pale and bloodstained. He had dark curly hair and a dark curly beard and a wide mouth; portrait of a Roman, perhaps. He had been stunned and thrown down into a well and was obviously confused and in pain, but he was neither unnerved nor suspiciously calm. His hands were long and beautiful, and he smelt of tweed and soap. She approved. He seemed to be self-possessed and alert which, in his situation, was remarkable. She said so.

'The s-stoics teach us, my dear Miss Fisher, that one should never react with too much enthusiasm to joy or with too much despair to pain.'

'When we are out of here and sitting in a suitable restaurant, my dear Professor Brazell, you may tell me all about the stoics. At the moment, we need to escape.'

'How?'

'I don't know at present,' confessed Phryne. 'But something will turn up. What happened to you? And you had better call me Phryne, perhaps.'

'My dear lady, I couldn't,' he said, shocked.

'Very well,' agreed Phryne, reflecting on the durability of etiquette. 'Tell me what happened to you, Mr Brazell.'

'I cannot account for my present s-situation,' he said simply. 'The last thing I recall is walking out of the s-side door of the library. The door was heavy and I s-shoved it open and then – nothing.'

'Hmm. They can't have carried you far without attracting attention. We must still be in the University. Can you think of somewhere? This looks like an old well.'

'That's not a comforting thought,' he said gravely.

'It isn't, is it? I can't find a crack in the bricks

which might let us remove a few, and even then there may not be anything but earth beyond them. Perhaps we can get out when someone comes to feed us.'

'Er ... Miss Fisher...' ventured Brazell. Have to tread carefully, he thought to himself. One never knew with women, even this bold specimen of the New Woman. Prone to hysteria, ladies.

'What?'

'Has it occurred to you that they – whoever they are – don't actually mean to feed us?' He readied himself for a scream and wondered if he remembered the correct form of words for soothing the frantic female. Was it 'There, there'? Or perhaps 'Come, come'? It really was too bad of Fate, always a s-saucy unreliable minx. Here he was alone with the delectable Miss Fisher, had her all to himself without a lot of other fellows bothering around, and all he was likely to be able to do was to s-starve to death with her.

'You mean, have I considered that this is a murder attempt?' She sounded quite cool.

'Er, well, not to put too fine a point upon it, yes.'

'I have considered it,' she answered composedly. 'It's possible. Some persons might shrink from actually killing their victim outright, and might consider leaving us to starve a less shocking pro-cedure. But I think it more likely that they mean to keep us here in durance fairly vile for a set period.'

'Why? I mean, why do you think that?' If Phryne was impressed by the stoic professor, he was impressed and not a little disconcerted by her. She didn't seem even disarrayed by being thrown down into confinement with a man to whom she had not even been introduced.

'Because something has to be done soon, and we might have foiled it,' replied this strange woman, calmly.

'But what?' asked Mr Brazell, helplessly. 'I'm the Professor of Anthropology. I've never done anything which might involve criminality in my life. Mind you, if I get out, I may join you in committing an indictable offence, Miss Fisher, but...'

'Then it is not something you have done, but something you know, and it must be something that I know, too. Give me another playbill, will you?'

'We might let the light go out for awhile,' he suggested. 'We don't know how long we are going to be here. Also, it uses oxygen.'

'We can talk just as well in the dark,' agreed Phryne. She spread her blanket and enclosed both of them in it. Mr Brazell leaned his aching head against a soft bosom and wondered how on earth he was going to concentrate. The stub of the playbill flared and went out.

It might have been the darkness. Phryne found that all of her senses were more alert. She felt Mr Brazell shrug off the jacket and slide an arm behind her. She felt the warmth of his chest and side as they snuggled together. She smelt tweed and soap as he leaned his forehead into her shoulder, and she caught the sweet-salt tang of blood as his wounded head fitted under her chin. The cocktail of scent was powerfully aphrodisiac and she was shocked at herself. She shrugged a little to bring the beard into contact with a stiffening nipple and cleared her throat.

'So, what is it that you know, Professor?'

'I know a little about s-sacred objects and tabooed words, but my field is manhood rituals in the tribes of C-Central and Northern Australia. You might have seen my article in the *AJA*, perhaps? It's called "On Death and Resurrection in Manhood Rituals amongst the Coast Murring Tribes". There's a god called Daramlun, you see, who s-slays the boys entering initiation, and then they are born again as men.'

'Not something that I know as well, so not terribly relevant. Was anything in the Dean's safe yours?'

'Yes, the hand axe. Can't understand why they s-stole that. Not worth anything except to an anthropologist, just a worked pebble.'

'Why did you have it?'

'I was going to give it to the Kruger collection. It's unusually well-made of a darkish green s-stone.'

'A sacred object?'

'No, a tool. I swapped it for a tomahawk. I can't approve of the way in which some of the fellows s-sic the missionaries upon innocent tribes and then harvest the s-sacred objects once the pastors have converted them and they've lost their old gods. Seems unfair. Fellows like the Murri have a perfectly good religion of their own already. Don't you think s-so? I remember a good s-story one of the Cambridge men told me. An Eskimo says to the priest, "Now that I know your religion, if I s-sin then I'll go to hell, is that s-so?" and the priest says, yes, that's s-so, and the Eskimo says, "But if

211

I had never heard of your Christ and lived a good life according to my old gods, I could have gone to heaven, is that not s-so?" and the priest agrees, yes, my dear fellow, righteous heathen and all that. And the Eskimo looks at the priest and s-says, "Then why did you tell me?" and you know, I bet the priest couldn't think of a good answer to that.'

Phryne couldn't either. The darkness was pressing against her eyes. Down in this pit, there was no light. Not just the darkness of night above ground, but absolute blackness. She could not see at all, and trying was making her eyes ache. She closed them and found her concentration centred on skin contact, and all that was palpable was male flesh. She shivered and Mr Brazell embraced her more closely, trying to ignore his body's enthusiastic response to her nearness.

'It is cold, isn't it,' he murmured.

'I'm not cold,' said Phryne, flooded with heat. 'Mr Brazell, let me put a hypothetical case. If I were to kiss you, would you object?

'Not in the s-slightest. Do you think that is s-something that – hypothetically, of course – you are likely to do?' he asked hopefully.

'It's the darkness,' she said, rearranging his embrace so that she could reach his mouth.

'The darkness?' Mr Brazell was powerfully aroused and compliant, delighted to acquiesce in whatever Miss Fisher desired, but he was a scholar and could not let a statement like that pass.

'Having no sight magnifies ... touch,' said Phryne. She unbuttoned her blouse and allowed his palm to slide over her breast. 'Doesn't it?'

'It does,' he agreed. He had never been so

acutely aware of how a breast felt: the skin so smooth and almost velvety, the nipple as hard as a pebble, the softness overlying the high ribcage. Phryne removed the rest of her clothes and then those of Mr Brazell, and felt him react to every touch. He did not speak again until she lay down beside him and he felt her all along his body; feet and calves and thigh and hip and breast and shoulder, and the wing of hair brushing his face.

'The oldest poem in the world,' he whispered. 'Babylon, five thousand years ago: "Naked into the dark we come, naked into the dark we go. Come to me, naked, in the dark."'

Phryne felt that she should have glowed in the blackness. Her skin was all nerve-endings, over which the scholar's sure hands ran like trails of fire. His mouth was soft and tasted of salt. His beard tickled as he bent to kiss her breast; he tongued the nipple and heard her gasp. The contact was so general that it didn't seem strange that it did not at first involve any of the usual features; Phryne realised that she was rubbing herself against her lover like an amorous cat, tumbled in his arms. Darkness took away all the usual cues of expression; she had to either speak or feel what would give pleasure. Her voice had deserted her. She could only feel.

Sweat broke on his skin. She licked his chest. They locked in a hold like wrestlers, striving not to break away but to get closer, closer. Phryne wrapped her thighs around him and screamed aloud at the sensation, which sent her over the edge of a climax which seemed to be indefinitely prolonged.

Nothing in his previous amatory career, which was as extensive as he could make it, had prepared Professor Edmund Brazell for Phryne Fisher. The darkness magnified touch but delayed his usual over-eager response, and he had no need to recite the Babylonian pantheon to delay ejaculation. This love-making was desperate, fierce and prolonged. The invisible woman in his arms seemed to have mythic force. He had spoken to tribes who believed in spirit-lovers; in Europe they were called succubi. 'She came only in darkness,' they had told him. 'And the man who lay with her pined forever after for her embrace.' He knew he would never feel like this again, he knew that he might die here in the everlasting night, he knew that the scalp wound had split and was bleeding again, and he did not care.

Phryne lost all sense of time. Her body had taken over and was reacting and moving without her orders. She was possessed, elevated, electrified. She felt her lover as though he were in her bones, as though they shared tendon and tissue. She tasted his blood on her tongue. When he climaxed she felt her own thighs tremble and the rush of fire along the spine.

She might have passed out. When she came back to herself the curious twinness was still there. But she was naked, cold, wet, cramped, and a little shocked. She felt around until she located the wall, then the edge of the blanket. On it was lying a naked man who groaned when she touched him.

Phryne wrapped them both and asked, 'Are you alive?'

'Perhaps,' he said. He coughed and his voice

214

grew stronger. 'Yes, I am definitely alive, and very s-surprised. And gratified. Did you feel ... that closeness?'

'As though we were one flesh? Yes. Curious. I still feel it. I know where your feet are, for instance. In relation to mine, I mean.'

'Yes. One flesh. Very biblical. Miss...' he laughed. 'I s-suppose that I can call you Phryne, now, can't I?'

'Yes, Edmund dear, you can. I think this constitutes an introduction.'

Twelve

'The flying foxes having nipt my piches, I distild 400 gals of strong cider from the damaged fruit ... after frumentation one glas put parson in the wheelbarrow.'

Settler, Lane Cove, quoted in Ruth Park,
A Companion Guide to Sydney

'Entrancing as it is to be down here, Edmund,' said Phryne, 'I think we'd better get out.'

'I s-suppose so,' agreed Brazell, who had never been so thoroughly aware of the meaning of the term 'ravished' in his life. 'How do we propose to do that?'

'It's about ten feet, and I heard the scrape of a lid just before those children of unmarried parents threw me in,' said Phryne. 'If I stand on your shoulders...'

'Phryne, don't you think they, whoever it was, put us down here because we couldn't get out?'

'Yes, of course. But that doesn't mean that we have to comply with their wishes,' said Phryne. 'Tell me, if Ayers gets the archaeology money, what will you do?'

'Oh, go back to the desert,' said Brazell. 'It would be nice to have some lolly, but I can always use my s-sabbatical. I've been owed it long enough. My main difficulty with Ayers isn't him. I mean, not him himself, if you s-see what I mean. Nice enough chap, we don't s-see eye to eye on what constitutes a desirable mate but that could be s-said of any s-set of fellows. No, my quarrel with him is that he is always looking to Egypt for worthwhile projects. If he doesn't want to s-study the S-Stone Age Murri, that's one thing, but what about the Malays and the rich, complex c-civilisations of Japan and China? We're not part of the Empire any more, Phryne, that's what I tell them. We're part of S-South-East Asia and we'd better be getting on with it. And them. Not that they pay any attention to me. All for King and Country and Empire, and look where that got us, hmm? What did you s-say?'

'I said, if you stand over here by the wall and I climb on your shoulders, I can at least find out how far it is to the top,' said Phryne impatiently. A lot of things had just become clear to her and she was anxious to get out and test her hypotheses.

Brazell stood by the wall, resting his back against cold stones, and Phryne ascended him until both her stockinged feet were on his shoulders and he could hear her swearing to herself.

216

'Damn, damn, damn,' she said.

'What have you discovered?'

'That it's only about ten feet, all right – I have both hands on the lid – but the lid is immovable. I wish I could remember whether it slid or pivoted.'

'I can't help you,' said Professor Brazell. 'I didn't notice when they threw me in. But from my own knowledge, if this is a well, it should s-slide.'

'Dashed unsporting of them to bolt it or put a rock on it,' muttered Phryne. The professor staggered under her impetus as she shoved with all her might.

Nothing happened, except the professor was reminded that he had a terrible headache and was not as young as he used to be.

'Aha,' said the voice from above.

'Aha?'

'Maybe I've been shoving the wrong way. Ready for another try?'

'No, but I'm still s-standing.'

'There's a good professor,' said Phryne. The lid was smooth, but rust had pitted it somewhat and she managed to dig her fingers into it and lift it a trifle. Her shoulder muscles twanged.

She shoved with all her might in the exact opposite of a sensible direction and was rewarded with a creaking rasp. The lid moved. A little light showed. Phryne pushed again, broke three fingernails, toppled forward and fell, landing with more bruising. Professor Brazell sank against the wall and groaned.

But the lid had moved aside. Light came down into the well. Phryne gathered her possessions, re-assumed all available clothes, and patted Ed-

217

mund on the cheek.

'I'll be back in a moment,' she promised. Brazell lifted her again and saw her get both hands on the lip of the well. Then she sprang upward, inflicting more damage on his shoulders, and he saw a strange flash of thigh and foot as she vanished over the edge. Like those ships that fall off the edge of the world, he thought, vanishing one bit at a time.

There was a crash and a cry. Brazell held his breath. Of course, they would have left a guard. Then a body came hurtling down, landing with a thud.

It was not Phryne – it was a man in a dustcoat. He appeared dazed, which was not unexpected. Professor Brazell was feeling fairly dazed himself.

To the noise of scraping and very unladylike language, a ladder appeared in the half circle of light. Brazell climbed it, not knowing what he would meet at the top. Phryne, panting, dragged the ladder up after him.

'Nasty piece of work,' she said. 'Tried to grab me as soon as I got to the top. Could at least have waited until I got out.'

'Most unc-civil,' agreed Mr Brazell. 'Are you hurt, dear girl?'

'Not more than a few extra scratches,' said Phryne. 'Do you know where we are?'

Professor Brazell squinted at his immediate surroundings. Wine racks loomed out of the darkness.

'Why, it's the wine c-cellar,' said the Professor. 'Under the Great Hall.'

'Don't know about you,' said Phryne, shaking back her hair, 'but while I'd like a bath and some more clothes, I'd settle for a drink. There must be a candle somewhere. I don't have a lot more in the underwear department to burn.'

'Always have candles for decanting,' said Brazell. The contrast in illumination after the pit was making his eyes sting, but it was not nearly light enough to, for example, read a label. He found a table and a cupboard by walking into them in the half dark. A rummage in a drawer produced a bundle of household wax candles. 'Yes, here we are. Care to s-sacrifice another match?'

'Certainly.' Phryne lit the candle and shadows leapt. The cellar was not large, but it appeared to be well stocked. Stone stairs led up to what apparently was a firmly locked door. Phryne ran up the steps, tried the door to no avail, then threw a big iron bolt.

'Why are you doing that?' asked Edmund. 'S-Surely we are locked in enough?'

'I don't want anyone else to intrude on us until we have had an intimate talk with our friend in the well,' she told him. 'Find us a nice bottle, will you? I want to summarise my investigation.'

'How about the Tahbilk '05?' he asked. 'Very good wine.'

'More expensive than that,' she said, combing her hair and drawing water in a bucket to wash her face. 'There are some nice glasses here. The cellarman obviously considers it part of his duty to make sure that the wine sent up to the high table is of merchantable quality.'

'I'm s-sure,' Professor Brazell said.

'Pity there isn't anything to eat. Are you hungry?'

'Miss Fisher,' asked Brazell, 'haven't you got any nerves at all?'

'No,' said Phryne. 'I was so angry I hadn't enough spare space to be afraid, then I was overcome with lust, and now we are out of that beastly well I see no reason to be. Unlike that person who is now down there,' she added. 'He has every reason to be very, very apprehensive.'

'I'm not s-sure that I haven't, also,' said Professor Brazell. 'I never in all my time met anyone like you, Phryne.'

'And won't again, I should imagine,' said Miss Fisher, complacently.

She washed her face and hands, bathed such scratches as she could reach, and put on her shoes to insulate her feet from the cold floor. The puzzle was, at last, coming together. She might be a little frayed around the edges by events and certainly needed some minor cosmetic attention, but she felt that she understood what had happened to the contents of the safe and who had poisoned Joss Hart.

And she had found Joan Thompson née Williams. That thought was sufficient to warm Phryne all over.

A further rummage in the butler's cupboards had disclosed a folded quilt in which not too many spiders were nesting, a tin of dry biscuits which were only a little mouldy, and a further cache of candles. Phryne lit three and by their light found a candle lantern and lit that as well. It was such a relief to be out of the black dark, and just lighting a candle was a luxury.

'How about this?' asked Brazell, returning with two cobwebby bottles. He set them down with appropriate care, then borrowed Phryne's bucket to wash his face, leaving her handkerchief plastered over his scalp wound. Apart from a thumping headache, he felt wonderful. Never before had he appreciated light and free movement so much.

'Excellent,' said Phryne, examining the bottles. 'Someone must have been travelling in the south of France and bought them home. How nice of them.'

'No corkscrew,' said Brazell. 'We s-shall have to break the neck, which is a pity.'

'I have here a selection of three corkscrews,' said Phryne. 'The only neck I'm intending to break is that of that wretch in the well. I wonder if he's woken up yet?'

'I wonder who he is,' said Brazell. 'He may be an innocent porter, and we are going to get into frightful trouble for assaulting him.'

'No innocent porter would have tried to use my head as a football,' snarled Phryne. 'See?' She pointed to a broken bottle of water and a loaf of bread on the floor near the well. She picked up the loaf and tore it in half, giving one piece to Professor Brazell. 'He was coming to feed us,' she said. 'As I suspected, we were to be kept, not killed. Unless that proved necessary, of course, or unless the well filled up with recent rains, in which case it would have been regrettable and he would have been very sorry.'

'Miss Fisher, am I going to regret it if I ask what we are talking about?' Edmund Brazell bit off a piece of bread. It was real, fresh baked, and made him feel more stable. He opened the bottle of Chateau Petrus and poured it roughly into a glass, allowing the air to mingle with the ruby fluid. 'No,

221

don't drink yet – in ten minutes,' he chided as Phryne grabbed for the glass. 'This wine is twenty years old, we don't want to gulp it.'

'Oh, very well.' Phryne put it down again. 'Assume that they were going to keep us until Monday morning, Edmund dear,' she said chattily, sitting down in the butler's chair. 'Put together a boy's natural desire to impress his father, who thinks he is a disgrace to a fine family, with the only thing in common between us, which is your knowledge of a green stone tool and my good idea of who stole the goods out of the Bursar's safe. We have to be put down a well and kept incommunicado until, I suggest, Monday.'

'What happens on Monday?' asked Brazell.

'The Mines Department opens,' replied Miss Fisher.

'Perhaps my old father was right,' said Professor Brazell. 'He always s-said I had no talent for deduction. I couldn't even do those jigsaw ones where you put in all s-sorts of coloured bits and end up with the Tower of London or s-something.'

'Tell me what else was with your hand axe,' said Phryne.

'Nothing. It was just a rather nicely s-shaped s-stone axe,' said Brazell.

'Would it not have been labelled?'

'Of course, all specimens are labelled. Pasted on the back was a label with the place of discovery, the time, my name and my reference number,' said Edmund, bewildered.

'Didn't do any geology, did you?' asked Phryne. 'Ten minutes can be assumed to be up, and I am now going to drink this wine,' she instructed him.

222

There was a moment's respectful silence as both appreciated the robust, full, peppery taste of a great Bordeaux.

'To love,' said Professor Brazell, raising his glass a sip too late.

'To love.' Phryne drank and held out her glass for more. 'When was the last time that you saw your axe?'

'Oh, must have been weeks. No, I'm wrong. I s-saw the package when S-Sykes dropped it about a week ago. Unwrapped it to s-see if it was broken, then rewrapped it and put it back. A week. By George, this wine is really rather s-special.'

'A week ago,' said Phryne, 'it was stolen, or rather, borrowed, and replaced with a paper and sealing wax package which weighed the same. Probably another rock. Stolen by someone who knew what that green stone meant and who desperately wanted to impress his father. In the beginning, Joss Hart went to Mr Hart and told him that the axe was malachite and, from the label, he knew where he could find an excellent deposit of copper. His father didn't believe him – or so I guess. His father demanded proof. So Joss stole the axe and left a package in its place. It was easy for him, his best friend is Adam Harcourt and he's often in the Dean's office, trying to sort out the accounts. It would not have been hard for Joss to make the substitution. His father, today, got the results from the geologist which confirmed that the stone was malachite and malachite only occurs where there is copper.'

'Why do you s-say, today?'

'Because Joss' father was sitting by his bed, saying that he was sorry. Why should he be sorry?'

'There could be a lot of reasons,' said Brazell.

'I may be wrong about that,' admitted Phryne. 'Joss, however, begged me to forgive him. In advance, perhaps, of this assault. He also tried to tell me to "stop Dad". I have no proof that this is what he meant. But I heard Hart tell Joss that he had to arrange something, and I suspect that this is what he had to arrange. To keep us out of the way while he registered a claim on that land.'

'Why would he want me out of the way?'

'My dear Professor.' Phryne leaned close and kissed Edmund Brazell on the mouth. 'He must have heard of your views. How would you feel about the establishment of a great big copper mine in the middle of your desert? The Aborigines, of course, don't matter. They aren't citizens. Their views on having their landscape demolished and desecrated are irrelevant. They can't effectively protest about Hart and Co. charging about, removing their landscape and sending it away in large sacks. Not a newspaper inch in the views of desert people – why should they have views, just because they live there? However, you are in a position to make a scandal, but only before the miner's right has been made. After that there would be nothing that you could do. Twig?' asked Phryne, and sipped from her third glass of Chateau Petrus.

'I'm unwilling to doubt your word, Phryne, but...'

'Just wait.' Phryne walked to the edge of the well.

'Hello down there,' she called. A stream of language replied, tinging the air blue. The speaker was unhappy about his confinement and was offering to do a number of biologically impossible things to the person who had caused him to occupy this blasted well.

'Don't be like that,' said Phryne, 'or I'll just put the lid back and I bet your knickers won't burn like mine. Getting wetter underfoot, is it? Happens in a well. Springs. But you'd know about that, wouldn't you? Being a geologist. Or are you a surveyor?'

'I'm a miner, lady, and if you don't get me out of here...' threatened the voice.

'What will you do?' asked Phryne. 'Tunnel?'

The reply could not have been printed in any reputable newspaper and Phryne walked away, to resume her seat on the butler's chair.

'I hope he comes around soon,' she commented.

'Why?'

'Because he's got the key to the door,' said Phryne. 'Do you reckon that pouring water on him might work?'

'Not unless it's a lot of water, and we've only got one tap and one bucket,' said Brazell, beginning to be convinced.

'Perhaps we should put back the lid. Then, when the well fills, he'll drown. However, I'm rather banking on him deciding to talk to us before that. I bet he didn't sign up for murder,' said Phryne loudly.

'Hey, lady,' said the well.

'Yes?'

'What d'ya mean, murder?'

'Would have come to that, you know. Put it to

225

yourself. Professor Brazell and I would be rather cross when we finally got out of the hole in which you are now sitting. We'd be likely to try and find out who put us there. And do you think that we wouldn't draw deductions and make inferences? I think we would. And when we did we'd be sending the cops around to interview Mr Hart.'

'Yair?' asked the voice.

'So he couldn't afford to let us escape,' said Phryne. 'Of course, he wouldn't put to himself like that. He'd know that if anyone traced the man who was last down here and shoved aside that lid, by fingerprints perhaps, it would be you and you could hang for killing two innocent visitors, and he needn't say a word. And you wouldn't be believed if you told on him,' added Phryne. 'You didn't pick up my handbag, did you? I dropped it when you grabbed me.'

'Nah. Sorry,' said the voice.

'Put it to yourself, my dear troglodyte,' said Phryne. 'Who would the cops believe? You, a lowly miner with a criminal record, or Mr Hart, head of Hart and Co., rich, powerful and terribly respectable?'

''Ow'd yer know I 'ad a docket?' demanded the voice.

'Stands to reason. You wouldn't get involved in something like this unless you had. In fact, Hart probably wouldn't have involved you unless you could be made the scapegoat.'

There was a pause in which Brazell opened the second bottle of wine. One more glass, he told himself, and no more. It wouldn't do to get drunk, of course. Chap needs his wits about him

226

in circumstances like these. But one more glass might ease his headache. The well heard the pop of the cork and asked hopefully, 'Yer ain't got any beer up there, 'ave yer?'

'Edmund, do we have any beer?'

'S-Should be s-some.' Brazell scouted about, searching the crates on the ground. 'We used to keep a few bottles down here for visiting bar- barians... Ah yes, here we are. Foster's s-suit you, barbarian?'

'Yair,' said the well, thirstily.

'Here we go, bit of string round the neck, lower gently, and – got it?' asked Phryne.

'Thanks,' said the well. There was a glugging noise and the string in Phryne's hand tugged. She drew it up, replaced the bottle, and lowered it again.

'What d'yer want ter know, lady?' asked the well, much refreshed.

'Who hired you? What did he hire you to do?' asked Phryne.

'Hart hired me,' said the well darkly. 'But not for any murder – murder didn't enter into it, not murder.'

'Why?'

'Boss was only paying me five nicker. Mur- der's...'

'Much more expensive?' asked Edmund Brazell, sweetly.

'Yair, well, yair, sort of. Boss Hart says to me, get the prof and the tart, sling 'em down the well, then lock the door and guard 'em till Monday, then yer can leave. Tol' me where yer'd be, too, 'im comin' out of the library and 'er standin' under the jacaranda tree. But now I thinks about it, 'e was makin' me inter the goat. Yer mightn't 'ave got out of the well in time, before the water rose. Then yer'd be dead, and who's in the frame? Me. Gotta docket, like yer say, lady, I'd be just nacherally pie for the jacks.'

'And he didn't tell you what was to happen to us after Monday?' asked Phryne.

'Nah. 'E didn't mention that. Along with yer being bloody good in a stoush and in the habit of kickin' a man's head in. Nah,' said the well bitterly, 'that's another one of them things he didn't mention, Mr Boss Hart didn't.'

'How much do you think you owe Mr Hart, then?' asked Brazell, interested in this anthropological specimen.

'Nothin',' said the well, spitting noisily.

'Feel like giving me the keys to the door of the wine cellar?' asked Phryne, hopefully.

'Nah,' said the well, spitting again. 'You'll just call the cops and then I'll be a gone gosling.'

'What if I make a deal with you ... what is your name?'

There was a long pause, then the well said, 'John Black. They call me Blackjack.'

'Mr Black, think about a deal. You give me the keys. I promise on my honour not to call the police. This is going to require delicate handling and I don't want to involve the police and neither does the University. Isn't that so, Professor Brazell?'

'Oh, indeed, that is s-so, Miss Fisher,' agreed the professor.

'The bad side is that you have to stay in the well

until I can finish my investigation. The good side is that we have – let's see – three cases of beer here, and you can have it all in return for the keys,' said Phryne.

'I dunno,' said Blackjack.

'Or I can just close the lid and leave you there alone in the dark until you either suffocate or drown,' said Phryne. 'Then I can come down and get the keys off the corpse; I won't even have to climb if you drown, just catch the body as it floats. And believe me, the dark down there is very dark indeed. Like being caught in a collapsed mine, in the blackness under the earth.'

Blackjack appeared to be thinking about this. Phryne raised her eyebrows at Professor Brazell. He nodded. Extensive research into the human animal encouraged him in his belief that this was working.

'You promise not to call the cops?' asked Blackjack from the depths.

'I promise.'

'The toffy bloke, too?'

'I promise not to call the police,' said Brazell, gravely.

'Send down the beer,' said the well. 'I'll tie the keys on your bit of string. But listen, lady, when are you gunna get me out?'

'Tomorrow night at the latest,' said Phryne. 'And on that you have my word.'

The exchange was made, the crates being lowered down on a sling to the raging thirst below. Phryne finished the glass.

'Shall we go?'

'Taking the keys with us,' said Brazell. 'Can I

offer you the hospitality of my College?' He bowed.

'Even better, you go and pick up a change of clothes and I'll offer you the hospitality of my hotel,' said Phryne. 'I need a bath and some clean knickers.'

'I will be delighted if you will let me watch you put them on,' said Brazell.

'My dear professor,' said Phryne. 'I will be delighted if you will then take them off.'

Professor Brazell began to wonder if he had – s-so to s-speak – bitten off more than he could chew.

Dot accompanied Mrs Hart, Professor Bretherton and a rather large porter to the infirmary. It smelt, Dot thought, just as an infirmary ought to smell: carbolic and floor polish. The starched sister led them to Joss Hart's room and opened the door.

A huge man rose from his seat at the side of the bed and stared at the woman in sober garments who looked familiar. He gaped at the respectable Dorothy Williams, who looked just like what she was, a good girl. He flicked his gaze to include Professor Bretherton, the epitome of academic presence, and a large economy-sized porter behind him in the University's livery. For a moment rage robbed him of speech. Then he managed a smothered shriek.

'Dolly, you dare!'

'I dare,' said Mrs Hart shortly, not even looking into the reddening face. 'I dare anything. You sit down, Viv. I'm not here for you. I don't care about you. I'm here to see my son.'

She walked to the other side of the bed. Dot

fetched her a chair and she sat down, taking one of the boy's hands in both her own.

'Now, Mr Hart,' said Bretherton. 'Let's not have a scene. Not here.'

'But she...' Hart strangled on his own shout, suppressing it with great difficulty, 'How dare she be here?'

'Is she the boy's mother?' asked Dot briskly.

'Yes, well, yes, she is, but she's...'

'I don't think there's any doubt about why she's here, then, is there?' asked Bretherton quietly. 'If I were you, Mr Hart, I would be thinking not of my own sense of outrage, but of Joss. How is he?'

'They say there's nothing to do but wait,' Hart groaned. 'He's no worse, they say, but I reckon he's quieter. He tried to speak a while ago but I couldn't understand him. All right. I won't go crook. But after this is over I'll have a word with you, woman!'

'You can have as many words as you like, Viv Hart,' said Mrs Hart implacably. 'It won't make a blind bit of difference. I got nothing to say to you. Now sit down, do, and shut up. I'll be all right, Professor,' she said to Bretherton. 'You don't need to stay. Nor your porter chap.'

'I'll just take my leave then, Dolly,' said Bretherton. 'I'll be back later to see how he is.'

Dot wondered if she should go too and decided to sit for awhile and make sure that Mr Hart wasn't going to cut up rough after all. She drew up a chair a respectful distance from the bed and the two parents, took out her best go-to-church pearl bead rosary and began to pray.

Dot did not subscribe to Phryne's view that the

best thing to be said for prayer was that it gave the bereaved something to do. In Dot's view, prayer worked. She had prayed for her sister and Joan had been given back to her, alive, whole and with her virtue intact. What else could one ask of any god? It sounded like prompt and efficient service to Dot, as expected of the best stores.

She had always found solace in the rosary, and began on the Five Joyful Mysteries. They all related, now she thought of it, to motherhood. The Annunciation, the Visitation, the Nativity, the Presentation and the Finding of the child Christ in the temple. 'For this my son who was lost now is found,' thought Dot from quite another part of the Bible, and began to recite: '*Pater noster, qui es in caelis.*'

Thirteen

Parties have degenerated these days. The old time shivoos and picnics where there was tea and scandal for the women, ginger beer and sticky toffee for the kids and beer and fights for the men, were better than the modern version… A fight livens up the evening and weeds out the undesirables, and if modern hostesses only had the enterprise to arrange a brawl among the guests the present boredom of the social round would not exist.

Lennie Lower, *Here's Luck*

Phryne dived into her bath, dragging the professor with her, and began to lather him with jasmine soap. His scalp wound had been examined by the hotel doctor and pronounced bloody but trivial. He was afloat on a cushion of aspirin and stolen Chateau Petrus and laughed helplessly as bubbles burst in his beard.

'What are we doing tonight?' he asked hopefully.

'We are going to have a brief but restorative nap,' said Phryne, surfacing between his knees, 'and then we are going to the Artist's Ball. Or at least, I am. Would you care to accompany me?'

Bruises were rising on her knees and her hands were grimed and torn by climbing walls, s-she had just flung a fellow human down a well after being abducted and imprisoned in darkness, s-she ought to be quite prostrated, and s-she was proposing to go to a ball, he thought. Every muscle in Professor Brazell's body, including quite a few of whose existence he had previously been happily unaware, twinged at once and he gave a complicated, wet, all-over wince.

'Would you mind terribly much if I just lay down and s-slept?' he asked. 'For about three thousand years?'

'Not in the least,' said Phryne promptly. 'In that case, I shall have a brief nap and you can go byes and I'll come back later. Dot!' she called, then remembered that Dot was not among those present. 'Of course, she must still be with Mrs Hart. Never mind.'

'Did you s-say Mrs Hart? I didn't know that Mr Hart had married again.'

'He hasn't, it's Joss' mother.' Phryne rinsed foam off her face.

'I thought Joss Hart's mother was dead.'

'No, she's been somewhere else.'

'Phryne.' Brazell grabbed the edge of the bath and wrung out his beard. 'S-So did Joss Hart.'

'What?' Phryne sat up abruptly and a bow wave sloshed onto the marble floor.

'His father told him that his mother went to London and died there,' said Brazell. 'It's a very affecting s-story. He told me all about it. S-She's been missing s-since he was a little boy.'

'That's what Adam told me, too, now that you mention it. Oh, lord, what a tangled web we weave,' sighed Phryne. 'Well, either he'll recognise her or he won't and there's nothing we can do about it now. Are you clean, Edmund dear?'

A face like a Roman coin turned to her and smiled bravely. Perhaps Brazell was a little mature for these athletic games, Phryne reflected. However, with any luck he would be back in mid-season form with a little rest.

Meanwhile she had a costume which would astonish even at the Artist's Ball and she meant to wear it. The silk body stocking would conceal her bruises and the costume itself was daring, verging on indecent, without being actually obscene enough to attract police prosecution.

She dusted herself with rice powder and slid into the body stocking. It was of milk-white silk and matched her skin. Over it she slipped the pleated Egyptian cloth, the heavy necklace, and the fillet. She loaded her left arm with bracelets, stiffening it to the elbow. On her feet she had flat sandals. She outlined her eyes with kohl and reddened her lips.

'You look wonderful,' said Brazell, reflecting that

it had been an interesting day. When he got up that morning all he had been expecting in the way of excitement was actually locating a reference which had eluded him, for a letter he was intending to write to dear James Frazer about an inaccuracy in *The Golden Bough*. There was a c-certain interest in s-such things, of course, though his private opinion was that the more excitable form of classical author wanted to be hunted across the hills and torn to pieces by the maenads, while in that event James Frazer would be up a tree, taking notes.

Being assaulted, abducted, pitched down a well, frightened half to death then ravished out of his remaining s-senses hadn't entered into his calculations. Nor had ending the day s-sitting on a luxurious bed in the Hotel Australia, clad in a fluffy towel and bruises, watching an astoundingly beautiful woman get dressed.

'Do you like it? Oh, drat. Someone at the door. Perhaps you might like to go into the bedroom, Edmund. If you hear me scream, do something brave.'

Phryne shut the door on Brazell and opened the outer door, little gun in hand. Professor Ayers was standing there. He blinked, dragged in a deep breath, and swayed like a palm tree.

'Miss Fisher, do you know what you're wearing?' he asked.

'Come in, Tom. I can only spare you a moment – my escort must be about to arrive.'

'Oh, you're going to the temple, then?' he asked anxiously. 'Do be careful, Miss Fisher, I know it must be an honour to be asked, but these are very dangerous people.'

'No, I'm going to the Artist's Ball, and although they may be drunken wretches I doubt if they are dangerous. What did you think I was doing?'

He leaned on a chair back and fanned himself with his open hand.

'That's all right then. I thought, when I saw you wearing all the badges of Isis...'

'Yes, Hathor might have been better, but I would rather be Mistress of Magic than Goddess of Love and Music, and in any case, I never will understand the Egyptian affection for cows,' said Phryne, who had researched the matter – in point of fact, from *The Golden Bough*. 'I have no intention of indulging in magic tonight, except the usual kind made of music and wine. What are you intending to do?'

'I'm going to write a little more of my paper on Khufu, lie back in the luxurious bed allowed me by your largess, imagine that I am a *houri* and invite the sandman in,' said Ayers.

'Just so long as it isn't the hall porter,' said Phryne, grinning at his shocked expression, and allowed him to leave. 'Good night, Mr Sanders.'

Bowing over her hand, Ayers said, 'Dance well, Lady of Spells,' and was gone.

Phryne went into her bedroom to collect her cloak and found Brazell tucked up in her bed, smiling.

'Are you sure that you'll be all right, Edmund dear?' she asked. Against the white sheet, he looked rather like a deceased pope: beaked nose, hollow eyes and black beard.

'Miss Fisher, you have transformed me from a S-

236

Stoic in good s-standing to an Epicurean in bad s-standing,' he said, without opening his eyes. 'And I don't know when I've been s-so happy.'

'Sleep well,' said Phryne.

She went out into the parlour, brewed herself a cup of café Hellenico on Dot's spirit stove, and drank it carefully, feeling the essence of coffee racing through her veins. This might prove to be an interesting evening. In any case, it was the social event of the season.

Chas Nuttall met her in reception and looked just as taken aback as Phryne would have wished.

'You look...' Words failed him. He was attired in a canvas smock and leggings which someone had painted like a playing card. He wore a Tudor bonnet and crown and a remarkably realistic pointed beard.

'The Knave of Hearts he stole some tarts,' said Phryne, walking around him. 'Very pretty, Chas.'

'Of course, I know I broke my word about shaving.' He grinned knavishly. 'But it'll come off tomorrow, I promise.'

'If you want to keep that spiffy little pointed beard, I release you from your oath. The uncut version looked like stuffing from a horsehair sofa, and I only wanted you to remove it in the interests of public amenity in Sydney,' said Phryne. 'Let's go, shall we?'

'You're going to make a stir in that dress,' prophesied Chas. 'Have you got anything on underneath it?'

'That's for me to know and you not to even think of attempting to find out,' said Phryne firmly.

The Town Hall was lit with electricity, a Romanesque pile with pretensions. Phryne wore her cloak into the building and into Centennial Hall and up to the balcony. The place was so full of people that it was hard to guess what it usually looked like. Hundreds of helium balloons were ascending ceiling-ward bobbing around the organ. Streamers hung from improbable vantage points. The noise of voices easily drowned the attempts of a jazz band to lend a little atmosphere to the ball. Notwithstanding this fact, a lot of couples were dancing. Some were dancing the Charleston, some the Bunny-hug, and some that indiscriminate sliding embrace known as the Nightclub Shuffle. Each, Phryne noticed, were dancing to their own private tunes and some were gravitating to corners and alcoves where other music was playing. The pipes of Pan, perhaps.

'Are you carrying anything?' asked Chas. Phryne wondered if he was asking for drugs and was preparing to squash him when she reflected that she was in Sydney, where there might be a dialect difference. Phryne had tried cocaine once. She had spent almost a day and night unable to shut her eyes, compulsively talking, and had woken from nightmares with the only real episode of depression in her life. The price, she thought, was too high for the rush. There were many other ways of getting thrills, and most of them were legal, available, and did not rot the nasal linings.

'What, precisely, should I be carrying?' she asked.

'Why, a little bit of a drink to wet the whistle,' said Chas. 'There's a bar in the basement but the price is ruinous.'

238

'Sorry, Chas. I have drunk quite enough for one night. I am not going to insult Chateau Petrus by adding punch on top of it. Go and buy a beer or three,' said Phryne, stuffing a note into the Knave's hand. 'I'll be down there if you are looking for me.'

'You're a good fellow, Phryne,' said Chas and rattled down the steps.

So now she was on her own, with an effect to make.

Phryne handed the cloak to a girl and received a ticket, ducked behind a solemn-faced policeman to straighten her cobra's head fillet, and came out to stand at the head of the stairs.

This had, of course, been done before, most notably in 1924 by Dulcie Deamer in a rather daring animal skin. But Phryne was a stranger. No one knew what to expect of her. The crowd on the dance floor shuffled to a halt. The band tootled itself into silence. Everyone looked at the shameless woman at the head of the stairs.

The poets turned as one man as she stood there. Jack gaped. Bill grabbed George's arm.

'Chris said she was Lilith,' he gasped.

Phryne seemed naked under the columnar fall of the Egyptian cotton gown, which descended in a straight line from throat to feet, almost transparent with the strong light behind her. The heavy collar of red and green faïence beads seemed to be the only thing holding the gown on (though this was not, in fact, the case) and her neat black head was crowned with Isis' symbol, a blue faïence construction rather like an L. Her face was white, her eyes circled in black. Her mouth was red as blood.

She lifted her chin to survey the crowd. Proud. Wise. Beautiful. Worshipful. The Mistress of Magic.

'She is not Lilith,' said Marrin, pushing George aside. 'She is Isis.'

Phryne smiled very slightly at the applause then began to walk slowly down the stairs, holding herself with regal stiffness. All of her bruises were crying aloud for attention and reminding her that she could have stayed in bed with Edmund Brazell, a man with whom it was definitely worth staying in bed. But not even the remarkable professor could have given Phryne that accolade: the moment of silence as all the men in the room desired her at once.

Worth stretching a few joints and leaving a lover for a few hours. Something she would only be able to do a few times in one lifetime.

Chas Nuttall fought his way up through the rabble with two glasses of beer in time to see her reach the bottom of the stairs and look around for an interesting person. None of the immediate human offerings seemed to attract her. Jack, George and Bill overcame their astonishment quickly and shoved through the mass.

'Miss Fisher? You look splendid,' babbled Bill. Phryne turned her head, having to move carefully under the headdress.

'You owe me a shilling,' she said to Jack, who looked puzzled.

'It hasn't been a week,' said Phryne, 'but our acquaintance is no closer.'

'Fair go,' said Jack, recovering quickly and aware that his pockets held exactly ninepence. 'I haven't seen a lot of you. Not as much as I'm seeing now,' he grinned.

'And this is as much of me as you will ever see,' said Phryne implacably.

'Besides, I say that to all the girls,' said Jack. 'Just in case one ... er ... wants to lose a bet. Well, it worked once,' he added. 'And you never know your luck in the big city.'

'Uniformly bad, I should say,' replied Phryne.

The jazz band had recovered from its amazement and picked up approximately where they had left off, more or less. It was getting late and the band were, along with the dancers, both tired and emotional. Not their fault, as they later pointed out to a policeman whose profession had hardened him against sad stories of human frailty. People kept buying them drinks. Bringing them drinks. And, naturally, they had drunk the drinks so charitably provided. People might have got offended if they hadn't, officer.

The drummer was playing in a time that was being estimated by his critics at two-and-a-quarter per bar, variable, the trombone player was yawning, the cornet was asleep and competent medical advice might have declared the banjo player to be clinically dead, except that he was still strumming. The fact that he was strumming 'Bye, Bye, Blackbird' while the rest of the band was playing 'Tiger Rag" was going unnoticed in the general clamour.

Phryne accepted an invitation to turkey-trot from George and slid away into the mass of dancers. George might have been a good dancer – there was simply no way of telling. Phryne wreathed her arms around his neck and tried to keep her feet out of the way of boots as beggars, rabbits, someone who was probably impersonating a pixie and presumably meant well and the poet Villon in someone's tights milled and swayed.

This crowd was drunk, thought Phryne, slipping a sandal out from under a descending thigh-high boot which belonged to a rather tasty Robin Hood. So far they were drunk and cheerful, drunk and amorous, drunk and morose perhaps but not drunk and belligerent or drunk and disorderly. Various policemen who stood around the walls were also blinking gently and had probably absorbed a good deal of the old familiar juice. One, in fact, was so glazed that he had allowed a large lady dressed as a kangaroo and carrying a whole bottle of gin in her pouch past him without saying a word. As Phryne watched over George's shoulder, he slid bonelessly to the ground and lay there unregarded, a small smile on his face and his helmet resting at the foot of a marble plinth.

Interesting, thought Phryne. I cannot imagine this happening in Melbourne.

The temperature in the hall was high. Phryne was glad that she was so lightly dressed, and that she had not worn greasepaint. Everyone who had was sweating profusely. Though it was educational to see just who was wearing make-up.

A young man in a toga, wearing rather too much eyeliner, slid Phryne from George's arms and carried her away into the crowd. 'Such a press,' he said into her ear. 'Would you care to come out onto the balcony?'

'Not at present, Caligula,' Phryne replied, fending off hands which showed a tendency to wander and conscious of Professor Brazell waiting in her bed at the hotel. 'I mustn't be greedy,' she added, to the young man's evident puzzlement. Then his mascara'd eyes widened and he stepped away from Phryne, allowing another to move into his place. Someone dressed in a black silk robe with moons and stars on it and a tall pointy hat. He removed it and bowed.

'Lady Isis.' Marrin smiled his shark's tooth smile, and Phryne spoke sternly to her skin, which crept under his clammy touch. Then the room went blurry, and Phryne heard her own voice speaking as though it belonged to someone else.

'Marrin,' she said sadly. 'I'm very disappointed in you.'

'Lady?' he asked.

'You are supposed to be my worshipper,' said Phryne, wondering what on earth she was saying and when this strange state would wear off.

'Lady, I worship you,' replied Marrin, alert for some trick but trapped by Phryne's persona and the strange gaze of her kohled eyes.

'Then you should have trusted me,' said Phryne, opening her mouth to see what came out. 'I never demanded human sacrifice, Marrin. To use my own serpent for such a purpose will defeat your working. You must come to Isis with a pure heart,' she went on, not knowing what was inspiring this line of dialogue but agog to hear what she would say next.

Perhaps it was more than a bottle of Chateau Petrus in one evening.

'Lady Isis, forgive your slave,' said Marrin. He did not have room to kneel, but he bent his head, revealing an unexpectedly vulnerable nape of the neck, shaven clean and shining.

'It is my will that you undertake what this woman asks,' Phryne heard herself say. 'Then, perhaps, what you seek shall be found. *Apocalypsos*,' she said. Phryne did not know the word. She shook herself and the room clicked back into focus.

'Marrin,' said Phryne, herself again. 'Did you do that?'

'No,' said Marrin. 'You were possessed.'

Phryne gave him a sceptical look and drew them both towards an alcove she had spotted under the stairs. The other couple there were far too advanced in the worship of Dionysius to pay them any attention.

'It is true,' insisted Marrin. 'You wear Isis' symbols and perhaps you yourself are a Mistress of Magic as she is. You are a woman of power,' he said.

'Nonsense. What does *apocalypsos* mean?'

'It's Greek for "that which is revealed",' said Marrin. 'She's here, all right, she chose you, and now I have sworn to do as you instruct. What is your will, Lady?'

'I want you to come to the University on Sunday evening at seven,' she said. 'I want you to duplicate something you have already done. Bring all your paraphernalia. I will assist you. And as long as Joss Hart lives, Marrin, I will not interfere with you or allow others to do so; but if he dies, all bets are off. Is that clear?'

'It is clear, Lady. But if Joss Hart lives and the papyrus is found, will you give it to me?'

'No,' said Phryne. 'It isn't mine to give. Not unless the Goddess makes me, of course. But she said that she would show you, and goddesses keep their word. If not by the papyrus, by another path.'

'That is true.' Marrin bowed and Phryne saw him move through the rabble. He did not have to shove. People melted away before him and he passed through their midst like a cold wind.

Jack bobbed up at Phryne's elbow and grabbed her by the shoulders. She repressed an urge to clip his ears.

'Are you sure about that bet?' he asked, shamelessly, grinding his groin into her stomach.

'Perfectly so,' she assured him. 'And whilst I know that this hall is very crowded, if you push that thing into my belly again, I wouldn't count on getting it back.'

Jack jumped as if he had been scalded, whined, 'You're no fun,' and yielded his place to George, who held Phryne very carefully, as though she might bite.

It was never wise to grope a Goddess.

An hour later she reclaimed her cloak and stood at the head of the stairs again, smoking a gasper and waiting for Chas Nuttall to swim back into view. The crowd was now definitely drunk and Phryne wanted to get out before any women were assaulted or fights broke out between rival clans. A sozzled clarinettist was attempting the difficult bit in 'Easy Street' and forgetting how many stops, or indeed, fingers, he was meant to use. Listening to him had a certain uncharitable appeal but it wore off quickly. Phryne could, of course, leave without Chas, but one of her firm principles was to always leave with the man who brought her to a function, no matter how many better offers had arisen during the evening and no matter how full her dance card was with addresses, assignations, and expressions of fervent adoration.

'Oh, dear,' said Phryne aloud, backing away to the outer door and dropping the gasper into a sand-filled ashtray. Principles were one thing but a punch in the nose was another, as she seemed to remember someone saying in Australian literature. Phryne was leaving, Chas Nuttall or no Chas Nuttall.

The fight was starting. It began with what was probably a minor altercation over against the Royal Box between two men who seemed to have a difference of opinion about with whom a woman in mauve satin and bunny ears ought to be dancing.

Man A swung a fist at Man B, who ducked. Man A thus found himself flattened by Man C, who additionally had had a dearly bought beer spilled down his shirt front to avenge. Man B, meanwhile, had retaliated by kicking the nearest pair of shins, which belonged to Man D, who resented this, and, aiming at Man B, struck Man E a sharp blow in the midriff, causing his partner (Miss F) to scream and bash Man G with a handbag which must have had a bottle in it, because Man G went down like a sand-filled sack and Man G's partner, Miss H, tripped Man I and sat on his head.

From then on, Phryne knew, as inevitably as a Greek tragedy or an Australian batting collapse, the action would become general and she didn't intend to be part of it. She slipped out of the door into the hot Sydney night. Outside there were only trams, cops, street singers, a few drunks yelling and the ceaseless tramp of feet, which was refreshingly serene after the inside of Centennial Hall. She hailed a cab and went home.

Edmund Brazell woke. A stab of pain went through all his misused muscles. Then a stab of delight went through some others. He opened his eyes into a dim light. Very classical, he thought. A naked nymph was inviting him to play.

S-Stoics, he thought, surrendering without a fight. What did they know?

Dot had prayed all the way through a corona of her rosary before either of Joss' parents spoke again.

'He's grown into a fine young man,' said Mrs Hart. The woman who looked twenty-five in a favourable light looked fully fifty in the harsh hospital illumination. She wore no make-up to fill her wrinkles. Dot had never seen anyone age so fast.

'No thanks to you,' snarled Vivian Hart.

'You must have fed him well,' said Mrs Hart, ignoring this comment.

'He eats like a horse, comes home and just wolfs down whatever the housekeeper puts on the table,' said Vivian Hart. 'Big strong boy, Joss.'

'You never married again?' asked Mrs Hart tonelessly.

'Never needed to,' said Mr Hart. 'Plenty of women around for a price.'

'I know,' said Mrs Hart without rancour. 'I'm one of them.'

There was a pause.

'Could have divorced me easy enough,' she prompted. Vivian Hart looked acutely uncomfortable. Mrs Hart laughed. 'Of course, that would mean you'd have to tell a judge that your wife was a prostitute.'

'Why ... why did you go on the game, woman?'

'I didn't have a profession,' she said. 'I didn't have a job. I married you when I was sixteen. By the time I left you I thought that was all I was worth. You told me I was a whore often enough,' she said, quite flatly. 'Not surprising that when you shut me out to freeze that last time I believed you.'

'I ... looked for you,' confessed Vivian Hart. 'But when I found you, it was too late.'

'You mean, I'd lost my virtue? So you couldn't ask me to come home and be tortured again? Wasn't that lucky,' said Mrs Hart, still in a flat voice. 'I've made a success out of my profession, Viv. Pretty soon, I'll be able to retire.'

'Don't talk about it!' said Mr Hart, and Dot half rose, ready to summon help. Hart felt her movement and waved her irritably back to her chair.

'Tell me about the boy, then,' Mrs Hart said soothingly, and Hart mumbled, 'Disappointed in him, to tell the truth. Didn't want to go into the company, starting at the bottom, of course, like I did. Got a craze for university. I never went to university. Pack of pretty boys, spending all their time arguing about philosophy. Told him he was wasting his life.'

'I bet you did,' said Dolly Hart with the first trace of emotion in her voice. 'Told him every day, if I know you. Every morning when he came down to breakfast there you'd be, reading the paper, and

248

over his porridge you'd say, "Off to that place again, Joss?" and he'd say he was, and then you'd say, "Waste of bloody time, you'll never amount to anything," and then he'd go out.'

'How do you know that?' asked Mr Hart, horrified.

'Because you did it to me,' said Dolly Hart, very firmly.

'No, it wasn't like that,' protested Mr Hart with waning conviction. 'It was only a joke in the end, Joss knew that. I thought he'd change his ways and come and join me, be Hart and Son.'

'It was just like that, Viv, you know it was. It drove me away and it'll drive him away. You haven't changed a bit,' said Dolly, with faint admiration under the loathing. 'You haven't learned a thing. Not in all these years.'

'Bet *you* have,' hissed her husband.

Mrs Hart was not perturbed by his tone and took it as a question. 'No, not really. Most men are unimaginative. Easily pleased. You taught me all the tricks I needed for a life of vice and crime. I've been lucky. Never poxed. Never jailed. Never pregnant. The doctor reckoned that that last kicking you gave me to remember you by – recall the night, do you? Dinner wasn't to your liking. I undercooked the broccoli, I think. Or maybe it was overcooked. When you felt like belting me you never lacked a reason, did you? Well, that finished my chances of ever having another baby. So this is the only one I've got, Mr Vivian Hart.'

'Dolly...' began Mr Hart.

'Don't you "Dolly" me, Vivian. Silly name. Girl's name, I always thought. I blame myself,' she mused, ignoring the bright red face close to her own, the angry vein pulsing in the temple. 'I should have taken a saucepan and donged you the first time you slapped me. Only a few days after the wedding, it was. You've got the makings of a real man, you know, if you hadn't been such a bastard.'

Mr Hart left the room abruptly. Dot looked at Mrs Hart. Then, at a sound, they both looked at the bed.

Joss had opened his eyes. He struggled to form words. Mrs Hart took the glass Dot handed to her and lifted his head so that he could drink. His hair was wet with sweat. Joss swallowed and managed to speak. Even a whisper conveyed his utter astonishment.

'Mum?'

'Yes, pet, yes, precious, it's Mummy. You're in hospital, Lambkin.' Her voice was the essence of all motherly voices, reassuring, calm, eternal.

'You're dead.' Tears ran down the pale cheeks as Joss fought for breath. 'I must be dying.'

'No, love, I'm not dead, I'm as alive as you are.' Mrs Hart leaned close. 'Feel. I'm warm, you can feel my breath.' She kissed his cheek.

'Dad?'

'I'll get him,' said Dot, and flung open the door to collide with Mr Hart's returning breastbone. He took two steps to the bedside and grabbed Joss' other hand.

'Is Mum dead?' Joss asked on a failing breath.

'Answer him,' said Mrs Hart, suddenly loud. 'He thinks I'm dead so he thinks he's dying. Tell the truth for the first time in your worthless life,

250

you bastard! Get a move on!'

'I lied,' mumbled Vivian Hart. His wife poked him hard in the ribs. 'I lied,' he said, louder. 'She ran away and I didn't know how to explain to you, son, so I said she was dead... But she's alive,' said Hart, and sat down suddenly. 'And you ain't dying.'

'Don't want to die,' murmured Joss, and sank back into a coma.

'Jesus wept,' said Dolly Hart. Dot crossed herself.

Vivian Hart put his head down onto the bed-clothes and began to cry.

Dot took up the rosary again. The Five Sorrowful Mysteries. The Agony in the Garden. The Scourging. The Crowning with Thorns. The Carrying of the Cross. The Crucifixion. 'Our Father, Who art in Heaven,' murmured Dot.

Fourteen

I would not come back to cricket for a season or two [after the Great War] and I think cricket itself could not come back at once. It had been dismayed; it did not guess in the golden days at things like world wars, or that its score-books should be splashed with the blood of the quiet men its votaries.

Edmund Blunden, *Cricket Country*

Phryne woke feeling marvellous, stretched, winced

251

a little, and decided that she still felt wonderful. A little battered, but wonderful. Sleeping next to her was an Ancient Roman, looking now perhaps more Ancient Greek, for the curve of the lips was definitely as close as the twentieth century was going to get to an archaic smile.

'Food,' she whispered into the nearest ear.

'Breakfast?' asked Professor Brazell. 'All of that, plus breakfast? I thought I'd died and gone to heaven when I s-saw you burning your underclothes in that pit, Phryne, but now I'm sure of it.'

'What shall I ask for? Bacon and eggs?'

'Not idyllic enough. Nectar. Ambrosia. On s-second thought, I'm starving. Earthly food will have to do. Eggs, bacon, tomatoes, mushrooms. And toast. A bushel or s-so s-should do.'

'And coffee,' agreed Phryne. 'We have a busy day ahead of us.'

'Oh?' Professor Brazell hoped that his powers would be equal to Miss Fisher's demands.

'We have to pay some Sunday calls,' said Phryne; she would not say another word until they were dressed, fed, had read the newspaper and were out in the street, with the porter hailing a taxi. Phryne had a list of addresses in her hand.

'Where are we going?'

'To visit the faculty at home,' Phryne replied.

'Not, I would venture, an ideal way to s-spend S-Sunday afternoon,' said Brazell.

'Look on it as an exercise in anthropology,' said Phryne.

She was dressed in neat, going-to-tea-with-a-maiden-aunt clothes: a dark blue linen suit of proper length as to skirt and looseness of cut and

252

a subdued cloche decorated with a small bunch of velvet pansies.

Sydney looked very appealing in the clear, after-rain light. The high Gothic buildings of the city receded and the taxi, with only the expected number of screaming contests of right-of-way, bore them out of the central city and into the green suburbs.

'First, we have Professor Kirkpatrick,' said Phryne. 'We should just catch him between lunch and afternoon service.'

'S-Should we wish to do s-so,' agreed Brazell. 'Why *do* we wish to do s-so?'

'To provide the answer to the rest of the riddle. I know who tried to kill Joss and I know who stole the papyrus and planted the exam papers in Harcourt's desk,' said Phryne seriously. 'I'm sure that Joss nicked your hand axe and gave it to his father. But I don't know about the other things.'

'And you think that they are going to tell you?' asked Edmund, as Rose Bay approached at speed.

'No, I think their wives are going to tell me,' said Phryne. The suspicion of a smug smile was hovering at the corners of her mouth. Professor Brazell decided, as others had before him, to just follow along in her wake and watch. It was, at least, going to be an interesting afternoon.

Professor Kirkpatrick answered his own door. 'I never allow the girl to work on the Sabbath,' he said with conscious virtue. 'Oh, it's you, Miss Fisher. And Brazell. Come in, will you?'

Phryne did not ask any questions. She looked around a small sitting room whose predominant colour was dark brown with chocolate highlights, drank tea as pale as straw and asked polite questions about the decor. Mrs Kirkpatrick, a meagre woman whose social manner was more than a little creaky, roused herself from contemplation of the sinfulness of not one but a whole bunch of velvet pansies on a blue hat, and displayed her treasures. There was a steel etching of the Monarch of the Glen, a fine Chelsea tea-cup and saucer in the shape of a lettuce leaf (safely locked behind glass where impious hands could not touch it) and an oil painting of Glasgow University, presented to Professor Kirkpatrick on the occasion of his leaving it and coming to Australia, a land, Mrs Kirkpatrick said, of frightful moral laxness and sin. What was to be expected, she asked, of a place originally inhabited by godless savages and convicts? Though the moral tone of the colony, of course, had improved with the arrival of her exceptionally noble, virtuous and upright husband, Professor Kirkpatrick, a man of unexampled probity and – of course – honesty.

Phryne agreed and smiled, told Professor Kirkpatrick to be at the faculty office at seven o'clock even if it was the Sabbath, and Mrs Kirkpatrick saw them out.

'Well, that didn't prove anything,' said Brazell, trailing his coat.

'Didn't it? Next address, please, driver.'

'You hirin' me for the whole day, Missus?' demanded the driver.

'If necessary,' said Phryne.

'It'll cost you,' warned the driver. Phryne dropped a banknote over the seat.

'I can afford it,' she told him. The note vanished with remarkable speed. One moment it was there, the next, only a disturbance of the air and the suspicion of a whisking noise.

'Right you are, lady,' said the driver with as much optimism as a Sydney taxi-driver ever displays. 'Next house.'

Fortunately, most of the faculty lived either in Bellevue Hill or Vaucluse, with the exception of the Dean, who had recently moved.

'The garden really is splendid, isn't it?' asked Phryne, as they walked up a winding paved path to a small house called – as Phryne knew it would be – Rose Cottage.

'Beautiful,' agreed Brazell, who preferred deserts. Gardens always seemed to him to be vaguely obscene. So lush. So urgent.

Then again, he reflected, he was in no position to be judgmental, considering the night and day he had just spent. He followed Phryne's neat back up the path. A woman in a thick skirt and battered tweed hat which had clearly belonged to her husband stood up and stretched.

'Come in,' she called, waving a hospitable trowel. 'Hello, Mr Brazell! Corny's just put the tea on. Soon have a nice cup. Hello,' she said to Phryne. 'I'd shake your hand but I'm a bit mucky. That couchgrass is a real curse in growing weather. It'd have all my beds overgrown in an afternoon if I didn't keep at it.'

'This is Miss Fisher.' Brazell introduced Phryne. 'I'll go and find S-Sykes, s-shall I?' Following the path towards the house, he was almost hidden under a tangle of weeping roses which dropped pink petals onto his shoulders.

Mrs Sykes cleaned her trowel, tucked a wisp of

255

straggling hair under her hat (in the process getting a smear of topsoil on her weathered cheek) and gave Phryne a considered look.

'So you're Miss Fisher,' she said. 'Nice to meet you. Corny's told me about the trouble at the University, and he says they all trust you to find out the answer.'

'It's a puzzle,' said Phryne, sitting down on a rustic seat made of lacquered tree branches.

'All I know about it is that poor Corny's nearly worried to death,' said Mrs Sykes, joining her. The seat groaned. Mrs Sykes was a solid, blocky woman, broad in shoulder and beam.

'He's never been a complicated man,' she said softly, pushing back the hat and wiping her brow. 'Sykes, I mean. Fond of the garden. Likes pottering about with the plants. He's writing a paper on azaleas for the *Gardener's World* magazine. I don't believe there's a dishonest bone in his body. But he worries, see, and that Dean makes him worse by shouting at him. I'm afraid he may have done something foolish.'

'If he has, I'll probably find out,' said Phryne gently. The scent of roses flowed over her, strong enough to make her sneeze.

Mrs Sykes produced a pair of secateurs from her pocket and snipped off an intrusive trailer.

'He could retire,' she suggested, cutting the severed creeper in half, then in quarters. 'With his pension and a bit of money I've got we'd be all right. Tending the garden. No more worries.'

'That could happen,' Phryne watched the trailer cut into eights and then sixteenths. 'The University doesn't want a scandal. Tell him to come to the faculty office at seven o'clock tonight and we should be able to fix everything.'

'Well, I hope so,' said Mrs Sykes. 'Come in and have some tea. We'll have it out in the gazebo, eh? Nice weather for it, Miss Fisher.'

'Nice weather indeed. How do you manage the wind? It must tear across your fence and blight your plants.'

'Planted that row of bamboo, oh, it must have been twenty years ago now,' said Mrs Sykes. 'Bamboo doesn't mind wind. Behind its shelter we've got all the most delicate things. Come and look,' she said.

Phryne went quietly.

An hour later they departed. Phryne got back into the taxi preceded by a huge bunch of roses of all colours, from pure white to a red that was almost black. She placed it next to the driver. He was about to protest when he thought of that nice crackly fiver under his waistcoat, and subsided.

'Nice feller, S-Sykes,' said Edmund. 'Knows a fearful amount about roses.'

'Yes,' said Phryne, giving nothing away. 'So does his wife. Next address, please.'

The next address proved to be just around the corner. Professor John Bretherton lived in a small mansion with green lawns and a gravelled carriage drive – not very long, but very impressive. Phryne and Brazell were announced by an aged maid in a black uniform and rigidly pinned cap. Mrs Bretherton was in, and would receive Miss Fisher. Mr Bretherton was in his study and would be pleased to see Mr Brazell.

Wondering if this was a policy of divide and

conquer or just a desire to keep Miss Fisher away from the susceptible Bretherton, Phryne was shown into a large parlour. The French windows were open onto a pleasant garden in which a small child was being pushed in a swing by a larger sibling. Squeals of joy rent the air.

'My granddaughters,' said Mrs Bretherton. She was a middle sized, middle aged woman with soft hands and a slightly tired smile. 'I don't know how it is, Miss Fisher, but I'm finding small children just a whisker less of a delight than I used to. I was once immune to noise. Now I find that it grates on my ear. Will you sit down? Nan will bring tea directly.'

Mrs Bretherton was longing to ask Miss Fisher to what she owed the honour of her visit, but it was far too early in the ritual to do so. Phryne sat down on a chaise longue and wondered how much tea she could drink in one day without serious bladder damage.

'John told me that you are looking into the burglary at the university, and the shocking affair of the Hart boy.' Mrs Bretherton made the opening bid.

'That's true,' said Phryne. 'I'm expecting it all to be cleared up directly. Can you tell Professor Bretherton to come to the faculty office at seven tonight? What a charming room.'

'It's a little battered, but so are we all,' replied Mrs Bretherton. 'The children leave their mark on furniture, of course, and I can't bring myself to replace, as it might be, the sofa that the little girls used to bounce on or the chair where my eldest daughter sat in her wedding dress.' Her

258

face shone as she spoke of her children. This was a woman, Phryne thought, who might not be very clever but who would die for her offspring, or murder for them. And what would life hold for her, now that she would no longer conceive? The answer was even now falling off the swing in the garden and screaming at the top of its voice.

Mrs Bretherton was out of chair and house at the speed of light, and returned carrying a tot who had bruised its topknot and lost its ribbon and was very unhappy about it.

'Hush, hush,' soothed Mrs Bretherton. 'What a bump! Grandma will kiss it better. That didn't hurt, did it? Now, Lucy, this is Miss Fisher come to visit Grandma. Say hello.'

Prompted, the small girl eyed Phryne, said 'H'lo,' obediently, then added, 'Flowers!'

'Pansies,' said Phryne, allowing the grandchild to ascend her chaise longue and inspect her hat.

'Nice,' decided the child. 'Nice lady smells good,' said Lucy, embracing Phryne suddenly. It was like being hugged by a puppy. Just as suddenly the child released her hold on Phryne's neck and climbed down with a great display of frilly undergarments. 'Lolly?' she asked.

'Choose,' said Mrs Bretherton, lifting down a tall jar of boiled sweets. Lucy sat down to consider it. Her bump was forgotten and her concentration total.

'The lolly standard,' said Mrs Bretherton, inclined to like Phryne now that Lucy had given her a vote of confidence. 'One lolly per bump. Of course, she may have fallen off the swing on purpose. Lucy really loves boiled lollies.'

'This one,' Lucy said, pointing. Mrs Bretherton managed to shake the jar so adroitly that the chosen sweet rose to the surface. Phryne saw that Lucy was choosing for size, not taste. Lucy left, smiling.

'My husband is a good man,' stated Mrs Bretherton. 'Oh, I know he's susceptible. He's a hot-blooded creature and would go anywhere, with anyone, at the drop of a handkerchief. But he always comes home.' She leaned forward to emphasise her point. 'There's no reason why he'd steal, Miss Fisher. If it had been a matter of some woman's virtue, well, then I might be concerned.'

'Indeed,' said Phryne. She drank her tea, when it came, asked for and got use of Mrs Bretherton's lavatory, and was paying polite attention to Mrs Bretherton's commentary on several volumes of grandchildren's photographs when Bretherton escorted Brazell into the parlour. They both bore that look of uneasiness which men wear when they suspect (and rightly) that women have been talking about them.

'Very nice to meet you.' Phryne shook hands and the Brethertons walked them to their taxi. The driver had snoozed off in the scent of roses, and woke abruptly.

'Next address, lady?'

'Next address,' confirmed Phryne.

'Bisset lives in College.' Edmund ticked them off on his fingers. 'Ayers also. Are we going to s-see him?'

'No, he's not at home,' said Phryne. Brazell accepted this.

'Not the VC-C, s-surely,' pleaded Brazell.

'No, not the VC.'

'Oh, good. Why are we going back towards the c-city? Are we going home?'

'No, dear boy, not yet,' said Phryne. 'We're going to see the Dean.'

'Oh, golly,' said Brazell.

The taxi roared on the journey back to the city. Phryne did not speak. Brazell looked at her, wondering what she was thinking. His mind drifted off to his own concerns. Joss had stolen the hand axe to please his father. Well, that was damnable nerve but no real loss to archaeology. Australia was rather rich in hand axes. The idea, however, that Hart and Co. were about to demolish the landscape of his favourite tribe was outrageous, absolutely outrageous. There was still a Protector of Aborigines. Let him do his job! Let him protect them for a change. The land was the life of the tribe, any fool knew that. Edmund Brazell began to muster his arguments. That axe had come from the territory of the Coast Murri Dreaming. Every stone was sacred, every waterhole, every cliff, every patch of greenish gravel which apparently denoted the presence of copper. If Hart and Co. thought that there was no one who cared about the Murri, then he was wrong. It was wise and far-sighted of Hart to order Edmund Brazell flung down a well, because that was the only way that he would not make a frightful stink about this plan. Hart would get his mining lease over his, Brazell's, dead body. That, in fact, had been the idea. A sobering thought. It was largely due to Miss Fisher that he was still alive to object. He took Phryne's hand.

Far too soon, the taxi arrived at a middle-sized house in an unfashionable suburb near the University.

'Where are we?' asked Phryne.

'Ah, well, this is Glebe. Called s-so because a lot of it belongs to the Church, I presume. A lot of the s-students live here. Used to be full of pretensions – Avenue Road, for instance, with Toxteth House and all those impressive Edwardian terraces – but most of it just grew. It's a bit varied. But I like it. When I move out of College, I'd like to live here. Nice variable population, too: Islanders, Turks, Arabs, Aborigines.'

'No, not grew,' said Phryne, a woman who valued precision of expression. 'I think the word is accreted.'

There was something of the coral reef about Glebe. It had been there a long time, and houses were almost never pulled down. Instead they were added to in a variety of bizarre ways. A lot of it was falling down. Loose galvanised iron flapped on decrepit roofs and blocked-in upper balconies. An old man sat smoking a foul pipe on his front step, the only part of his cottage which appeared to be both level and solid. Children skipped in the road, chanting the age-old fate of the daughters of Old Mother Moore.

Phryne remembered that she lived by the shore and had children three and four, having skipped to the rhyme herself. She was disposed to like Glebe. Glebe Point Road was broad (for Sydney) and pleasant. The poplar trees were in full leaf, lending a Parisian air to it. Glebe was gently crumbling into the sea, but it retained some of its original gracious tone, like an old woman in mended lace gloves, offering cheap tea in a bone china cup. We might be poor, said Glebe, but we'll be genteel or die.

What on earth was the Dean doing here? Phryne said as much.

'I don't know,' confessed Brazell. 'He used to live in Bellevue. Glebe is not his s-sort of place at all, one would have thought.'

'Onward,' said Phryne, straightening her hat.

Mrs Gorman was not pleased to see visitors. However, social duty was social duty, and she escorted her unwelcome guests into a parlour which was crammed with furniture.

'I will fetch the Dean,' she told them, and stalked away, closing the door with a suspicion of a slam. It raised dust and Phryne sneezed.

'I can think of more interesting ways to s-spend an afternoon, Phryne,' suggested Edmund Brazell. Phryne could also. She lifted the hand which he had slid onto her knee and held it for a moment.

'This is the last one,' she told him. 'Then we can go back to the hotel.'

Brazell brightened. After an uncomfortably long interval, Mrs Gorman swept back into the room, carrying a tray on which reposed a Crown Derby teapot, sugar basin and milk jug, four teacups, silver spoons, and a silver strainer. She set it down briskly on a large dining table.

'My maid left this morning without notice,' she stated. 'It's so hard to get reasonable servants these days! Milk and sugar, Miss Fisher? My husband will be here shortly. It is his practice to spend Sunday afternoon writing letters.'

Which was another name for lying back in an easy chair and catching forty winks, Phryne thought, as Mr Gorman stumped into the parlour and accepted a cup of tea. 'Well, Brazell, how's the investigation?' he asked. 'You seem to have wormed your way into Miss Fisher's confidence all right.'

He spoke over Phryne's head, as though she was not there. Phryne did not take offence, but watched Mrs Gorman. She did not blink.

'Oh, I wouldn't s-say "wormed", Dean. It is the duty of a gentleman to assist the Fair S-Sex in any difficulty,' said Brazell, who had been playing academic politics for many years.

'Duty of a gentleman!' sneered the Dean. 'Who are you to talk to me about the duties of a gentleman? Lot of gentlemen back at your college, are there?'

'A c-certain number.' Edmund was retaining his calmness rather well, Phryne thought. She intervened before the generalities became personal.

'I'm so sorry, Mrs Gorman, that you should have lost your garnets in this burglary,' she assured her. 'I'm doing my best to retrieve them for you.'

Mrs Gorman looked at Phryne. She was a large woman in a punitive corset. Her hair was dragged back into a bun and skewered with two vengeful hairpins. She was dressed in dull purple, which accentuated the red patches of her complexion. A thick line divided her brows. Prone to headaches, Phryne thought, or short-sighted. Of course, it could just be temper.

'Thank you, Miss Fisher,' she said.

'Were they family heirlooms?' asked Phryne.

'They belonged to my mother.' Mrs Gorman was no longer even looking in Phryne's direction, but was watching her husband. 'But you do not need to trouble yourself. They were insured.'

'If the Dean would care to come to the faculty office at seven o'clock tonight,' Phryne told her, 'the matter will be cleared up for good.'

'He'll be there,' said Mrs Gorman.

'And the move must have upset you,' insinuated Phryne. 'Such a dreadful undertaking, moving a whole house.'

'Terrible,' agreed Mrs Gorman. 'Trying to supervise the carriers, all careless fellows, sorting out all the china and glass, packing everything so carefully that even if they drop it it won't break. Then the mess! And the dust! I was quite prostrate by the end of it.'

'I'm sure,' sympathised Phryne. 'Are you going to cut down your curtains?'

'No, I won't cut that, it's good velvet. I suppose you have a modern house, Miss Fisher, all shiny surfaces?'

'No, I've bought an old terrace house in St Kilda,' replied Phryne. 'All mod cons, of course, but otherwise left just as it was. Plaster is the chief problem, I believe,' said Phryne, who had given the task to a builder and let him get on with it.

'Oh, yes, some of the plaster here is so fragile that it won't hold a nail. I'll have to get a man in,' said Mrs Gorman, who clearly didn't know a lot about it either. 'And me with no help...'

'Since your maid left,' prompted Phryne.

'Eh? Oh, yes. Of course. Since the maid left.'

Gorman and Brazell had not spoken to each

other. Phryne finished her tea and beguiled another quarter of an hour talking to Mrs Gorman about the difficulties of adapting furniture to smaller houses before she allowed Edmund to escort her to the door.

'Phew,' he said, shutting the taxi door.

'Phew.' Phryne leaned her head on his shoulder and he put an arm around her.

'Where now, lady?' asked the driver.

'Back to the Hotel Australia,' said Phryne. 'And don't spare the horses.'

'Right,' said the driver, seeing an unusually large tip evaporate unless he got back onto the street soon. The taxi roared away.

Dot had told the whole rosary twice. For hours the only sound had been the click of the beads as she passed a finger and thumb over the large Pater and the intervening Aves and the final Gloria. The Glorious Mysteries had passed under her busy fingers. The Resurrection. The Ascension. The Descent of the Holy Spirit. The Crowning of the Queen of Heaven.

'O Immaculate Heart of Mary, Queen of Heaven and Earth, and tender Mother of man, in accordance with thy ardent wish made at Fatima, I consecrate to thee myself, my brethren, this poor suffering boy, my country, and the whole human race. *Gloria Patri, et Filis, et Spiritui Sancto,*' said Dot, and let the rosary drop into her lap.

Joss Hart appeared to be asleep. On one side of him Mrs Hart was sleeping with her head on the bed. On the other side Viv Hart stared into the darkness.

266

'I didn't treat her that bad, did I?' he asked.

Dot felt that she should reply. 'She thinks you did,' she said.

'She was a wayward, flighty piece,' he said.

'Perhaps she was,' said Dot.

'Now the boy knows she's alive, what am I going to do with her?' he demanded.

'You don't have to do anything with her,' Dot informed him. 'Now, I got to go. Can you keep the peace, Mr Hart, or do I need to send a porter in?'

'Joss is going to die, isn't he?' asked Viv Hart.

'I don't know,' said Dot. 'Doctor said he'd be along in the morning with that new antivenene they've been trying. And it's morning now. That's why I have to go. I'll be back as soon as I can,' said Dot.

Hart laid his head down on the bed and closed his eyes.

Dorothy Williams took the first tram to the Women's Prison and joined the crowd waiting at the gates. Six o'clock in the morning, exactly, was the release time for prisoners. The iron gate creaked open at six on the dot, and released into the street a chattering mob of dishevelled, shrilling women and a plump figure in an evening dress. Mrs James Thompson was wearing what she had been wearing when she was picked up in the sweep on Palmer Street. It was a nice dress, apricot silk, but noticeable on the street at that hour. Joan's face was drawn, her hair was dirty, and her fingernails were in mourning for her lost virtue. The prison had given her back her possessions in a paper bag, and she was scrabbling

267

through it for tuppence tram fare, wondering how on earth she was going to get home without everyone in the world knowing where she had come from. Sharkbait would come with the car to pick up the other girls, but Joan knew what her husband would say if she was delivered home in a Bentley.

'Joanie!' exclaimed Dot, pushing through the crowd.

'Dot?' Joan appeared bewildered. 'So you got here, after all. Who told you I was in this place? Does Jim know? Are the children all right?' she demanded, grabbing her sister's arm.

'Mrs Ryan is minding them, but you might have a bit of difficulty with Jim. He ... well, the night I saw him, he was pretty crook,' said Dot.

'Men,' said Joan. Dot nodded.

'I'll call us a taxi and we can go back to the hotel. You need a bath and some clothes. You can borrow some of mine. Come along, Joanie.' Dot guided her sister into the street and summoned a cruising cab. She gave the address, glared the driver into silence and ushered Joan into the hotel and, finally, into Phryne's bath with a good deal of Phryne's lavender bath salts.

Joan sank herself abruptly underwater and rose to scrub her body until her fair skin flushed red, as though she was scrubbing off something more than ordinary dirt. Then she selected a severe suit from her sister's wardrobe while Dot read a note which had been left on the hall table.

Joan wondered what her sister was doing as Dot tiptoed to the bedroom door, opened it a crack, seemed to be counting, then screwed up the note

268

and dropped it into the wastepaper basket.

'Well, she's got herself out of trouble again,' Joan heard Dot say with quiet pride. 'Joanie? You decent?' Dot wondered to hear a shake in her sister's voice as Joan assured her that she was, indeed, decent.

'I know what you've been doing,' declared Dot, as Joan tried on a pair of low-heeled black shoes.

'Do you?' Joan seized a towel and muffled her head in it, sick with apprehension. Dot had always been the good girl. God knew what she'd say about this escapade. Or what she'd tell Mum, who'd brought them up to be children of Mary.

'Yes, Mrs Hart told me. Dolly Hart.'

Joan's astonished face emerged from the towel. 'Dot, how on earth did you meet Dolly Hart? For a good girl you've got some strange friends!'

'She came to bring me your message. She told me you've been teaching deportment to Tillie's girls. She's sitting with her son at the University infirmary. It's a long story,' Dot informed her sister. 'You look real nice, Joan.'

Joan Hart looked at herself in the mirror. In Dot's well-made black suit and hat she did indeed look respectable and smart – an improvement on her previous appearance. It was all right. No one knew about those men in the alley. Dolly Hart hadn't told Dot. She was a good woman, Dolly was. Relief flooded through Joan, strengthening her stance. Her drying hair fluffed around her shoulders. No one can see it in my eyes, she thought. It didn't happen. I'm just a teacher of deportment. And I might – by the grace of God – have been saved. Saved for my children. Even for my husband. I must have loved him once, I suppose, and I wouldn't want to hurt him. Joan vowed a candle every week to the Mother of Mercy and took a deep breath.

'Come on,' she told Dot. 'I want to see the children. And Jim,' she added. 'You stay out of the way if he cuts up rough, Dot.'

'I'm not afraid of him,' said Dot, and she wasn't.

Jim Thompson had been informed of his wife's situation through a message delivered by a huge bloke with red hair and the calm, considered tone of the real hard man. It had told him that Joan was in jail, that she was morally blameless, and that his business still existed because he had a wife of unparalleled refinement and delicacy. It also told him that if he so much as spoke a cross word to Joan, Sharkbait would reduce him to the small pounded up remains of those who crossed Tillie Devine, an offence which no one committed twice because after committing it once they no longer had the capacity for rational thought or, indeed, any thought at all. Jim Thompson knew that previous persons had been foolish enough to disobey Tillie's edicts and that they had regretted it for as long as it took for them to say their last words, which were along the lines of 'Ooh! Look at all those pretty fishes!'

But he could not have been said to be happy. A graduate of the school of What Will the Other Blokes Think, Jim Thompson was an ironmonger with a position to keep up. This could not be done if his wife was associated with Tillie Devine.

He was hammering listlessly at a piece of copper destined to be house numbers when his mate Tom came in, joined by Crosscut Smith, Curly and Big Josh. He stared at them glumly.

'Heard that Joanie's coming back,' said Crosscut. 'Bit of luck, that.'

'Luck? Findin' out me missus is a pro?' growled Thompson.

'She ain't a pro, yer know she ain't. Always been straight as a wire, your Joanie. She's a teacher. Yer wouldn't grizzle if she was teaching dancin' to schoolgirls,' put in Tom. 'I reckon it's a good deal.'

'Yair?' asked Jim Thompson, looking like an older and grimier version of the Dawn of Hope, a lithograph which his mother had placed over the piano.

'Too right,' said Curly. 'I wish my missus'd find a job. Things is crook, and what are we goin' to do when the bridge is finished?'

'Yair,' said Big Josh, who didn't talk much. 'Joanie be home soon?'

'Yair, must be. Her sister was pickin' her up,' said Jim Thompson, who had been on the receiving end of a telephone call from Dot to the corner shop. He hadn't enjoyed Dot's warnings much either. But if his mates didn't mind, why should he? 'I'd better go and get the tea on,' he said, and went into the house.

His mates sloped away, coins jingling in their pockets.

Tillie Devine knew a lot about men. They were, after all, her business.

When Dot and Joan arrived at the little house, the tea was on the table, somewhat stewed, and there was fresh milk in a jug, a packet (unimaginable extravagance!) of bought biscuits and the good cups. Both children had been collected from Mrs Ryan's. They flung themselves towards their mother and grabbed her by the knees.

'Mummy!'

'Darlings,' said Joan. Jim Thompson grinned at Dot. It would be nice to have Joan home again. Mrs Ryan would stop looking at him with that Irish compassion which he found irritating. The place was a shambles without Joan. He couldn't cook. The kids had cried for her every night. Half the crockery had smashed itself in the washing bowl by some porcelain perversity and he had no clean shirts. He had missed her. And there was absolutely nothing wrong with teaching dancing, was there? Whoever you taught it to.

Fifteen

Creatress of Green Things, Lady of Bread, Lady of Hame, Mistress of the House of Morning, Lady of Abundance, Mother of Corn, Queen of the Wheat Field, Lady of Storms, Star of the Sea, Slaughterer of the Friends of Evening, Mother of Horus the Revenger, Wife of Osiris, She Who Weeps, Great Queen of the Gods.

James Frazer, 'Titles of Isis' from
The Golden Bough

Phryne had time for a refreshing nap with Professor Brazell, though actual sleep was not part of it. She had refused to answer any questions, and after awhile Professor Brazell had stopped asking them.

Around six, Phryne heard the door open and called, 'Dot?'

'Yes, Miss? I've just taken my sister home, and they made me stay for tea. I reckon Joanie'll be all right now. And I'm going back to the University to see how that poor boy is getting on, if you don't want me for anything.'

'Joss? How is he?'

'I reckon he's about the same,' said Dot. 'Not dead, at any rate. But you don't know about what Mrs Hart said to Mr Hart...'

Swiftly, Dot gathered and folded Phryne's discarded clothes while she told her the tale of Vivian Hart, Joss Hart and Dolly Hart.

'Gosh,' said Phryne's voice. 'I've got a visitor with me, Dot. This is Professor Brazell. Dorothy Williams, my companion.'

Dot smiled at the gentleman. Nice looking man, like one of them old Roman emperors, thought Dot. Her opinion was confirmed when she heard his voice.

'Delighted to meet you, Miss Williams. Your mistress must be a s-sad trial.'

Dot loved the small catch in his assured voice.

'She's found me sister,' said Dot stoutly. 'The cops couldn't do that. I read your note, Miss. You got out of it all right, then?'

'Yes, with the assistance of Professor Brazell. Never underestimate the value of inflammable underwear and a strong pair of shoulders, Dot

273

dear, when thrown into a pit. Now we need to find Adam Harcourt. Was he with Joss when you left, Dot?'

'No, but he was coming back. That friend of his, Clarence, took him away to get some sleep in a spare bed in the infirmary. Unless the poor boy's passed on, he should still be there.'

'Good. Now, I need to get dressed for a magical working, so I need the Isis costume and... What's wrong?'

'Miss, what are you intending? Something blasphemous?'

'No, something which may clear up the whole mystery of the burglary. The only magic in it will be mesmerism.'

'Like that bloke at the Tiv who made a man think he was a chicken?' asked Dot, her frown clearing.

'Somewhat like that. Did I bring another blouse?'

Dot cast a despairing glance at Professor Brazell, who shrugged.

'But if you think my immortal soul is in peril, Dot, you can pray for me. If you would like to go back and sit with Joss, you can come with us. We're due at the faculty office at seven and we'd better get a wriggle on.'

The faculty office contained a full complement of professors, including Bisset, who had come in response to a cryptic note; Harcourt and Clarence had been dragged away from Joss, the Dean Mr Gorman was in a flaming bad temper, Professor Kirkpatrick was in defiance of Sabbath and Sykes in defiance of couchgrass. Bretherton was leaning

274

against a bookcase, smoking a cigar. Juvenal would have enjoyed this gathering, he thought. And what had Miss Fisher and Brazell – the lucky dog – been doing? They looked altogether sated and very happy.

On the other side of the room, perfectly composed, were Madame and Marrin. Madame was wearing her usual bright gypsy clothes. Her bangles clashed like a percussion section every time she moved. Marrin was wearing a black robe figured with occult symbols. Above his unreadable gaze was painted an Egyptian symbol, the Eye of Ra. He was carrying a short black rod. A basket of assorted candles and dishes rested at Madame's feet.

'Really, this is mummery,' puffed the Dean.

'On the contrary, this is black sorcery, satanism, and the path to hell,' announced Kirkpatrick, glaring at Marrin, who returned no immediate response. After a minute, like a cat, he yawned.

The sight of those filed teeth appalled Kirkpatrick, but he stood his ground. Phryne, as she entered with Brazell and Ayers, was reminded of a Scotch terrier contemplating into what part of a Great Dane it is going to sink its teeth. It would probably die in the attempt, but the Great Dane would know that it had been in a fight.

'Gentlemen,' said Phryne, 'we are going to solve this puzzle by means which may strike you as strange. However, I must ask you to bear with me. Once this is started, please do not interrupt or make any loud noises until it is finished. I must ask you to trust me. Besides, if it works or it doesn't work, you'll have a story to dine out upon for years. Professor Bretherton, are your arrangements complete?'

'Yes, Miss Fisher,' answered Bretherton, who had complied with a set of unusual requests to the best of his ability.

'I don't like this!' protested Clarence. 'Professor Kirkpatrick's right. It's sorcery!'

'So it is, laddy, but even diabolical means can sometimes be used to reveal the truth,' said the Scotsman, gravely.

'Adam, let's go back to Joss. You don't have to do this!' cried Clarence Ottery.

'Put a s-sock in it, Ottery,' advised Professor Brazell. 'You don't have to s-stay and watch if it offends your s-sensibilities.'

'Professor Ayers,' pleaded Clarence. 'Can't you stop this abomination?' Ayers shook his head. Clarence grabbed Harcourt's arm and tugged. Harcourt did not move. His eyes were full of terror, but he had something to prove and a Golden Dawn amulet around his neck.

'Come with me, Adam, if you want to get to the bottom of this,' said Phryne. 'Do you?' Adam nodded. 'Good. Come with me. We will be back in a moment. Marrin, will you prepare?'

Phryne and Adam Harcourt vanished into the Dean's office. Clarence subsided, muttering. The Magician laid out a series of brass dishes on the floor, filled with incense. He lit it. The smell suggested that you would not want to know what it was made of: it had an odd, organic scent.

The faculty was disturbed. Most of them were fascinated.

'I can't do it!' wailed Adam Harcourt, clutching

276

at his breast.

'Yes, you can, because I will be here,' said Phryne, costumed as Isis. 'I will not let anything happen to you. I give you my word. I am a woman of power, even Marrin admits that,' she said. Harcourt, sitting on the floor, looked up the slope of her body to the penetrating green eyes under symbols he had been taught to worship.

'If I fall into it again,' he whispered, clutching at her knees in the manner of a suppliant, 'kill me. Don't give me back to Marrin.'

'I will not,' said Phryne. Harcourt allowed her to assist him to his feet and unbuttoned his shirt.

'Don't fail me,' he pleaded.

'I will not fail you. I will not leave you. And by this act, I will free you,' said Phryne, wondering if she was being dictated to again.

Adam Harcourt nodded, and continued to undress.

The lights were extinguished. Madame lit her array of candles. Into the half-dark Adam Harcourt came walking, escorted by a goddess, putting each foot before the other in a parody of a dance. He came to Marrin and extended his arm, and Marrin jabbed once with a spike which drew blood. Harcourt swayed, his eyes glazing.

A *grand guignol* scene, Phryne thought, a naked young man with just one trail of blood running down the inside of his right arm. *The Golden Bough* had a whole chapter on the use of intoxicants to induce trance.

'You remember what I said to you before,' she murmured to Marrin, who grinned and raised his voice.

277

'In the name of Osiris, in the name of Isis Mistress of Magic, her number is seven and seven candles are before her set. Her incense is burning. We prostrate ourselves before her. She puts her hand in ours. We follow where she leads.'

'We follow where she leads,' repeated Harcourt.

'She orders that you repeat the movements you made in her service last Saturday night,' said Marrin, putting a black-handled knife into the boy's hand. 'So mote it be.'

'So mote it be,' repeated Adam Harcourt.

Marrin stepped back against the wall and raised his wand. Harcourt went out of the office and shut the door. Phryne grabbed Bisset and hustled him into the wardrobe. He went, biddably. The door handle rattled.

'He's miming the unlocking,' whispered Brazell. The door opened. The fascinated professors watched Harcourt as he walked into the main office, avoided a chair which was no longer there, and went into the Dean's sanctum. They saw him kneel and remove the back of the safe with the knife, gathering an armload of things.

'The ledgers,' whispered Sykes.

'The Book of Hours,' breathed Bisset.

'The papyrus.' Ayers' voice was just on the edge of hearing.

'My hand axe,' said Brazell.

Harcourt stood up in one fluid movement. As he passed the wardrobe in which Bisset was concealed, he looked down as if something fell from the pile. Then he passed on.

He laid his armload on the desk and sorted through it. Phryne, who could see his face, thought it as pale as marble and completely devoid of expression. Harcourt looked dead, except that he was still moving. He picked up the ledgers and pushed them into the bookcase, amongst the folios on the bottom shelf. He dropped the hand axe behind them. He added the jewel case and the petty cash tin. Then he stood up with the mock papyrus and a sheaf of typed papers in his hands and walked out of the door.

The whole faculty followed him like hounds on the scent. Marrin walked beside the acolyte, waving his wand as though he was conducting. Barefoot, Harcourt paced down the steps and out into the main building, then up another flight of steps into the Fisher Library.

He threaded through the maze of bookcases without incident. He opened a carrel and laid the sheaf of papers inside. Then he walked back, towards the door.

'But where is the papyrus?' asked Ayers, in agony.

'Dad?'

'Joss?' Vivian Hart woke at the sound of the voice.

'Mum?'

'I'm here, lambkin.'

'I thought I imagined you,' said Joss sleepily. 'Can I have a drink of water?'

Dolly Hart held the glass as he drank. Colour was coming back into his face. He plucked at the pressure bandage, which was uncomfortably tight, and Dolly took his hand. He tried to sit up. His father assisted him.

'I feel so tired,' said Joss. 'What's happened to me?'

'You were bitten by a snake. But you'll be all right now,' said Vivian Hart. 'I'll go and get the quack. Just hang on for a moment, son.' His feet made echoes as he ran from the room.

'Mum?'

'Yes, precious?'

'Why did you leave me?' demanded Joss, and burst into tears. 'If you hadn't left I never would have got into trouble. Now I'm in big trouble. I stole something, Mum. And I let someone else be blamed. One of my friends. And I gave it to Dad and I don't know what he's done...'

'Ssh, pet. Hush now, lamb. We'll explain. Your father always was a hasty, stupid man. I'm back now, Joss, and I'm not going away again. I've missed you for ten years,' said Dolly Hart, 'and I'm not going to lose you now. Whatever you've done.'

She sat back, retaining her grasp on the boy's hand. After all, she thought, I'm not in a position to cavil about wrongdoing. Dot, from her chair on the other side of the room, laughed with relief and put down her rosary.

Entranced, Adam Harcourt walked away from the library.

'Where's he going?' asked Madame in Phryne's ear. 'He was supposed to come to the gate where we were waiting, but he never came, and this is not the way to the gate.'

'Adam, don't do it!' A loud voice jolted the acolyte so that he staggered, clutching at his heart.

280

Phryne turned and clamped a hand over Clarence's mouth. He struggled. Marrin glared. Professor Brazell seized the young man and locked his arms behind his back.

'I learned this hold in Broome from a pearl fisherman,' he said gently. 'If you make another s-sound, you'll be really s-sorry, plus you'll go through life being called "lefty", do you understand, Ottery?'

'I understand,' muttered Clarence.

Adam stood bewildered with the papyrus in his hand. He wailed in pain, shaking from head to foot. The interruption had almost killed him, but he still breathed in short, hard gasps. He turned north and south, wavering. Marrin waved his wand.

'Continue,' said the magician. 'Isis is with you. All hail her name, Lady of Storms, Star of the Sea.'

'All hail,' replied Adam in his dead man's voice. He steadied, then began to walk along the corridor, keeping to the left.

'He's walking with someone,' commented Sykes. This seemed to be true. Adam was allowing his companion room to move. He stopped at a door. He tried the handle. It opened, and he went in.

'But this is my room,' snapped Kirkpatrick.

'Keep your voice down,' scolded Phryne.

Adam Harcourt dropped to his knees and hauled out a large book. He opened it and laid the papyrus inside. The paper which Professor Bretherton had prepared exactly to Phryne's instructions lay on top of a real leaf of papyrus.

'Good. Now, Marrin. The demonstration is

complete. Bring him out of his trance,' ordered Phryne.

'Give the papyrus to me,' demanded Marrin, forcing the others out of his way. 'I command you, acolyte! Isis commands you!'

Adam Harcourt jerked. Before anyone could stop him, he straightened and handed the papyrus to Marrin. The magician grabbed, turned and, followed by Madame, ran in a jingle of bracelets and a flapping of robes like sails. They were round the corner and plunging down the steps in a moment, Marrin flourishing the papyrus in one hand. His black rod had fallen unregarded to the floor. Phryne picked it up. Bisset leapt to follow them. Ayers cried out in torment.

'Wait,' said Phryne, 'let them go. Everyone stand still. Drat the man! I don't know the right words to break this trance and if I make an error I could lose Harcourt – or at least everything we have been used to knowing as Harcourt. Give me some room, gentlemen. Edmund, put that young hound into a chair and Professor Bretherton, just bash him with something if he makes any noise, will you? There's a lovely copy of John Knox's *Commentaries on the Bible* over there. Sock him one, is my advice. Edmund darling, come here. Get behind Adam and catch him if he falls. Now, may all the goddesses help me. I can't afford to get this wrong.'

The affronted faculty were pressed into the corridor as Phryne stood before Adam Harcourt, trying to remember the words of the prayer to Isis.

'I am Lady of Flame, Mistress of Wisdom, Star of the Sea, I am Isis,' she said clearly, and Adam

282

replied, 'All hail to the Mistress of Magic, Isis.'

The amulet between Phryne's breasts seemed to wriggle a little, like a small animal settling down to sleep. Warmth crept into her body. Words came to her.

'I am your lady, your goddess, your protector from all that might harm you,' she said, improvising wildly. 'I resurrected my lost Osiris, I cast down the serpent and broke the power of the crocodile.' She grabbed at all she could remember of Isis from *The Golden Bough*. Sir James Frazer should be here, she thought, he'd be better at this than me. Phryne ran dry. Harcourt was listening to her, standing naked, entranced. His eyes were unseeing. Phryne/Isis wavered. She did not know what to say next.

Then Ayers, his face set in lines of complete despair, chanted in his clear voice, 'Slaughterer of the Fiends of Evening, Lady of the House of Morning, all hail, Isis!' and Adam flinched a little at the change of voice, but repeated, 'Hail!'

'Your task is complete, we are well pleased with you,' said Phryne, again feeling a strange sense of dislocation. 'You are freed, child, from all commands or bonds.'

'Your *ba* is returned, your shadow is tied to your body, your *ka* is with you,' chanted Ayers, looking as if he wished to weep. 'Wake! Wake! Wake! We are with thee, thy sisters and lovers. Thy world awaits thee.'

'You will wake and be joyful, knowing that she who has seen all your deeds, the Lady Isis, forgives you and frees you from domination,' said Phryne. 'Wake! Wake! Wake!'

Adam Harcourt opened his eyes and saw the compassionate gaze of a goddess bent on him. He gulped, took one step, and fainted into Professor Brazell's arms.

While Bretherton rallied around with his brandy flask, Kirkpatrick proclaimed that it was all sorcery and they would all go to hell for it, the Dean scowled blackly and Sykes repeated, 'I knew I locked the safe. I told you! I locked the safe. I definitely locked the safe. Of course, I locked the safe. I *always* lock the safe.'

Phryne was hefting the book in which the papyrus had been hidden: the *Proceedings of the 1902 Synod* of the Church of Scotland.

'Come along, gentlemen,' she said, lifting the book in her arms. 'It's time for tea and a few recriminations.'

'Well, remarkable effect,' said the doctor, who had been woken abruptly and was still sleepy. He seldom got woken to hear good news and was beaming. 'They said that antivenene would work quickly if it worked at all, but it was only because we found out what sort of snake it was. Not a very potent poison, fortunately. Black snake. Might have been a different story if it had been a tiger, eh? But you'll be all right. I'll take off this bandage now, young man, free the limb a little, eh? How does that feel?' he prodded and Joss winced.

'A bit sore,' he confessed.

'It might cramp a little, you've been lying still for so long. You want to move it as much as you can, but gently, mind. Still, one thing, you've got both parents with you, and I'm sure this young lady's prayers have had an effect.' The doctor bowed slightly to Dot, who smiled.

'Doctor?' asked Joss.

'Yes?'

'I'm going to be all right, really?'

'Really.'

'Then I'd like something to write on,' said Joss. 'There's something I've got to set right.'

'Joss, no...' said his father.

'Dad,' said Joss, for the first time in his life. 'Yes.'

'I know, I know,' said Phryne. She had doffed the Isis costume and was now dressed in her own clothes again. Adam Harcourt, a little dazed, had been reclothed by Ayers and was sipping tea and brandy with heavy emphasis on the brandy.

'We don't understand,' summarised Professor Bretherton. 'Yes, I see that that scoundrel Marrin put poor Harcourt into some sort of trance and made him rob the safe. No blame attaches to Harcourt. He was a pawn. He has been completely exonerated by this fascinating demonstration. I'm sure the faculty agrees?'

There was a murmur of agreement, even from Professor Kirkpatrick.

'So there won't be a Senate hearing tomorrow and you aren't going to expel me?' asked Harcourt, beginning to grasp the essentials.

'No, laddy, it was not your doing. Though I shudder to think of the state of your soul,' said Professor Kirkpatrick. 'And the evil of it was, that you placed those papers in your own carrel. They wanted you disgraced, perhaps to put you more firmly in their power. God knows where they've gone,' said the dry Scottish voice, 'but the Lord will deal with them in his own time, wherever they run.'

'Oh, I do agree,' said Phryne.

'But what became of the other things in the safe?' demanded Bretherton. 'The papyrus is gone, divine retribution aside, no offence, Kirkpatrick. But where are the books, the jewels, the petty cash, the Book of Hours and the hand axe?

'Cast your mind back to Adam's movements in this office,' said Phryne. 'He looked down as though he had dropped something when he passed the wardrobe. Well, there was someone in the wardrobe. He had come here on some entirely proper errand I have no doubt, had been surprised by Adam's entry, and had hidden in the nearest place available. I smelt him when I was first here. He uses sandalwood soap. I couldn't pin it down at first because all I could think of was San Barnabo in Venice, but then I had it. Italian churches use...'

'Sandalwood incense,' said Bisset. 'Here's the book. It fell off the stack as Harcourt passed. I didn't take it to keep it or sell it. I just picked it up when it fell. It seemed to be meant, you can understand that? I was going to give it back once I had convinced the librarian at the Fisher Library to display it. Beautiful things should not be hidden. It was meant to be looked at, admired. It cried out to me in its iron prison,' said Bisset. 'And people kept dropping it. It was bound to be damaged sooner or later. No one cared about it but me. And, yes, that's how I knew it was Harcourt who stole the exam papers. I'm sorry, Harcourt. I didn't realise you were in ... an unnatural state of mind.'

There was a rustle amongst the faculty, but no voice was lifted in denunciation.

'The hand axe should still be here,' said Phryne, and groped behind the folios. She gave Professor Brazell two wrapped packages with a nod. He said, 'Ah, yes, well, the Kruger collection will be glad to have it at last.' They waited until he had unwrapped both. He coughed politely. 'Er, Phryne, I don't want to put a damper on this exposition of the detective arts, but neither of these is my axe,' he said. 'This is a piece of sandstone and this is an unworked river pebble of no distinction whatever.'

'Nevertheless, it is what was in the safe when Harcourt emptied it,' she replied. 'As you recall, I already explained it to you, and for the rest we'll get to the hand axe later. Where are the ledgers, the jewels and the petty cash, you are about to ask? Consider the scene in the office on Monday morning. Mr Sykes, what was happening?'

'The Dean was shouting and I was in a flurry and we couldn't find anything,' he replied in a tight voice.

'The Dean discovered the ledgers and the other things in the bookcase,' Phryne said, to the accompaniment of dropping jaws. 'He's broke. He had to move from Bellevue Hill to Glebe. He's addicted, I suspect, to gambling. I am positing gambling because he shows no signs of alcoholism, is clearly unfamiliar with the underworld, and is not the man to spend all his wealth in the pursuit of women. So was it horses, Dean, or cards?'

'I never heard such a suggestion in all my life!' bellowed the Dean. The rest of the faculty observed him with curiosity.

'He's gambled it all away,' said Phryne. 'His wife's jewels, the income, the big house – he even nicked the petty cash. And, of course, you had to make sure that Harcourt was blamed, didn't you? You had already employed poor Mr Sykes to do the books, a man utterly unfitted to be an accountant – though he's wonderful with roses – hoping he wouldn't notice that you were embezzling the funds. But Harcourt had been helping Mr Sykes out of the goodness of his heart, and he was beginning to notice discrepancies in the books. He's a thorough worker, Harcourt. He traced a lost sum back to the previous Monday. He'd notice if the Dean's fund was empty, wouldn't he? And the money for the archaeological expedition about which Mr Ayers and Mr Brazell were arguing – that's gone too, hasn't it?' She stalked the Dean across the office, until he was backed up against the wall. His face had drained of colour and he looked about three hundred years old.

'He was ... he was going to find out.' The Dean stumbled over his words. 'Sykes could have been bluffed or even blamed, but not Harcourt. I had a system,' he mumbled, 'but it has to have capital to work. And I had a run of bad luck at blackjack.'

'And the people who run gambling in Sydney are not nice in their methods of retrieving lost funds, are they?' demanded Phryne, coldly incisive.

'They would have killed me,' faltered the Dean. He scanned the interested faces around him, searching for compassion. He had made enemies of them all by cruelties and humiliations great and small. They all looked at him without charity.

'You will tender your resignation, Gorman,' said Bretherton. As senior professor the duty fell to him. He said it with less pleasure than he would have thought possible if the matter had been put to him a week ago. 'The Senate will have to be told,' he added. 'Tomorrow. At the meeting which would have expelled Harcourt here.'

'What did I say about retribution?' asked Professor Kirkpatrick. 'Is there more, Miss Fisher?'

'Just a few things. I would like to go down to the wine cellar, but it can wait for a moment. By the way, Dean, why didn't you sell the wine? There's some valuable stuff down there. Professor Brazell and I drank two rather good bottles of Chateau Petrus while we were held captive last night.'

'The inventory is kept by the butler,' said the Dean. 'I couldn't bribe or befool him. There is an end to my career, Miss Fisher, and it is all your doing!' A flash of the old arrogance sparked through the air.

'Shut up, you ... criminal,' said Sykes.

The faculty stared at Sykes. It was not every day that one saw a worm turn. He was shaking with righteous indignation.

'Did you say "held captive", Miss Fisher?' asked Bretherton.

'Yes, let's just go and release our prisoner, eh, Edmund dear?'

'C-Certainly.' Professor Brazell held out his arm and Phryne took it, tucking the *Proceedings of the 1902 Synod* under the other arm.

They had already left the office when they heard footsteps hurrying towards them and stopped. Marrin, perhaps, returning? Dot held out a paper to Phryne.

'Miss, Joss Hart is getting better, and he insisted on writing this,' she said. Phryne scanned it and handed it to Professor Bretherton.

'Good Lord!' he said after he had read it, handing it to Professor Kirkpatrick, who fumbled for his glasses.

'Perhaps I'd better read it out loud,' said Bisset, leaning over Kirkpatrick's shoulder. 'It says: "I wanted to please my father so I stole Professor Brazell's axe because I knew it was copper-bearing ore, malachite, and my father's a miner. My father sent a man to kidnap Miss Fisher and the Professor and keep them in the old well in the wine cellar until he could register his mining claim. He's sorry. So am I. Jocelyn Hart." By George!' said Bisset. 'How did you escape, Brazell?'

'I had the intelligence to be trapped with Miss Fisher,' said Brazell. 'My advice is, always take Miss Fisher along on any perilous enterprise. S-She tipped our captor into the well, and it is about time we got him out, I s-suppose.'

'Unless the well has filled up,' commented Bretherton. 'In which case the rescue is immaterial.'

'But we should find out,' said Bisset.

'Always verify your facts,' said Brazell, leading the way down the stairs. 'A good s-scholarly principle.'

The well was occupied by a very thirsty gentleman who was swearing the air blue. Phryne yelled down to him, 'That's enough! I told you I'd come back by tonight and I'm early. Now climb up that ladder, and after one of these gentlemen takes your statement, you can go.'

'Fair dinkum?' asked the voice.

'Fair dinkum. In fact, everything is ryebuck on a straight wire and there's a ladder in front of you. Climb out, there's a good bloke,' said Phryne.

A bleared figure climbed slowly out of the well, dictated and signed a statement which exonerated him and blamed his boss, and was conducted out of the cellar into the hands of a porter who was instructed to see him out of the University grounds.

'Well, there we are,' said Phryne.

'Magic,' said Edmund Brazell. 'Pity about my funds, though.'

'I would have got them,' said Ayers, 'if I could have found my papyrus. But there it is,' he said. He raised his head and looked Phryne in the eye. 'And you haven't solved my little problem, Miss Fisher.'

'Oh, yes I have,' said Phryne. 'You wouldn't tell me who was blackmailing you, and you were so frightened of him that you began to sweat when you thought of him. Why are you sweating now, Mr Ayers?'

'It's a hot night,' he muttered, passing a hand over his high forehead.

'No one else is sweating. I think your blackmailer is here. And since this is a cleansing of all hearts and nothing of this will be produced before the Senate tomorrow morning, we will ask the Dean to take a short walk outside. He doesn't need to

291

hear this. Perhaps Bisset will go with him and make sure that he doesn't take to his heels?' Bisset and the Dean left reluctantly.

'We come now to the exposition of another little puzzle. Why did Adam Harcourt not hand over the papyrus to that bounder Marrin? Marrin was in complete control of him. He had to do as Marrin said. But Marrin wasn't actually here. The papyrus ended up in Professor Kirkpatrick's office because someone else intervened. You saw it happen. Someone led the entranced Harcourt down the corridor to the office of the one member of staff that no one, however hysterical, could possibly suspect of stealing anything. Someone walking beside him. Someone who had no scruple about allowing Adam to be expelled. Someone crafty enough to leave the papyrus there until it could be safely removed and sold to the highest bidder.

'Now, what do we know about your black-mailer, Mr Ayers? Someone who has come into possession of knowledge which could destroy you. You haven't been stealing. The Dean was the thief. You knew something about the magicians, so it might be that. And in dealing with Marrin and his form of magic, it must be sex – good old sex. If we became hermaphroditic the profession of blackmailer would cease to exist. Who would know about you? Who would manage to terrify you so efficiently? One of your lovers, of course. What could ruin a university lecturer faster than the testimony of one of his male students whom he had seduced? And who would do anything that didn't involve any effort for a beautiful life? And who tried to ruin this demonstration, not

292

caring that by that loud yell he risked Adam's sanity and perhaps his life?'

Clarence Ottery rose to his feet. 'All right,' he said insolently. 'You've got me bang to rights, Miss Fisher. You've really done terribly well, you know. When Joss wanted to bring you into it I went along, because not to agree would have seemed suspicious, but I never expected you to find out what really happened.' He smoothed back his hair, immaculate as ever. 'There's nothing you can do to me, you know,' he told the assembly. 'I know that Ayers will support anything I might like to suggest, eh, Ayers?'

Ayers was leaning against the wall. 'Why?' he asked through white lips.

'Because it amused me,' sneered Clarence. 'I liked watching you hanging onto your job and your life with one finger over the abyss. It took me so long to seduce you,' he added, in his light, careless, boy's voice. 'You were frightfully moral to begin with, weren't you? But then I took you to see Marrin, and just one night at the temple and you were mine. I didn't love you, of course,' he said, matter-of-fatly. 'I could hardly bear your con-taminated touch, your wet kisses, ugh! But Bisset kept avoiding me and Kirkpatrick was a waste of effort, though it might have been amusing. But all I had to do with you, Tommy, was listen to your nauseating prattle about love and Ancient Greece and Egypt and then wait until I had you in a suitable state. Didn't you get a shock when I told you that I had kept all your letters? And didn't you cry buckets when you found out that I was going to tell? I had to wait until Adam was expelled, then

293

I would have produced the papyrus and either you or Marrin would have given me enough money for a life of complete idleness as befits a gentleman.'

'I haven't got the money,' Ayers choked. 'You knew I didn't have any money.'

'Oh, but you would have given me the Dean's grant,' said Clarence airily. 'Or perhaps I would have gone with you to Egypt and found the tomb. Antiquities sell well on the American market. And now this meddlesome female has destroyed my nice little plan. *C'est la vie*. I'm going now. And you had better not try and stop me,' he added, before turning his back, 'because I know it all, and given the slightest difficulty, I'll tell it. Might sell rather well to one of the more sensational papers, at that,' he said.

He sauntered towards the stairs. No one moved for a moment. Then, outraged and horrified, Adam Harcourt, without thinking, stooped, grabbed and threw a bottle at the back of his immaculate head. Clarence was halted in mid-air, then knocked off his feet. He clawed for the edge, missed, and fell down the well. There was a soggy thud, then silence.

Ayers cried out and sank to the floor, sobbing wildly. The faculty stood astounded. Brazell, shuddering with disgust and pity, went to Ayers and raised him to his feet, patting his shoulder. Phryne heaved the ladder across the floor and lowered it into the pit.

'I'll do it,' said Bretherton. 'I was a stretcher bearer on the Somme.' He climbed down into the well, reappearing moments later, shaking his head. 'Broke his neck. Dead as a doornail.'

'I'd be happy,' said Ayers into Brazell's handkerchief, 'if the papyrus wasn't lost. He's been torturing me for months, months. He was mad.'

'He came to my room,' said Professor Kirkpatrick. 'To talk about his soul. I thought him in earnest. But he knew where poor bespelled Harcourt had hidden the papyrus, and came to make sure that it was still there. And to practise his wiles on me! Such wickedness,' he said sadly.

'He was my friend and now I've killed him,' said Adam blankly. 'They were both my friends. Joss is a thief and let me be blamed. Clarence was a blackmailer and let me be blamed. I don't know who to trust.'

'One of the burdens of being free,' said Phryne. 'I suggest that we report this tragic accident to the police. He came to lift a bottle of wine and fell, breaking his rotten little neck, and not before time, the slimy little serpent. You are released, Mr Ayers, and soon will be on your way to Egypt. I suggest that you put to the Senate that both your project and Professor Brazell's be funded. I think they'll agree.'

'What's the use of going to Egypt?' asked Ayers, wiping his face. 'The papyrus is lost.'

'What did Marrin say to Adam?' asked Phryne, opening the *Proceedings of the 1902 Synod* to page 666. '"Give me the papyrus", he said. But Adam was in a trance state. For Adam, Professor Bretherton's fake was the real one. So he gave Marrin...'

'The fake,' whispered Bretherton.

Ayers received the original into his hands as though it was the Host.

'And now, as Sherlock Holmes would say, "I think we will have an amnesty" in the direction of Bisset and the Book of Hours.' They nodded. 'And Ayers and Clarence?' They nodded emphatically. 'And Joss Hart? I'm willing to forgive him if you are,' she offered. 'And I was the one in the pit. Edmund, how about you?'

'S-Since his theft meant that I met you, Miss Fisher, I am willing to s-state that I have been over-rewarded for merely being thrown into a pit,' said Brazell.

'Oh, very well, Miss Fisher, since you and Brazell have forgiven the boy. No harm done, I suppose. But not the Dean,' said Kirkpatrick, firmly. 'The Dean has stolen in breach of his trust, and not only has he broken that commandment, but he has borne false witness, and if that was not enough, he has shown no remorse. He must face judgment.'

'Certainly the Dean is not to be excused,' she agreed. 'And now, a bottle of wine, I think. Will you join me, Professor?'

'You may do as you wish,' said Professor Kirkpatrick. 'But I never drink wine on the Sabbath.'

Fortunately, everyone else did.

Sixteen

Of all the English athletic games, none, perhaps, presents so fine a scope for bringing into full and constant play the qualities of both body and mind as that of Cricket. A man who is essentially stupid will not make a fine cricketer.

John Nyren, *The Young Cricketer's Tutor*

Adam Harcourt struck lustily. The ball whistled past deep mid on and continued unchecked to the boundary.

'Very pretty,' said the aged Professor Jones, clapping both veined hands together. 'I'm rather relying on Hart, though. Very sound, Hart. Holds up his end like a good 'un, generally. Just the chap to support Harcourt's aggression. And six again! Very good.'

Phryne settled back lazily to watch the game. This was, after all, why she had come to Sydney. After belting his way to a solid thirty-two, Harcourt miscalculated a Chinaman from that cunning Scotsman, Professor Kirkpatrick.

'Wrong 'un!' exclaimed Professor Jones, as the ball unexpectedly rose and caught the outside edge, and was collected with efficiency by Sykes, who appeared perfectly confident when he kept wicket. He was crouching behind the stumps like a small, greying tiger.

'Well done. As I said, there's Hart: not wasting a ball, nudging one to give the strike to Harcourt. Next man in is Tommy Smith. Good stroke player, but rather rash. I've had a full account of your doings, Miss Fisher, from Brazell. Nice chap, Brazell. Of course my lips are sealed, he knows that. Never been one to gossip. Have to be sorry for poor Ayers. Imagine not appreciating sitting here in the shade and talking to a pretty woman, eh?' He chuckled and patted Phryne's knee. 'Some chaps are just made like that, I suppose. It's a hard road for them, and there's always the chance that they'll be put in Ayers' position. Well, well, the wretched boy has gone to his reward and it will probably be a hot one. But there are several things I don't understand. Who put the snake venom in Harcourt's shoe?'

'Marrin. But it wasn't meant to kill. He'd been using diluted snake venom on poor Harcourt, to make him malleable and put him into trance. He knew that something had gone wrong with his attempt to steal the papyrus, and he wanted to put Harcourt back into trance, but Harcourt had broken with him, so he had to do it by stealth. I imagine that the wretch Clarence stole the shoe for him. They were hand in glove, those two. We found some very nasty publications in his room. Harcourt was meant to go back into a trance state and repeat his movements on the night he stole the papyrus. But he was out practically first ball; the inner sole of his shoe was thicker than Marrin had anticipated, poor Joss got the dose instead, and he wasn't used to it. It was nearly death before wicket, Professor.'

'Hart seems to have recovered well,' remarked Jones. 'We'll miss Ottery, of course. It's a terrible blow to learn that someone with such a beautiful cover drive could be a wicked person. Still, we can make do,' he said philosophically. 'Is that a six?'

'Yes,' said Phryne, watching the umpire.

'Rash,' said Professor Jones. 'I always said so. See? I don't know what they teach young men these days.'

The hapless Smith, having belted his six, had played on entirely the wrong line to Bisset's most vicious ball, which pitched and instead of rising fizzed through at knee height and demolished the middle stump.

'That was a very good ball,' offered Phryne, attempting to mitigate Professor Jones' wrath against T. Smith.

'Yes, Bisset's fast. He can only bowl that one once a match, but it always works. Who's next? Ah. Smith's brother, Mike. Something of an oak tree. Always think we should have an oak tree at number four. Steadies the side and tires the bowlers.'

This Smith was cautious. He played forward rather than back and down rather than up, and after a couple of overs Bisset was beginning to pant and was replaced with Ayers, who wore his county cap and bowled left arm finger spin with occasionally amazing force and ingenuity.

'Ayers can't keep his mind on his game, or he would have been a Test player,' grumbled Professor Jones, watching him run up with the grace of a large cat.

The oak tree Smith stood firm and Joss Hart played with great caution, picking off singles as

299

they came. The serenity of a day's cricket floated down on Phryne, and she suppressed a yawn.

'The other thing I don't understand,' the aged man said, continuing the conversation where he had dropped it, 'was that Brazell says that you knew it was the Dean from talking to his wife. How did you know? Did she tell you?'

'No. Partly I was considering the house. It was clear that a once wealthy family had come down in the world. The furniture was good but it was too big for the rooms. If Gorman had just had a fancy to live in Glebe, there were houses in good repair which he could have bought – unless, of course, he couldn't afford it. And it was not one of those strange relationships where both parties want to renovate an old house,' said Phryne, to whom renovation was a signal to rent another house for six months. 'Because Mrs Gorman didn't know one end of a nail from the other. Also, she lied about her maid leaving. She had no servant. And she'd been used to having one. There was an appreciable delay while she remembered that there was no one else to answer the door. Poor woman. But it was not that she told me anything. All the other women knew that I was investigating the theft and tried to tell me that their husbands couldn't have done it because they were dear good chaps, but all of them considered it. Mrs Gorman didn't say anything of the sort. She knew that he was guilty, and she couldn't think of a thing to say to exonerate him.'

'And she was the cause of it, I should think,' said Professor Jones sharply. 'Greedy woman, always nagging him about his social standing. He might have taken to gambling as the only way to get enough cash to satisfy her?'

'He might,' said Phryne. 'Anyway, he's gone.'

'Good riddance,' said Professor Jones. 'No use as batsman or bowler and couldn't field.'

They watched Hart and M. Smith patting back dangerous balls and occasionally making one or two until tea was brought for the academic staff and Phryne accepted a cup.

'No, there he goes,' she said to Mrs Sykes, as M. Smith followed his brother with an injudicious stroke worthy of T. Smith off Kirkpatrick, who was cashing in on the terror at the other end. The batsmen played Bisset with difficulty, and misjudged the slower spinner. He had two wickets to prove that this was unwise.

'They take this so seriously,' sighed Mrs Sykes. 'But I suppose gentlemen must have their fancies. Who's in next?'

'Oberon,' said Professor Jones. 'A strong young man with no fear. Not a lot of judgment either. You watch him take on Bisset!'

Phryne watched. Oberon was a young giant and stood up to the bowlers, opening his chest and belting the cover off the ball. The faculty were leather-hunting, hot and unhappy. Oberon hit both Bisset and Kirkpatrick out of the attack, bringing on Ayers and Bretherton and finally Cummings of Physics, a quick but wild fast bowler. 'What a fine analytical head you have on those pretty shoulders, Miss Fisher,' commented Professor Jones in another interval caused by the ball having gone over the pavilion again. 'Always said that they ought to make women detectives.

301

You could rival that Sherlock Holmes chap. Are you travelling down to Melbourne by train, m'dear? I might be travelling with you. I'm going to the Melbourne Test.'

'A triumph of hope over experience?' asked Phryne. 'We lost the Sydney Test almost as disgracefully as the Brisbane Test. I mean, can anyone make up a margin of six wickets?'

The old man's eyes gleamed. 'There's a change coming,' he prophesied, holding up one hand like someone from the cast of the Old Testament. 'Only takes one man to change the whole team. You mark my words, Miss Fisher.'

Phryne nodded. Oberon, completely above himself, danced down the pitch and skied a ball which spun unexpectedly at the last moment. There was a scurry of fielders sorting themselves out. Edmund Brazell stood underneath. The moment stretched out. Then the ball slapped both palms, the fingers closed, and the crowd clapped Oberon as he returned, out for 31 made quickly.

'Brazell says that Harcourt got young Ottery on the back of the head with a bottle,' said the old man. 'Hard things to throw straight, bottles. Always said he was a good cricketer.'

The tail departed rapidly under the renewed assault of Kirkpatrick and Bisset. Joss Hart was still there. Professor Jones was doing sums.

'There, m'dear, we have them all out for 151, not a bad total at all, and Hart not out 35, having carried his bat. A good boy.'

At lunch, Phryne went for a walk around the grounds. The grass was green and littered with students, some of whom had bought picnics and girls. She spied Mrs Hart sitting on a rug. Dolly got up and walked with Phryne until they stood under the trees.

'I've left Tillie,' she said. 'Bought myself out, all sweet, she even kissed me goodbye and hoped I'd do well. But I haven't gone back to Viv. I'm not a fool! I've seen him in these moods before. Weep like a crocodile and within a month it's back to the old ways. But I've accepted an annuity from him. All paid for, so he can't change his mind. I can afford my little house with the money I've saved, and it will be all mine and in my name. I won't need to work, and I was getting a bit sick of it to tell you the truth, Miss Fisher. I'll have to find something to do with myself.'

'Why did you agree to take money from Mr Hart?' asked Phryne.

'Well, dear, I'm not as young as I was,' said Dolly. 'I want my son back, and I can't have him while I'm a working girl. Not that I mightn't take a private client, just the one,' she said, as Professor Bretherton saw them and waved. 'Not for money. For...'

'Love,' said Phryne gently. 'Why not see if you can help someone?' she asked. 'There are plenty of charities. Churches. Lots of people who could do with a listener, a cup of tea, maybe a salutary clip over the ear.'

'Since your friend prayed my son back, I been thinking about that,' said Mrs Hart. 'I heard her, all night, the click of the beads and the murmur of the prayers. I'll see,' said Dolly.

She paused near Joss Hart and his father, who was saying, 'I'm impressed, boy. That was a good

303

innings, an innings for your team. I noticed you giving away the strike to Harcourt and Oberon, and farming it to try and protect the tail. I'm proud of you, Joss. Maybe this university lark isn't so useless after all.'

Joss Hart smiled. Phryne strolled on. Joan was taking her sister Dot to a hairdresser. Phryne wondered if Dot would reappear shingled, and thought it unlikely. Professor Brazell was mopping his brow, looking like an Ancient Roman playing cricket. The white flannels suited his dark hair. Though the strange closeness which had come with the dark underground had not returned, he was a definite find as a lover and Phryne was trying to decide whether she would stay on in Sydney for awhile. The University Senate had cleansed itself of the Dean, accepting his resignation and packing him off. They had funded both Ayers' Egyptian journey and Brazell's outback trip. No mining lease had been registered for a copper mine in the Northern Territory. Mr Hart had apologised and endowed rather a large scholarship for the faculty of Arts. Joss Hart and Adam Harcourt had recovered. Nothing had been seen of Madame and Marrin in any of their usual haunts, though a landlady was pursuing them for unpaid rent. The police had investigated Clarence Ottery's untimely death. The Coroner had said some severe words on the subject of student pranks, and the boy was safely buried. And just in case, Phryne was still wearing Bretherton's amulet. Against her skin, it still felt warm.

The afternoon session began with the academic openers, Bretherton and the large Budgen. Jeoffry

Bisset, relying on not being called for awhile – he batted at number five – climbed into the pavilion and sat down next to Phryne. Professor Jones was conferring with an even older colleague, doubtless discussing how far cricket had fallen from the good old days of the Hambledon men.

'The Book of Hours of Juana the Mad is on display in the library in a glass case,' said Bisset.

'I've seen it. Lovely thing. I can understand why you stole it,' replied Phryne, watching Budgen lumber down the wicket for a risky single. Harcourt flung the ball back and shattered the stumps, but the engineer was home. He leaned on his bat, panting. 'There's nothing like cricket, is there?'

'"Pavilioned in splendour and girded with praise",' agreed Bisset, quoting a hymn in a manner which would have brought a sharp reproof from Professor Kirkpatrick. 'Damn, Mike Smith really is the cleverest of the students! Look at that ball. Tweaked at the last moment and spun in completely the wrong direction. He'll have Budgers if he doesn't look sharp. Australians are good at wrist spin.'

A roar announced that Budgen had not looked sharp enough, and Ayers strode to the crease, bearing a resemblance to Lawrence of Arabia. He took guard as though he was about to command a regiment of Bedouin to attack, and scorned Mike Smith and his infidel wrist spin. He began to score freely.

'It was nice of you not to mention...' Bisset faltered.

'No matter, dear boy,' said Phryne. 'Give my

305

best regards to Dora.'

Bisset displayed shock. 'How did you know it was Dora? I mean, I can understand how you knew I had been there with a woman, you must have seen my face when you suggested it, but how did you...'

'From something she said.'

'She didn't give us away?' gasped Bisset.

'On the contrary. She told me about how all of them could have done it – except you. One can glean an awful lot from what women don't say. I could discount her knowing the name of the Book of Hours, she would have heard it often enough. But she left you out of the possibles, Jeoffry. Didn't even mention your name. In fact...' Phryne laughed suddenly.

Bisset stared at her. There was something uncanny about her intuition and he wondered what else she knew about him and Dora.

'What?'

'She asked me to make it the Dean,' Phryne laughed again. 'And I *have*.'

'I'd better get back,' said Bisset, as Bretherton hopped and grimaced. 'He's going to need a runner.'

Even with a runner, Bretherton was aware that he was failing. Deciding to go out with a bang if possible, he swung wildly at a fast medium cutter, which missed his stumps by a whisker, hit the next ball over cover for four, then holed out to backward point attempting to repeat the stroke.

Batsman followed batsman. Bisset misjudged the speed of a deceptively lazy Harcourt ball, strode down the pitch and heard the bails whipped off behind him by T. Smith. He liked Bisset, so he refrained from whooping too loudly. Besides, his French essay was overdue. Kirkpatrick applied his strong Presbyterian principles to dismiss the ball from his presence as though it was heretical, and made seventeen before his downfall was brought about. Professor Jones sniffed, 'Should never underestimate Oberon. Rash, yes. But sometimes he has remarkable application. He's been plugging away at Kirkpatrick all this time, waiting for him to play forwards, and the one time he does it, it tempts him out of his crease and that's the end of him.'

'He will have to call Christian resignation to his aid,' agreed Phryne.

Ayers, stalwart and free from fear at last, held on heroically as the tail crumbled around him, managing a very creditable fifty-three, the highest score of the match. When he was finally devoid of partners, he walked off to cheers.

Professor Jones, Phryne saw, was adding up again as the last player left the field to quench their thirst in champagne cup. No one had told Professor Kirkpatrick that it had real champagne in it until he had drunk two glasses, and then he was feeling too elated to complain.

Phryne watched Professor Jones add a figure into the bottom of his scoresheet, total it, and rule a line underneath. She did not comment aloud, but pointed.

'Oh, it's a tie, dear girl. These matches are always a tie. This one was, too. Did you see how Ayers held up the side when all those ferrets were popping in and out?'

'Heroic,' said Phryne. Cricket really was a gentleman's game.

The scene was positively ill with happy endings, and Phryne was trying to make up her mind when she should leave Sydney.

The city had its own magic, from the brawling Darlinghurst rabble to the heat, the steamy tropical excitement which made criminals bold and flowers huge and scents unsubtle, and above all the harbour and the salt smell, the glimpses of water at the bottom of age-old steps. She had still to extract some erotic poetry from the crowd at Theo's. She might even start a literary magazine. She had a pressing invitation from Brazell to stay. The grass was lush, the day dreamy, and Phryne was walking around the picnic which marked the end of play waiting for a sign. Just a small omen to tip her decision either way.

She had only walked a little way further when a figure bustled up to her, panting.

'Oh, Miss Fisher, I'm glad I caught you,' said Sykes breathlessly. 'It's not the season for it but we managed to coax it into bloom. My wife's very good at them and we wanted to thank you.'

He thrust a terracotta pot into her hands and stood back, waiting anxiously for her reaction. In the flowerpot was a single azalea, perfectly white, perfectly beautiful. Stuck in the pot was a wooden marker on which was written the azalea's name. Phryne read it and laughed in delight. She had received her sign.

The azalea was called 'Phryne'.

Select bibliography

Althan, H.S. *A History of Cricket,*
  George Allen & Unwin, London, 1962
Arlott, John and Trueman, Fred. *On Cricket,*
  BBC Publications, London, 1977
Baker, Sidney J. *A Dictionary of Australian Slang,*
  Robertson & Mullens, Sydney, 1943
Barnard, Marjorie. *The Sydney Book,*
  Waite & Bull, Sydney, 1947
Butel, Elizabeth and Thompson, Tom.
  Kings Cross Album, Atrand Pty Ltd,
  Sydney, 1984
Carr, J.L. *Carr's Illustrated Dictionary of
  Extra-Ordinary Cricketers,* Quarter Books,
  London, 1983
Cooper, Ashley. *Old Sydney,*
  Horowitz, Sydney, 1970
Dutton, Geoffrey. *Waterways of Sydney,*
  J.M. Deant Pty Ltd, Melbourne, 1988
Fairfax John. *Historic Roads Round Sydney,*
  Angus & Robertson, Sydney, 1937
Frazer, Sir James G. *The Golden Bough.*
  A Study in Magic and Religion,
  Papermac, London, 1987
Frewin, Leslie (ed.). *The Poetry of Cricket,*
  MacDonald, London, 1964
Geeves, Phillip. *Phillips Geeves' Sydney,*
  Angus & Robertson, Sydney, 1981
Glaister, John. *The Power of Poison,*

Christopher Johnson, London, 1954

Harmsworth, A. *Harmsworth's Home Doctor,*
Amalgamated Press, London, 1922

Haskell, John. *Haskell's Sydney,*
Hale & Iremonger, Sydney, 1983

Illingworth, Ray and Gregory, Kenneth.
The Ashes, Collins, London, 1982

Kirkpatrick, Peter. *The Sea Coast of Bohemia,*
University of Queensland Press, Brisbane, 1992

Lawton, David and Steele, Jeremy.
The Great Hall Guide,
University of Sydney, Sydney, 1981

Lower, Lennie. *Here's Luck,*
Angus & Robertson, Sydney, 1961
— *Here's Lower,* Hale & Iremonger, Sydney, 1983

Mendelssohn, Joanna. *Letters and Liars,*
Angus & Robertson, Sydney, 1996

Mercier, Emile. *Wake Me Up at Nine,*
Angus & Robertson, Sydney, 1950

Nyren, John. *The Young Cricketer's Tutor,*
Davis-Poynter Ltd, London, 1974

Park, Ruth. A *Companion Guide to Sydney,*
Collins, Sydney, 1973

Park, Ruth and Emmanuel, Cedric.
The Sydney We Love, Nelson, Melbourne, 1983

Symonds, John. *The Great Beast: Life and Magick
of Aleister Crowley,* Mayflower, London, 1973

Turney, Clifford, Bygott, Ursula
and Chippendale, Peter. *Australia's First:
A History of the University of Sydney,* vol. 1
Hale & Iremonger, Sydney, 1991

Waite, A.E. *The Pictorial Key to the Tarot,* Rider &
Co., London, 1910

This Large Print Book for the partially sighted, who cannot read normal print, is published under the auspices of

THE ULVERSCROFT FOUNDATION